Intrusions

Sal Hunter

For my dad, and all those library visits together.

Contents

Chapter 1 – Tuesday 10th December 1

Chapter 2 – Wednesday 19th November.. 4

Chapter 3 – Saturday 31st May... 7

Chapter 4 – Lana, Monday 2nd June... 15

Chapter 5 – Munro, Monday 2nd June 22

Chapter 6 – Tues 3rd June and Wed 4th June... 29

Chapter 7 – Friday 6th June.. 35

Chapter 8 – Wednesday 11th June... 39

Chapter 9 – Friday 13th June 48

Chapter 10 – Mon 16th June and Wed 18th June.. 56

Chapter 11 – Saturday 21st June.. 65

Chapter 12 – Lana, Tuesday 1st July.. 75

Chapter 13 – Munro, Tuesday 1st July... 86

Chapter 14 – Wednesday 2nd July 90

Chapter 15 – Saturday 5th July.. 98

Chapter 16 – Wednesday 9th July.. 105

Chapter 17 – Saturday 12th July 111

Chapter 18 – Friday 25th July 119

Chapter 19 – August.. 126

Chapter 20 – Monday 25th August 134

Chapter 21 - Tuesday 26th August... 140

Chapter 22 – Wednesday 27th August.. 147

Chapter 23 – Sunday 31st August.. 154

Chapter 24 – Thursday 4th September 162

Chapter 25 – Tuesday 16th September 169

Chapter 26 – Saturday 20th September.. 179

Chapter 27 – Monday 22nd September.. 187

Chapter 28 – Autumn 193

Chapter 29 – Thursday 16th October 199

Chapter 30 – Mon 20th Oct to Wed 22nd Oct 206

Chapter 31 – Thursday 23rd October 216

Chapter 32 - Saturday 25th October 223

Chapter 33 – Monday 27th October 230

Chapter 34 – Wednesday 29th October... 238

Chapter 35 – Thurs 30th to Wed 5th November.. 246

Chapter 36 – Monday 10th November... 256

Chapter 37 – Saturday 15th November 264

Chapter 38 – Sunday December 14th 274

Afterword 280

About the Author... 281

Chapter 1 – Tuesday 10th December

An intense hush blanketed the room. Ranks of terraced seats rose into the darkness, each white tie or ballgown-clad occupant motionless. Chatter had stilled some time before, but no one could have anticipated how much noise the softest shifting of silk, wool, sequins and gems had been making. Some moments before, a gentleman in the sixth row had cleared his throat, and a shockwave of nervous twittering had bubbled briefly before the blanket resettled. Royalty commands silence.

From her seat to one side of the podium, Bev felt everyone's eyes turn to her. She willed her face to still and grounded herself through her feet, pressing unfamiliar heels into the deepest, most malleable of carpets. Her breath fluttered in her chest, butterflies bringing all their winged cousins to the party. Peter lightly brushed his finger against hers, letting her know he was there.

"For your work reclassifying Human Psychology and your Psychological Factorisation process: Dr Peter Bryant, Dr Beverly Cargill, the Swedish Academy congratulates you. Please step forward and receive your Nobel Prize from his Majesty the King."

After the long foreword describing their work and its implications, hearing the award announced so starkly was profoundly affecting. It was unquestionably the proudest moment of Bev's life, and her slim limbs trembled as she approached and accepted the honour. Looking back out over the audience of dignitaries, she felt a slash of disconnection from these glamourous and polished people who applauded her so fervently. There was more wealth displayed here than had been invested in all their work so far. The student loans she would carry for years could easily have been settled by the daily earnings of many in this room. Even groomed as she was, Bev remained a dainty but dishevelled figure; more comfortable in jeans, knitwear and her lab coat than the dress she'd chosen for today. Yet they applauded her.

As she returned to her seat, she smiled ruefully and shook her head in disbelief. There had been so many doubts over the years – the uncertain results of their experiments, the enormous workload they were committing to, defining the practical applications of what they were uncovering, the ethical nuances of the processes they had created. To bring the fruits of their labour out of the realm of academia, to see it deployed and successful in mental health services across Europe, had made it all worthwhile. This award, however, this somehow made their work seem more significant than even they could ever have anticipated. She caught Peter's eye, and the smile they shared was as much relief as joy. Nearly imperceptible beads of sweat peppered Peter's brow as his smile turned to a triumphant grin.

Later that evening, once the formalities were completed and more relaxed celebrations were under way, Bev observed as Peter shook hands with everyone in his orbit. She winced minutely as she remembered the Covid outbreak years and yet again reflected on how glad she was that lockdown hadn't forever ended such casual human contact. Bev was more reserved than most and would happily have never shaken a hand again. In contrast, Peter had always been the tactile and sociable crowd-pleaser of the team, and now he was beaming as he pinballed his way from group to group of well-wishers. She followed some steps behind, struggling to calm nerves which had been habitually taut for far too long now. The publicity this award would bring should clarify how their technology worked, educate the public to its benefits, and hopefully would put an end to the media scaremongering that still dogged them. Peter labelled the over-reaction to their processes as Luddism, but she could understand the caution. This was a breakthrough of unprecedented proportion, the first time the medical community could accurately assess a patient's mental strengths and weaknesses and prepare in advance for what would ail them through their lives. For some, that predictive diagnosis was alarming enough without the laboratory-based reality of wires and electrodes, scanners and monitors which were required to perform the assessment.

No, she reaffirmed to herself. Now, the undertaking they had started as post-graduates would be understood and accepted. Certainly, their work should be safe from the establishment interference or misappropriation that had concerned her most. As the weight of worry started to leave her shoulders, she joined Peter in his celebrations and thanked God he had been right all along. It was time to celebrate.

Chapter 2 – Wednesday 19th November

It was a still, bright, bitterly cold morning. The sun was still low in the palest of winter skies, not long clear of the hills over the water. The tide was retiring, leaving the near shore gleaming and slippery with weed and pools, and here and there an oystercatcher prodded tentatively, hoping for a morsel. A quiet figure watched it all from her doorstep, warm in layers of thick knitwear, her mug steaming in the crisp air. She had been here for two weeks now, and the changeable weather and quiet solitude had made her a creature of impulse rather than routine. Today she had risen early, and braved the choppy, chill waters for a swim, feeling at home in the dawn light with the seabirds and a distant otter. Two seals had watched her curiously, and she had found herself as curious as they were; how very unlike her this was, how very reckless. Now, she warmed herself and appreciated the view. In the freedom of her first week, she had attempted to draw the shoreline and had created accurate but pitifully unbeautiful imagery. She would stick to other creative pursuits from now.

From the north, she heard an engine approaching; a car by the sound of it, perhaps a warden coming to check on the neighbouring campsite, which would lie unused until March. She turned indoors and moved to the nearest southerly window, leaving the door slightly open. She held her breath and tipped her head to listen as the vehicle approached on the main road; it caught in her chest when she heard it slow and turn into her driveway. Swiftly, she threw her tea down the sink and filled the mug with cold water, glad she had not yet lit the stove. Grabbing her emergency bag of belongings, she pulled on boots and crouched below the level of the window ledge, ready to break for the back door if she needed to.

The large white SUV pulled around the drive and into view, weaving around potholes, the two occupants jolted by each bump. Red mud speckled its otherwise pristine paintwork. She didn't recognise the car; now would be the time to leave and head through the woods to hide further up the hill. The plan was unequivocal. Her legs remained locked in place, however, panic warring with uncertainty and reducing her to simply watching and breathing and feeling the thump of her heart as she hoped the people would turn and leave. Who could it be? No one should come here, not just now.

As the car slowed and crunched to a stop in the gravel outside the front door, she realised she had waited too long. She wouldn't make it to safe cover before they were out of the car. She trembled, knowing that only one door was locked; the other still standing ajar to allow the swift, quiet, escape she hadn't been decisive enough to make. Raising her head a little, peeking through the window nearest the car, she watched as the driver stretched and slammed her car door. She recoiled in sudden recognition. What was that woman doing here? How could she have possibly known where to find her? Swiftly, realisation and betrayal struck in fierce tandem. She fell back from her crouch onto the floor, and leaned against the kitchen units, sucking in breath and fighting back acid tears. Everything was over.

Chapter 3 – Saturday 31st May

"Get in there, you... blimming thing! Oh...!"

Lana Knight thought there was nothing so unsatisfactory as pointless, polite profanity. It did little to ease her pain or frustration, only granting her time to ponder all the other truly effective swearwords she could have used. But she was trying to get out of the habit of bad language, her last resolution standing since New Year.

"Darn-nabbit!" That was one of her late grandmother's favourites, and at least those fond memories made her smile a little as she wobbled at the top of her inadequate stepladder in her high-ceilinged lounge. Neighbouring homes had an ornate plaster rose and chandelier in this room, but a previous owner of this flat had over-zealously modernised: now modern socket spotlights brightened the room but added no character. Thankfully the beautifully detailed double cornice remained around the edges of the ceiling, as well as a high picture rail. These, along with the antique tiled fireplace and broad bay windows looking out over the river Tay, had sold the flat to Lana. Right now, she wished she still lived with her parents, and could pass the responsibility of upkeep to someone else.

Her situation was her own fault: she had known this job would test her temper, but she had chosen the lesser of two evils. Her dad is due to visit later in the day, and if he notices something as obvious as unchanged spotlights, he'll step in and do them for her. That would suit a lot of people, but Lana is trying to be more independent and doesn't like to deliberately take advantage. She doesn't need that on her conscience.

Lana is someone very much defined by her emotions: sensitive moods, frivolous moods, but mostly either great moods or black moods. When she was young, her mother used to call her contrary, fickle, hormonal - all in a semi-teasing fashion - and she was right. An ex-boyfriend had once called her an unpredictable bitch, and he was right, too. He was wrong in many other ways, but he was right about that. Self-knowledge isn't always helpful, she knows.

Just as she started to weary of her own churlishness, it all came good. Click, clip, done, and she was free to wash up and start preparing the seafood chowder she has promised her father. She stopped herself for a second, unearthed a smile, and put some music on. Pottering in her cheerful kitchen, her mood switch suddenly flipped, and the sun came out. She briefly wondered if it was the other way around but resisted the temptation to overthink when she was feeling so blessed. This evening she had good company to look forward to, she had true soul food simmering, and a bottle of Viognier chilling. Tomorrow would be a long lie day, and her time would be her own.

"So, are you still thinking of going for "The Good Life"?" Peter Knight winked as he dunked a hunk of bread into the aromatic, golden creamy mess in his bowl. His tall, thin frame gangled awkwardly in the old wooden dining chair Lana had upcycled beautifully, but he smiled. It wasn't that he thought Lana couldn't succeed as a crofter – the warm, sunlit kitchen and cramped but comfortable dining area stood testament to her capable hands and ability to craft. He just believed the isolation and relentlessness of it wouldn't suit her. The fridge freezer hummed, and the old sunburst clock ticked languorously on the wall. He gave her time.

Thoughtful, she sighed. "No, not really. I know it's not realistic. But just think about it, how nice it would be to decide your own plan for each day? All that time in the fresh air, eating well and getting your daily exercise by working outdoors instead of in the gym?" she countered.

"Hah! More like a daily grind. Getting up at the crack of dawn, digging muck all day, no nice nails or delivery pizza? And you wouldn't believe all the diseases chickens can get..."

Lana saved herself the gruesome details of do-it-yourself hen dissections by focusing on homemade bread and butter and crisp white wine. Peter knew she would listen and consider what he said but would go on to form her own opinion no matter what his advice; but Lana always appreciates guidance from him when it comes to her latest whim. Without it she would be penniless and jobless, and her compact home would be stacked shoulder high in exercise equipment, craft supplies, DIY gear and hobby tat. As it is, she is constantly reselling bits and pieces online. But she remains unready to resign herself to the humdrum. Deep inside, she wishes she had a true vocation in life, a north star of her own.

"I just want something... else. Something more rewarding, something I can be proud of. Something that isn't plodding away at the bank and classes at the gym afterwards, with only a night in the pub every so often to let off steam. I feel like I could really do something spectacular if I just knew what it was." Lana struggled to find the words to explain what was missing from her life. "Do you never feel a bit lost, like you don't know what exactly you would wish for...?" She failed to express herself and shrugged it off disconsolately.

Her father smiled sympathetically. "That was lovely as always, let me get these dishes for you," he offered. He would always talk things over if he knew they were important, but feelings are not his comfort zone. For him, practicalities are preferred, and he and Lana have covered this same ground many times before. Lana understood entirely, and there was nothing she would change about their relationship. She watched as he criss-crossed the kitchen, covering leftovers and gathering empty dishes, and for a while she simply appreciated the time together.

"Nah, leave them," she interrupted, as he started to rummage for dish liquid. "We can rinse them, and they'll be okay in the sink until tomorrow morning. The quiz will be starting soon, we don't want to be late: the others will be there by now. And no buying raffle tickets this time, I'm still trying to give away that dodgy vodka you won last time."

It was a glorious but fresh early summer evening as

they left the flat and stepped out onto the stairs leading down to the strip of front garden Lana tends. They crossed the narrow river-front road and descended stone steps to walk along the stony beach towards the centre of their bustling hometown, Lana's long dark hair flipping lightly in the breeze. Plump purple mussels and glistening bottle green weed glinted in the evening sun as they crunched, slipped and stumbled. This is where Lana grew up, and she's known this beach her whole life. Some years ago, the addition of flood barriers and a broad walkway had rearranged its landscape significantly, but nature rebounds and they still preferred the changed beach to the pavement when it was possible.

"How's Mum today?" she asked.

"Not bad! She's been more cheerful again today; she's not been as..." he paused to consider, "...annoyed with it all." Lana's mother was side swiped by multiple sclerosis some years ago. Each time her condition worsens, she struggles to re-adjust, railing against a cruel god. She's a proud woman, who previously suffered no fools and now worries too much about what those same fools will think of her as she feels diminished. It's rare that she leaves their family home, hating the crutches she needs, spending her time pottering online and watching soaps and old movies to distract herself from a reality she feels has betrayed her. "She says she might come out with me one day this week, maybe for lunch or a cake and cuppa someplace. It would do her good. And she's looking forward to seeing wee Robbie soon, of course." Lana nodded. She knew his plans were unlikely to work out but was glad to hear that her dad was bearing less burden than usual.

"It always feels so odd to be on the beach without the dog," Lana mentioned as she saw her dad looking bemused and embarrassed to have picked up a tangle of dried wrack. He shrugged and threw it back below the tideline. "Todd won't forgive you quickly when you get home, going out without him," she laughed.

But Todd, a handsome black Labrador and German Shepherd mix, is still young and puppy spirited. He's banned from quiz nights, when everyone wants to be able to focus on something other than him. Occasionally he will want to bother other dogs; more often he simply asks out to the loo just before tricky questions only Peter can answer. On one mortifying occasion, he had launched himself between tables like a shark attack, stealing a crisp from some poor tourist's hand. That was a while back, and he's settled down a lot since then, but he's still banned.

The sun was just setting as they passed the lifeboat shed and turned back into town, heading past shops, cafes and rows of outside tables to reach the bar entrance. The Bell was a town stalwart and had been in business since the 1860s. Unlike some other local pubs, it had survived the lockdown years by delivering takeaway bar food and relying on loyal locals to visit whenever they were allowed. It was split into two main areas, with a smaller, starker bar area which in Peter's youth used to be the province of old men and their overweight dogs. The larger, warmer and more welcoming lounge hosts the quiz nights. The days of social rules about who sat where are over, but the lounge still has a softer and happier atmosphere, the results of age-old architecture and interior design still lingering. In the day, sunlight sparkles through stained glass windows and makes kaleidoscope patterns on the polished bar. This evening the sun was already low, extra lighting in odd corners compensating for the gloom.

The lounge was busy, but genial and not too noisy.

Peter's elderly neighbour Brian was in the corner with a pint, but the father and daughter headed over to Colin and Sanj, old friends of Lana's from school. They had just arrived, too, choosing a rectangular table in the farthest nook of the lounge, filling the bench corner with the coats they would need for the walk home. Lana had once had a thing for Sanj, but both were too young to realise that good friends can make the best partners and so they kept the status quo. Laughter spiked from a large table in the window, where a group of fashionable women were surrounded by gift bags, sharing jokes and blushes. Glasses chimed and earrings sparkled as they toasted the birthday girl.

"Ailsa's just gone up for a round," Colin offered. "Get in there before they ring it up, Lan." Lana caught Ailsa's eye and waved – they had no real need to talk, they all knew each other's favourites well.

"Lana's still thinking of becoming a crofter!" laughed her dad, and the jovial cheek started. There was never any malice, but briefly Lana had the uncomfortable burden of being the centre of teasing discussion.

Ailsa returned with the first drinks and cut them off before it all became too nippy. "Have you heard Colin's news?" she asked. "He got the promotion!"

They settled into their seats as Colin was made to re-tell the whole story, his friends smiling and telling him he had always been the right one for the job. None were entirely sure what it was that Colin did for a living, but he was now a senior consultant something, rather than an ordinary one. Lana's sister Jen works in IT as well, so she would probably understand, but she and her husband live near Brighton, where they met at university. She was due to bring their new baby home for his first visit next month.

"Can I tell Jen, or would you like to tell her yourself, Colin?" Lana teased lightly, not needing to remind everyone of Colin's youthful crush on her older sister. Ailsa mocked affronted jealousy before she laughed fondly with the others, nudging Colin lightly to undo any offense. "She'll be here the last week of the school term, before it gets too busy," Lana continued. "I dread to think how many bags she and Cal will bring this time, what with nappies and sterilizers and toys. They were bad enough before they had Robbie. Did I ever tell you about her getting stopped at the airport for having too many heavy Christmas presents in her suitcase? She thought she'd broken some law or was going to be charged a fortune for overweight baggage, but it turned out the security guy just wanted to know who was getting candlesticks for Christmas!"

They continued to share their news before the quiz started, Lana trying not to dominate the conversation in her excitement at seeing everyone. No one minds her chattiness, but Lana often worries that she dominates, or reveals too much of herself, or sounds like a terrible gossip. Peter usually leaves straight after the quiz, heading home to walk Todd and spend time with Lana's mother, but the others like to make the most of being out. Saturday night just wasn't complete without hearing last orders rung at the bar, the barman getting annoyed with them for lingering too long, and a quick stop for food on the way home.

Chapter 4 – Lana, Monday 2nd June

Lana gazed out of the kitchen window at the rear of her flat, eyes wandering over her neighbours' gardens while she savoured her breakfast and first cup of tea. It was a dry but grey morning, though the view was still cheerful with early flowers and birds at feeders. Her schooldays had taught her a few of their names: she recognised blue tits and a chaffinch amongst the sparrows, but she noted one she'd have to check up on at some point. Her legs ached from an ambitious run the day before, and she stretched her calves while watching an equally ambitious cat unsuccessfully sneaking up on the bird table.

It was unusual for her to be ready this early, but today she had woken keen for a fresh start. The rest of her weekend had passed pleasantly enough – a long lie, a run, and a lazy afternoon with tea, toast, and her book. She'd even summoned the energy to tidy her flat and make a supermarket run in the early evening, so she was as prepared as she could be for her working week. As prepared as you can be for forty hours of sheer tedium and snide banter, she thought, and sighed. She briefly revisited her Sunday evening, and the sudden tearfulness that had started about a sentimental romcom and somehow became about her, and every hurt she'd caused or suffered. When she had finally scrubbed her face and shut the curtains, she was exhausted and grateful for the cool pillow she pressed her cheek into. She really needed to stop overthinking. For once, she was glad she had her work at the local bank to keep her busy.

Banking may not have been what she had planned when she went to university, but her four years there had convinced her that accountancy was too stifling for her. Until she decided what else she might prefer, the routine days of being a bank officer suited her. Including the fact that it wasn't particularly challenging yet paid enough to cover her bills and simple tastes, it mostly suited her - Monday mornings aside. If only her manager wasn't so dour and critical, she might even enjoy her job. Instead, she habitually bribed herself through her workday with thoughts of her evening – what she'd eat, what she'd do, who she'd see. "Working to live" had become her motto.

Steeled, she locked up her flat and headed along to the branch, stopping at the local supermarket to pick up a packet of shortbread for her desk drawer. Low blood sugar was unpredictable, inducing either anger or depression, and her lunch break tended to be late. Perhaps she'd had time for tea and toast this morning, but she could never be bothered making packed lunches like the others did. Limp salads, boring soups and squashed sandwiches just didn't appeal, so she needed to have the energy and willpower to choose the healthier options from the local bakeries and cafes.

"Morning, Lana!", called a cheerful voice as she arrived. This morning, Lind was as immaculate as always, with a distinctly eighties trend to their hair, makeup and accessories. Lana was happy to see her friend, but unsure she wanted to chat. Lind was lively company but sometimes a little too overbearing for first thing. She forced her brightest smile and knocked out a quick "Morning, Lind!" in reply before scuttling through the staff door to the moderate privacy of her desk. Lana was fortunate to have a spot in the back office, out of sight of the public areas of the branch; being on view made her tense and she couldn't have borne that all day the way the tellers did.

It was close to lunchtime when her manager unexpectedly called her to his upstairs office. Unlike the modernised customer areas, this floor had barely been touched since the 1980s, sporting balding magnolia woodchip wallpaper, a swathe of peeling wood veneer furniture, and the smell of rejected business loan applications. He fitted in perfectly.

"Ah, Lana, come in. Sit down, don't worry. Just wanted to check in with you, just a little concern. We've noticed that you have seemed, hmm, a little unlucky with your health, hmm, quite a few sick days again so far this year."

Some days, Lana finds it simply impossible to leave the house. Depressed and exhausted, it's taxing for her to get dressed, never mind be cheerful for scores of customers who still can't work out their online banking. Certain that this would be futile to explain - and entirely unacceptable to the bank if she did – on those days she tended to call in sick with a believable excuse. She perched on one of the visitor chairs, a hot lump of resentful gall solid and ungiving in her stomach, a poisonous toad waiting to awaken come spring.

She interrupted him before he could bluster much longer and anger her further. "I have been a bit unlucky, yes. A couple of colds, and that bad stomach I had. Thankfully nothing serious or recurring!"

"And two migraines, I see. That puts you very high on the Bradford score, the HR screen is showing you as red. Try to be careful, make sure you're rested for work. Maybe not so many nights out, hmm? Maybe some vitamins might help. That's all, keep up the good work."

Flushed and resentful, Lana headed downstairs and grabbed her jacket before bolting for the exit. In the stark light of a cloudy midday, she stalked past shop fronts and familiar faces, trying to burn off the hot hard anger in her chest. She didn't go out often mid-week, didn't stay up late, nothing that would impact her performance at work. Some of the staff were always out and about and regularly came into work hungover, and she resented being bracketed with them. Breathing deeply and evenly, she tried calming and distancing herself from the discussion, and finally stopped off at her favourite takeaway bakery to pick up a bacon roll and some lentil soup. Hoping for some peace in the staffroom to focus on her treats, Lana skulked past the others in the offices and opened the door softly.

"What did you go for?" asked Lind, ensconced in their favourite seat at the table, and somehow eating toast and jam without impacting a perfectly painted pair of lips. The staffroom was starkly lit and unwelcoming, and Lana was sure this was deliberately done to discourage lingering. A kettle, toaster and microwave cluttered the small counter, the sink surrounded by used mugs, plates, and crumbs. Without waiting for an answer, Lind launched into the details of a drama-laden weekend with a new partner and his ex. Lana sat, dismayed to miss out on some peace and quiet. She slowly ate and listened and tried to school her face, but inside she had really hoped for some time to herself to break up the day. Lind's recent years had been a repetitive pattern of crises and exciting but doomed relationships, and while Lana truly felt sympathetic and wished her friend some happiness, it had become painful to watch, and she simply couldn't empathise today. Nor could she keep quiet on the subject any longer, it appeared.

"Honestly, Lind, why do you put yourself through this? When you meet someone great who really likes you, you say they're boring. But anyone with a huge list of red flags, and problems coming out their ears, and you throw yourself into it like they're the catch of the year. What is it about all the drama and tension that you enjoy? Because you know that in two weeks' time, you're going to be complaining about it and miserable but still take months to drag yourself out of the mess!"

Microseconds, and Lana knew it was a mistake. Her friend was not someone to take harsh truths well. The lifestyle Lind had chosen came at enormous personal cost, and criticism from what they called the "norm seats" was unacceptable, even from a good friend. Lana watched in horror and shame as the emotions played out on Lind's face: shock, brief hurt, a flaring of anger, then pointed frost.

"Well, aren't you in fine form today. It must be marvellous being so perfect, Lana. Screw you!"

"Lind, sorry, I... it just slipped...." But it was too late; dishes were already crashing in the sink, and the door was slowly groaning to a close. And what could Lana have said, anyway? She was sorry, but she still believed in what she had said. She briefly heard her grandmother's voice, saying "Not all truths need to be said!" and knew the wisdom in it. Lana looked down at her lunch, the little appetite she had felt now gone.

Much later, as she ate a sparse dinner, Lana pondered calling her dad to talk through the day, but she knew what his response would be. Don't fret so much. Make something better for yourself instead of being bored in that bank. Lind would be fine in time. Stop worrying so much about other people's problems and try to be happier yourself.

Lana just wished she knew what might achieve that. She felt a grim tide of self-pity starting to rise and knew she should go for a walk or a run but instead she poured herself a drink and settled into the corner of her oversized sofa. She picked up her book but couldn't concentrate on the text. She gazed aimlessly about the room, photographs and bookshelves blurring in a film of bitter tears. She hopped through TV channels listlessly, praying for a distraction. Sometimes depression closed around her as fast as a hummingbird's wings; sometimes it was a slow mudslide she just couldn't combat, and it was best to let it happen. She did.

...

Lana realised her phone was ringing, her father. "Are you okay? You sound like you've been asleep or something? You took ages to answer."

...

"I've got some bad news, Lana. It's old Brian from number 27, he passed on yesterday, his son found him this morning. Worse still, he seems to have been ill for a while and hadn't wanted to tell anyone. They're saying it probably could have been sorted if he'd spoken up, or someone had noticed. Such a shame, his poor family. I'm not sure when the funeral will be. Will you get time off? Lana? Are you okay? Have you been drinking?"

…

Selfish. Stupid. Obsessed with her own problems. Imagine feeling sorry for herself when other people had real problems.... Cruel. Nasty. Judgemental. Lind was spot on, what right did she have? Why did anyone put up with her?

…

Later, the late news was on. Lana blinked slowly at the footage from her sofa, bleary wine glass lolling to one side and emptied bottles lying haphazardly on the floor beside her. She squinted at an audience of wealthy, shiny, smug looking people in tails and tiaras, in a fancy theatre or something. They were clapping, reminding her of an episode of The Muppet Show but jarringly chicer and more expensive. Waldorf and Statler were both missing, she thought, giggling abruptly. The glossy newsreader was discussing the government's new psych testing programme, and Lana realised that she was watching footage of the doctors who had won an award for it all. An unpleasant envy kindled through her drunken haze: they must be doing something right.

She collapsed into bed, barely able to keep her eyes open, room spinning as blackness enveloped her.

Chapter 5 – Munro, Monday 2nd June

Munro Alexander was dozing comfortably when his bed started to bounce, and he woke to the happy sounds of his six-year-old son Stuart. Bleary-eyed and a little confused, he grabbed his son around the middle and hugged him to stop the commotion.

"Morning, sunshine!" he managed.

"Would it, Dad?"

"Would what, what? I was sleeping..."

"Would a friendly T-Rex be able to help protect us if the dinosaurs were here too?"

Dinosaurs were a lasting passion for Stuart, but protection was his latest obsession since his school friend's house had been burgled. Burglar alarms, handy weapons, safes and hidey-holes were frequent topics. Munro was starting to worry about how unnerved Stuart had been by it.

His son had coped so well with the death of his mother two years ago, but Munro knew well that delayed reaction was common in children so young.

"Well, firstly dinosaurs are never coming back.... Yes, yes! I know.... But if they were here with us, then I think I'd let someone else try taming a T-Rex first, to see how they got on."

"Would a cattle prod help? Mrs Meachan told us about cattle prods last week, she said they'd help us get to class quicker."

Taking a mental note to worry about Mrs Meachan's teaching techniques, Munro rose and ruffled his son's hair. It was a light toffee brown, a different shade to both his parents but the softest and shiniest hair Munro had seen. His wife, Ann, had been so proud of it that she had lightened hers to try and recreate it, but it hadn't worked well, and she'd dyed it back to her natural shade. The pair made their way downstairs, companionably bickering about the strongest and smartest dinosaurs for training purposes, and whether one should be allowed to sleep in the house. Breakfast was never a rushed affair for them as Stuart always woke early, but Munro didn't want to push bedtime out any later. He needed that evening time to catch up on admin he brought home from his work. They took their time eating and preparing for their day, happy in each other's company.

The bright grey sky still hadn't cleared by the time Munro dropped Stuart off at the school playground, so he left the sun cream in his schoolbag. He stood and admired the old stone building where Stuart's mother had also gone to school; he had heard that little had changed over the years. The frontage was still large and imposing, anachronistic carvings claiming entrances for boys versus girls. Stuart and his friends were running around in random patterns, roaring and snapping their teeth. He smiled and headed off to work, mulling over his schedule for the week. He was still working full days at the doctors' surgery, part of his contract as a partner, so relied on a childminder to collect Stuart after school and take him home for his snack and homework. He usually made it home in time for them to make dinner together, but this week he was covering the surgery's Tuesday early evening clinic. He would salve his conscience by bringing home takeaway food. This lunchtime was also the partner's meeting. These were nothing like he had expected when he bought into the partnership four years previously, when Ann was still alive and Stuart a toddler. For a caring profession, general practitioners could be very business focused.

Munro locked his consulting room door, and passed through the draughty ground floor hallway, via the cluttered reception, and up the creaking balustraded side stairs. This building had once been an impressive home but had since been cut and moulded to make way for the demands of the medical profession. The impressive central staircase had been removed to make way for a longer corridor and a patient washroom, and large reception rooms had been divvied to form four consulting rooms, a reception, and a waiting area.

As he ascended, he predicted that today would not be an easy meeting. He could hear Maria's tone rising as she firmly put an end to Mark's hopes of including his need for a personal assistant in the day's agenda. The dimly lit meeting room took up the back half of the first floor, leaving the front half of the building, with its bright bay windows and corniced ceilings, for the kitchen and the staff room. The three reception staff, nurse, and practice manager should appreciate that, Munro thought. Each meeting they had in the jaded gloom of small windows and energy saving bulbs made him more tempted to swap the arrangement.

"Munro, welcome. Haven't had a chance to catch you today, fine weekend?" Dr Maria Gillies was abrupt but kind, and a natural organiser. She also ran specialist clinics in women's health at the local hospital. It was she who had found Ann's Stage 3C ovarian cancer, when the symptoms showed up just too late. "Busy week ahead," she added, without waiting for a reply, "best crack on."

The regular agenda only took twenty minutes, and after reviewing the most concerning patient cases, they turned to any extraordinary business. Munro had considered revisiting his request to reduce his weekly sessions in his contract but knew he needed to prove himself before asking for something which would impact the other partners so much.

"Did you see we've had the system update for Bryant-Cargill come through?" asked Theresa Clark, a misleadingly attractive woman and the next most junior partner in the surgery pecking order. "The referrals are pretty standard, but there's no choice of location as all the testing has to be done through in Edinburgh. In-patient for at least two nights, apparently. The results are passed for review to the new Central Care team and added directly to the central record. Looks like the only way we'll know the results, or the treatment plan, is to check back in on our patient's record after their processing is complete. It's ridiculous."

"Let's not go there," interrupted Mark Clegg, senior

partner after 28 years at the surgery. "It's done, we no longer get a say in where records are held, and I for one am glad to have the help of the Central team, they're welcome to manage it all. Especially when we have so few admin staff to assist. How am I supposed to type up everything myself as well as care for patients?"

"Right, that's us then! Have a good afternoon, all!" Maria's disapproval was evident in the pinched lines of her mouth. It softened as she turned to Munro. "Can I borrow you for a minute?"

The others took their cue and headed to the kettle to grab fresh tea before surgery restarted for the afternoon. Munro raised an eyebrow in curiosity. "What can I help you with, Maria?"

"I was expecting you to ask about your commitments again. I'm glad you didn't, nothing has changed. We all feel for you, looking after Stuart on your own, especially after losing Ann so suddenly.... but we just can't cover your sessions between us, and decent locum GPs are like hens' teeth nowadays."

"That's okay, I do understand. I just... I worry about him all the time, and I feel so much guilt for not being there enough. It was alright before; Ann was home with him all the time... but now he gets passed from pillar to post, school to childminder. Laurie is great with him, but it's just not the same as a parent. It must affect him."

"Yes, I guess that must be hard for you. But your career will be long, and before you know it, he'll be a teenager and he won't need you around so much. I know that sounds harsh, but honestly my girls hardly know I'm there. We're all concerned with what's best for you, as well as Stuart... Yes, and us, and the surgery. Maybe if we can find another way to cover your sessions, maybe in a while. Let's keep it under review. And keep up the good work, the others are aware of your commitment to your patients, you know."

Later that evening, Munro sat at his kitchen counter, surrounded by paperwork and making notes on his laptop. Like most family doctors he knew, he used extra time in the evening to catch up with everything he needed to do outside his packed appointments schedule. The news burbled in the background quietly, Munro enjoying focusing after a busy day and a lively dinner, play and bath time with Stuart. Glancing up, he was momentarily confused by a face he knew well, entirely out of context.

"Bev!" he cried out in recognition, then jumped and glanced guiltily to the stairs, where his voice could easily have carried to where Stuart slept in his room. Hearing nothing to indicate his son had heard, Munro relaxed and smiled. He'd heard about the Nobel prize, and sent congratulations to his friends, but it was still fantastic to see people he knew being honoured in such a historic way. And now they were almost famous, their names heading the mental health overhaul planned to utilise their discoveries. So much had changed for them all since they'd attended medical school together in Edinburgh. He had enjoyed the research work he had done, and often pondered whether another path would have suited him better, but always concluded that he loved working with patients and still believed general practice was the best place for him. To be on the very forefront of research like Bev and Peter, now that would be both rewarding and stressful in such different ways to his career. Munro wondered if he would ever catch up with them again, and ruefully accepted it was unlikely.

Intrusions

remembered her dad's adage – "you can never have too many friends". Sanj was especially curious about Lind and pointed out that they would certainly have more exciting chat than Lana. ""Not done much this week!"" he scoffed. "Where's the craic in that?"

"Well, okay, if you're really interested..." Lana had meant to keep her sick day quiet but found herself sharing the whole gruesome story. "After that was fine. Wednesday and Thursday were quiet, and today we finished early because the branch is being deep cleaned over the weekend. But... Well, the end result is that I've promised I'll go to see a doctor, and I have no idea what I'll say. "Sometimes I get a bit down or maybe drink too much, so I take a sicky" doesn't seem valid use of their time."

The faces around the table were understanding, but sombre, and Lana felt a pinch of guilt for having flattened the atmosphere. "Sorry, ignore me. This is meant to be fun."

The three others exchanged looks.

"Lana..." Colin started, and stalled, looking to Ailsa for silent support. "Lan, maybe... Maybe you should talk to them about how often you feel down. We all understand, we get it, and you're fine - but maybe they could help? Didn't that bloke at school mention that counselling might help?"

"They decided it was all just hormones that caused those problems," Lana replied miserably. It wasn't a time she liked to dwell upon, when anxiety, anger and depression had first reared their cruel heads and made her temperamental and difficult in class. Worse, the tumultuous changes of mood had resulted in her girlfriends gradually turning colder towards her, until eventually she was very much a loner. Weeks on, while leaving an English class one afternoon,

Colin and Sanj had made an impromptu adoption. With their shared love of science fiction and fantasy, and the boys' easy acceptance of her moods, the three had quickly become inseparable.

"I still say he was an idiot. He told my parents I lacked ambition!" Colin also had some grudges to bear, although his had driven him to succeed.

"What about that new testing they're doing?" Ailsa asked. Despite being newer to the group of friends, she had seen for herself how Lana could tear herself up over so little. "They're looking for early adopters, it said on the news. They do health checks and brain scans or something, and counselling, and then they can tell you where you might need help. It might be cool. You might meet a doctor, the guy in charge was quite..." She tailed off as Colin raised an eyebrow. "...convincing," she concluded firmly.

"Good save," Lana laughed. "Ugh, I'll see. Thanks, guys. But I'm not sure volunteering to be prodded and poked and re-programmed is such a good idea. It's all a bit too Frankenstein for me."

And with that, they moved on to discuss the latest adaptation of the classic tale, and whether it had been ruined, reimagined or honoured. No one agreed, but that was part of the fun.

needs more than his own career. He would reconsider it after he received her results.

Chapter 9 – Friday 13ᵗʰ June

Lana and Lind burst from the bank doors like children escaping into their summer holidays, giggling and shoving. "I can't believe you just said that!" Lana wheezed. "I nearly ended myself trying not to laugh. Who knows what they think we're up to now?"

Just as the branch closed to customers, Lind has asked Lana how much time she needed, and what she would like Lind to bring that evening. Ears had pricked terrier-like throughout the office, fear of missing out spreading virally. It was a time of day when everyone should have been at their busiest, balancing cash and closing down systems, but most still found the time to stop and listen. When Lana had asked Lind just to bring the outfits, interest had turned intrusive.

"What are you two up to?" demanded the head teller.

"Games night!" they had chorused, their giggling making it appear far less innocent than it was. "We're dressing up for games night, Cluedo characters," Lana had elaborated. "Lind is Miss Scarlett, obviously."

"And Lana is borrowing some of gran's things to be Mrs Peacock!"

That explanation had largely calmed the curious, until the moment they were leaving. Lind had deliberately projected, "I can't wait to see what you can do with those feathers when it comes to the poker later, Lana!" Outside, Lind giggled. "I honestly think I heard one of them get whiplash." They hurried off to prepare, agreeing to meet at Lana's flat in an hour's time.

Later, they were decorating Lana's lounge, getting ready for the others to arrive. Printed posters of game boards adorned the walls, snacks were scattered in bowls, and spare seats had been pulled around the large coffee table, unusually blocking the view of the TV which sat in the south-west corner to avoid the evening sun. Lind had supplied the playlist, announcing Lana's taste in music to be too serious for any fun occasion. The oven was warming for hot snacks later, the fridge was full of drinks, and they were both ready in their costumes.

"So, who's all coming? Tell me again," Lind prompted.

Lana smiled. "Sanj: single, book and comics nerd, still lives with his parents, been working as a postman because he hated social work after uni. Colin: lives with Ailsa, IT type, loves sci-fi. Ailsa: Colin's girlfriend, really lovely, she's a school librarian, loves fashion and celebs but keeps that quiet most of the time - into her books, too, obviously. My dad, Peter, you met him before when we were having lunch in the Riverboat that time, remember? My mum won't come - she wouldn't normally anyway, but today she really is busy sorting the house out for some friends visiting tomorrow morning. And then us. You sure you don't want to ask Kenny?"

"Nah. Thanks, but it's not his thing and I'm not so sure about him meeting everyone just yet. Not that you were right about him being a mistake! Well, I'm not totally sure about that, but I'm still waiting to see. There are only so many nights I can sit and talk over his old relationships, I'm no counsellor!" Lind laughed it off, but Lana could see it was an unhappy thought.

"He might snap out of it," she offered. It was the best she had.

"I hope so," Lind sighed. "I put so much effort into relationships, and then it's wasted every time. For me... I don't know, it's just not as simple as going for dinner, or a few drinks or a walk, and getting to know each other gradually. People see all this," gesturing, "...and assume so much. It takes a lot of time and work to adjust their expectations sometimes."

Lana had never considered it that way. If pushed, she would have thought someone attracted to Lind must surely be open-minded and therefore not a problem. Perhaps any preconceptions about Lind's character were equally unfair and difficult to deal with, whether coming from bigotry or admiration. Everyone made some assumptions about the people they met, but maybe more extravagant characters suffered more presumption. Watching her friend shrug off their thoughts and move to drape domino bunting across the fireplace, she appreciated Lind all the more.

As guests started arriving, they cooed over each other's outfits, with Peter stealing the prize as the epitome of Colonel Mustard. Lana watched Lind every so often, seeing a quieter and more uncertain aspect to her friend than she was accustomed to.

They played Cluedo first, in honour of their outfits, but after a few games they moved on to tag team Jenga, an early evening favourite for its ice-breaking commotion and banter. For the last few turns, Lana had one eye on the kitchen, not wanting to burn the party food she'd assembled; she had made some effort rather than buying in. Last night she had prepared devilled eggs, leek and cheese tarts and sausage rolls, and tonight she had quickly assembled salads, rice paper prawns and chilli-filled mini tortilla cups. The kitchen was redolent with the aroma of pastry and cheese. Dips and salads, napkins and crockery, adorned the pastel-painted vintage sideboard. She moved the hot food over to serving platters on the dining table and hollered through for the others.

"Ah, Lana, this looks a triumph as always!" Her dad loved rich food, belying his stick thin frame. He grabbed some of his favourites, looking pleased she had made them. The others were topping up drinks first, while arguing over the team wins and how they affected the score count so far.

Lana quickly grabbed the shabbiest examples of each appetiser, leaving the platters a little emptier but tidier. She was especially pleased with the prawns, rich with garlic and perfectly cooked in crispy jackets. Whenever her local takeaway delivered them, they had gone soggy in their plastic tubs during the journey. The chilli cups were a little unwieldy to handle, but no one seemed to mind. For a time, they simply ate, and the quiet reflected the quality of the fare.

"I might just take some of this home for your mum and leave you young ones to it," Peter suggested, looking to Lana to check her reaction while already grabbing containers from a drawer.

"Of course, Dad," she replied, "Take as much as you want while it's still fresh. There are always things in the freezer if we get hungry again later. Tell Mum we missed her."

"Yes, yes, course." He bagged his containers and grabbed his jacket from the hooks by the front door. "Lovely seeing you again, Lind, don't let this lot cheat you out of our Jenga points!" he concluded and headed out the door to the stairs.

"Should we go and wave?" suggested Lind, not sure how to react to his seemingly sudden departure.

"Already on it!" called Sanj, who stood with Ailsa at the broad sunset-lit bay windows in the lounge. "He's been stopped by someone to talk, but he's waving the food about and stepping past them already!" Sanj laughed.

"I really like your dad, Lana," admitted Lind, "he's nothing like my parents. He was just like one of us, really, except for leaving early. Was he fine?"

"Yeah, he just likes an early night. I'm lucky with him, I know. We always got on well, while Jen and Mum were closer. Mum feels left out now Jen isn't back so often; I think he's careful not to spend too long away from her. Are you okay? You seem a bit quiet..."

Lind dismissed the worry with a flourish and flick of hair, "Fab-u-lous, darling. Now, you never mentioned how

you got on with the doctor. Who did you see, was it one of
the old grumps? Or that cold witch Clark? You didn't get
the fantastic young lumberjack with the face to die for?"
they asked, mocking a swoon.

The others were back in the room now, and all eyes
were on Lana.

"It was Dr Alexander. He was really kind; they're
running some tests to see if there might be a problem with
hormones or glands or something. He said not to worry too
much, he'll call me back when they have the results, and we
can look at options then."

"Oh, you lucky, lucky, lucky…. Literally everyone is
talking about him. Well, maybe not everyone," Lind added
sheepishly, absorbing the bemused glances around the
kitchen. "He's a widower, and some sort of genius
according to the chat, but he always wanted to work as a GP
so he turned down all sorts of opportunities. The family
moved here to live near his wife's parents, but then they
moved to Spain or somewhere after she died. Some sort of
cancer, poor thing; she left a wee kid, too, I think. You must
tell me everything!"

"Oh no!" cried Colin, "It's games night, we game.
What do we all fancy next?"

The night spun on, a mix of games and gossip. By
eleven o'clock, Sanj was at the top of the leader board, hotly
pursued by Lind. Colin and Ailsa were bickering amiably,
Colin claiming the games had suited Ailsa better and so she
wasn't truly beating him. Lana was happy to languish in last
place, laughingly claiming she was focussing on her role as
host and therefore hadn't been paying full attention. Lana
was amused to watch Sanj's alarm as Lind tried to talk him

into arm-wrestling to determine the evenings overall winner. Lind had a speculative gleam in their eye, and Lana wondered if Sanj realised he was being pursued in more ways than one.

"When does Jen arrive?" asked Ailsa. "Will we get a chance to meet up?"

"Good idea," replied Lana, "I'll talk to Mum and Dad, maybe see if they fancy a barbecue or something. They arrive next Saturday for a week and a bit. I think Jen is hoping for a bit of a rest: babies just sound exhausting. And Cal is back to working all hours, so she's juggling it all herself. She says she'd rather he took the bulk of the parental leave instead of her, but his project is about to go live, while her team can manage without her more easily. It must be a pain working for the same company, she doesn't even really get to complain about him working so much."

Ailsa glanced quickly at Colin, "Yeah, babies definitely need both parents to muck in. I'll not be rushing into it, anyway. Plenty time once we've lived a little."

Lana noticed a slight flush rising across Colins neck and realised they must have been talking about starting a family. It sounded like it was a while off, but she was still excited for them; they made a great team, and both seemed happy.

"Have you met Jen, Lind? She looks like Lana, but quieter and more of a homebody," continued Ailsa.

"More of a homebody?" repeated Lind, who was elbow-deep in the blanket box full of games. "More than this woman who cooks and bakes, and loves to clean, and gardens, and makes to-die-for furniture from castoffs, and hasn't been out to a club in three years? More homely than that?" Lind laughed, but kindly.

"Jen is just a bit quieter around people," Lana explained, "She's more like my mum – a bit reserved, I guess - whereas Dad and I would talk to anyone. And she's not much of one for socialising, or the gym, or anything. She did say she was going to a baby club, though, and had made some friends at antenatal classes. I wonder what she'll be like as a mum," she tailed off, struggling to imagine her sister singing nursery rhymes or playing with bricks.

"Hopefully fine," announced Ailsa, before being distracted by a shriek.

Jumping to their feet, Lind was flourishing Twister. "Now this is the way to end games night!"

Chapter 10 – Mon 16th June and Wed 18th June

Tensions and tempers were both high in the practice this morning: another system error had corrupted the appointment books for the next six weeks, and the clinician rotas would need to be recreated by hand. In the meantime, the usually precise schedule was imbalanced, and the partners were left at risk of doing more or less than their committed hours. It was a sore point and left the staff on tenterhooks: as a result, Munro chose to spend his break in his consultation room, reviewing and filing test results.

Methodically pursuing his task list, Munro paused in recognition; he was reading the results of the blood tests he had requested for Lana Knight. Pleased to see there was nothing of any concern, he was ready to mark the results as "Please call, no further action required", when he realised that this wasn't entirely the case. Given how concerned Lana has been, being told nothing physical was causing her problems may not be completely reassuring. He chose the option, "Please call to make further appointment", hoping this wouldn't worry her more, and moved on to his next task. He could hear raised voices in the background and didn't intend leaving his room until his next patient was ready.

Two days later, Lana returned to Room Four. Munro turned in welcome, pleased to see she looked well and healthy. Today, she wore her hair up in a sleek ponytail, and it revealed the fine bones of her face, and surprisingly delicate ears. Around her neck was a fragile gold chain with a honeybee pendant, and he fleetingly wondered if it had been a gift from someone. Nonplussed by his distraction, he gestured to a seat and thanked her for coming back in to see him.

Lana sat carefully, a little nervous about her results, and failing to avoid picturing Dr Alexander as a lumberjack. Inwardly cursing Lind, she asked, "Is there a problem with my blood test?"

"No, not at all, I didn't mean to worry you. Everything was fine, you're physically well. I just wanted to check in with you, see how you were doing and how you wanted to proceed." Munro felt flustered; had he asked her back just to see her again? No, he was following up on a valid concern for a patient, second guessing himself was unnecessary.

"Ah, umm, so I've been fine this week, I think. I had a nice weekend, and I'm looking forward to seeing my sister and her family next weekend when they come up from Sussex. As I said, the moods don't happen all the time, just every so often." Lana felt foolish for wasting the doctor's time and started to rise from her seat.

"Please, wait. You are still concerned, though?" he checked. She nodded.

"Okay," Munro continued. "Have you ever tried counselling? Perhaps cognitive behavioural therapy, which can help you manage negative thoughts and feelings as they crop up?"

Lana shook her head gently. "No. There was a counsellor at school, but they just listened and hmmed and said they thought it was my hormones. It wasn't very helpful, to be honest."

"No, I imagine not." While school counsellors had a vital role in protecting the wellbeing of the young, they were often responsible for too many children, and when overworked could fail to recognise those with less obvious issues. "I think we can certainly look into ways to help."

He glanced back at the Bryant-Cargill literature by his filing cabinet, knowing that a simpler solution might be at hand, but excited at the prospect of being involved in something new and ground-breaking.

"Another option is this," he added, grabbing a copy of the patient leaflet before he changed his mind. "It's a new form of analysis called Bryant-Cargill Factorisation. It's been in the news, have you seen any of the reports? It's a combination of tests and therapies - using MRI and other scans to monitor brain activity, along with full-body monitoring, while using a mix of video footage and talking therapies to elicit emotional and logical responses from the patient. It's incredibly clever - but used in conjunction with more traditional assessments to correlate results. It's been thoroughly trialled and makes diagnosis so much easier. It is an in-patient process, but that's just to monitor you throughout, it's not invasive or surgical in any way. You would be in hospital for roughly 2 or 3 days, working with several specialists and having your sleep monitored as well. They come up with what they call a psychological factorisation profile, showing any tendencies towards depression, mania, psychosis and such like, as well as determining the patient's emotional triggers, for example. They then work with the Central Care team to agree whatever therapies may or may not be needed. It could even help prevent some mental health issues from developing if they catch them soon enough. Each person's treatment will be completely different, of course, and they continually evaluate for any tweaks they think are needed. As it's so new, once you're referred you receive lots of info and have a video call with them, just to make sure you're happy before committing to the process. Do you think that's something you might like to consider?" Munro stopped suddenly, realising he may be pushing Lana too hard.

She was very still in her chair, holding the paper in her hand like a lifeline. "Do you think I have something serious wrong with me? One of those things? Is it going to get worse?"

"Oh no. Not at all," Munro hurriedly soothed. He had worried her, shouldn't have rushed into the discussion. "I just wondered if it might reassure you to have been through this testing and know exactly where you stand."

"I would need to think about this. I'm sorry, I am grateful, but it just seems... so much. So serious. Like it's for people who are really unwell - not me and my moods and weepiness. I... I can't say for sure how I feel. How would I find out more?" Lana looked directly into Munro's eyes, and his calm, kind features settled her.

"Why don't I arrange for you to get the extra information? Then you can organise the video call if you want to know more. You can stop the process at any point if you wish."

"Thank you, I really appreciate that Dr Alexander. Will I have to come back here, or will they get in touch?"

"They'll get in touch with you directly, it's run through Central Care. Let me check we have the correct address and phone info for you, first. But feel free to make an appointment at any time if you want to discuss it further." Munro found himself wishing she would. He made the referral there and then, the system completing most of the form automatically with details from Lana's record. When asked for a reason for the referral, Munro summarised Lana's concerns and left the option for "patient has previously been referred for mental health therapy" unchecked.

"That's done then. You should hear from them shortly. Please, don't worry. Think of this as a health check, it's more to put your mind at rest than anything else."

"Yes, yes I see that. It would be nice to know everything was okay. Thanks." Turning, she stopped before the door. "No new dino pics this week, I see?" she added with a smile.

"No, he's busy modelling a dinosaur village from Lego," Munro explained. "I haven't been able to hoover that room all week."

"Ah, it's good he has such an active imagination. A lot of kids would just want to watch TV or sit on devices all day; he sounds great. Well, I'd better get back to the bank.

Have a good day."

Munro watched the door close behind her, and wondered if he had done the wrong thing, or possibly just the right thing for the wrong reasons.

The rest of the workday passed uneventfully, a rare occurrence for a busy family doctor. Munro was last to leave, locking up the surgery for the night and feeling buoyed by the prospect of a fun evening with Stuart. Tonight, they were making homemade pizzas; Stuart loved kneading the dough while the tomato sauce simmered. Munro had left money so that he and Laurie could stop off at the local delicatessen and choose toppings, another favourite treat. The staff were now used to the boy pondering and picking meats and cheeses and olives; his first visit with Munro had caused quite a stir. Not everything he picked was a success, but Munro considered that a small price to pay for encouraging his son to be more adventurous with his food. As he walked through the quieter back streets towards home, he smiled and lengthened his stride.

"Dad! Dad, I've made a Spinosaurus pool, come and see!"

Munro swung the door shut behind him and dropped his work bag onto the monk's bench in the hall. "Just coming!" he called, smiling a welcome at Laurie as she appeared in the kitchen doorway. Tall and spare, the former schoolteacher was a friend of Ann's family and an adoptive aunt to Stuart.

"He's been desperate to show you his progress," she added. "He had an apple and some milk when we got in but didn't want anything else in case he accidentally filled his pizza tummy," she laughed. "Do you mind if I head off straight away? I have the girls coming around tonight." Munro knew that the girls were all retired Girl Guide leaders, and that Laurie liked to have everything ready for their arrival.

"Of course! Do you want a lift over tonight, save you some time?" he offered.

"No, thanks, but I'm mostly organised and it's such a nice night for a walk. I'll have plenty time. You two have a good evening! Bye, Stuart!" With that, she headed out the door, double-checking she had her keys in her pocket for the next afternoon.

The Spinosaurus pool was impressive; Stuart had dismantled a number of other builds to source enough blue and green bricks to make it. With a viewing platform full of spectator figures, and a central island covered in small trees, Munro knew it must have taken all his time since getting home.

"This is pretty cool, mate!" he exclaimed. "Did you skip school this afternoon to build this? I can't believe the detail, look at this fish pattern in the bottom!" Stuart loved nothing more than praise, especially when it came to a build.

"I'm going to put another platform over here," he replied, "so the keepers can feed him and teach him tricks like they do with the penguins and seals at the zoo!"

"Sounds great," Munro agreed, "but how about we make tea first? I'm starving. Then we can maybe do a bit more together before bath time? What did you and Laurie pick up from the deli?"

Chattering happily, they moved into the kitchen, where Laurie had laid out scales and utensils and ingredients, and the matching aprons she had gifted them for Christmas. For a time, Munro put any other concerns behind him, and just enjoyed making a mess with his son.

Once he had tucked Stuart into bed, Munro returned to the kitchen to finish tidying. He was lucky with Stuart, who enjoyed doing everything with his father, even cleaning - but he was still too young and too small to do a thorough job. Munro habitually returned to finish up afterwards; tomorrow morning he would comment on what a good job they had done, how the kitchen was gleaming in the sun. He loved to see the pride lighting Stuarts face. As he polished the work surface, his phone rang.

"Bev! What a surprise! Congratulations again on your award, I saw you and Peter on the news again last night, they were talking about the testing getting started. This is so strange; I was just thinking about you today. I made a referral to the Edinburgh clinic. I'm not sure the patient is 100% on board, but..." Munro stilled, and listened intently.

"Oh! Oh, I see. No, don't worry, I don't mind you catching me at home, I often work in the evenings anyway. So, you saw my referral? Yes, that totally makes sense, you'll want to make sure everything is running the way you want, it's so early in the process, it's an important stage. Oh, now that would be fantastic. I think Ms Knight would feel reassured to be dealing with you directly, she's a little uncertain about it all. Why don't I fill you in, then you can arrange to speak to her yourself? She's very open about her concerns about her mental health, quite remarkably so. I don't think she has much to worry about but thought factorisation might put her mind at rest. At the moment, she's so worried about her moods that she's putting unnecessary pressure on herself and that will just make things worse. Yes, exactly."

Munro briefly summarised Lana's concerns, and how she had presented herself at the surgery. Although Bev had access to the medical notes, a first-hand account made those clearer, and in discussion Munro could be more forthcoming about his impressions of Lana. By the end of the conversation, Munro felt much more confident that Lana was in good hands; he had done the right thing in recommending the process to her.

Chapter 11 – Saturday 21st June

Lana's mother had been sitting at the window since mid-afternoon, unable to resist the urge to watch for Jen's arrival. The drive from Brighton would take around ten hours, so she knew they wouldn't arrive until much later, but was too excited to relax. She missed Jen immensely. The last few months had been hard, although not as difficult as when she had first left home for university. That her eldest child had gone through her first pregnancy and birth without her help was exasperating, and she meant to make up for it now. The spare room had been prepared the week before, a pile of new toys and clothes awaited Robbie, and Peter had cleaned the house from top to bottom today. Todd's dark hair and damp nose and pawprints accumulated too quickly for them to have prepared any more in advance. Lana had come over to help, but now wished she was at home where she could relax. She considered suggesting a movie to distract them but decided instead to walk off both her and Todd's excess energy.

"I'm going to take Todd out for a good long walk, tire

him out so he behaves later. Do you need anything while I'm out?" she asked.

"Hang on!" her dad shouted from the kitchen. "We need a few wee things from the shops, so I'll come as far as that with you, then head back. If that's okay?"

Lana's mum sighed. "How much more food do we need, Peter?" she asked. "The fridge is full, and they've already asked for a takeaway for tonight anyway!" This had been a sore point: returning children should be desperate for their parents' homecooked food. Lana suspected Jen was trying to save her parents some effort but secretly thought she should have known better.

"I thought I'd pick up some things from the bakery, just wee treats, things for breakfast tomorrow. Nothing much, honestly," he reassured her. "And I can pick up your prescription today, save having to do it on Monday when they're here." He rapidly changed the subject before she could disagree further. "Wednesday evening looks like the best weather for having everyone over, by the way Lana. Do you think that will be okay for the others? Check and let me know. Your mum wants to make a cheesecake, so she'll need to know in advance."

Lana smiled and agreed, heading out to the hall to collect shoes and her hoody; today the onshore wind was cool. Todd wagged and bounded excitedly at her feet, knowing the signs. His tail whap-whapped against the doorframe.

"Have you got bags?" called her mother, always a worrier. "There's a pile in the drawer there!"

Father and daughter headed out into the bright

afternoon, glad to be done with chores for the day and looking forward to the evening ahead. The fresh breeze from the firth was cleansing, and for a while they simply walked contentedly towards the town centre. As the houses and gardens gave way to flats and businesses, the pavement became more crowded, early holidaymakers joining the locals as they busied back and forth. Roadside flower planters were in bloom, brightening the streets and frustrating drivers who had lost parking spaces to accommodate them.

"Did I tell you I'd been to see the doctor, Dad?" Lana finally braved.

"No, what's wrong? Are you not well?" Peter stopped and grabbed her shoulder, concern rising in his eyes.

"No, I'm fine really. I'm thinking of doing that new psych testing thing, though, see if they can help get to the bottom of these bad moods I get. I'm tired of it affecting me and everyone else, you know?" Lana shrugged disconsolately.

Peter kept his hand in place as she spoke and squeezed her arm gently before letting go. "Lana, you're fine. No one sensible minds that you sometimes get a bit teary or down, and it doesn't affect anyone else at all. You're just a very bright, very emotional person. And there's plus sides to that, too, like everything. Everyone loves you just the way you are, you don't want doctors meddling with you, giving you pills that make you some featureless zombie plodding through your day without caring about anything."

Lana startled at the strength of feeling her dad was voicing and was touched by his support. "It's okay, Dad, I'm just going to speak to them. I wouldn't agree to anything that affected me too badly like that. It's just a chat."

Peter still looked sceptical but had already said more than he had intended. He didn't want to pressure his daughter out of something she believed in, especially if she was feeling vulnerable. "Aye, true. I still think you're fine as you are, though. "To see oursels as ithers see us!" and a' that!" he quoted. "Burns knew! The only people that have ever complained about you are the idiot at the bank and that lad who couldn't cope with you being smarter than him," he concluded forcefully. Since Lana separated from her ex-boyfriend, Peter had never referred to him by name, preferring to write him out of their family history. In betraying Lana, he had betrayed them all.

A large family group ambled towards them, happily absorbed children eating ice creams from the local gelateria. Lana tightened Todd's lead as he started to pull towards them, then stopped off to one side and commanded him to sit.

"He's definitely getting better," she reassured her dad, as she scratched his ears, the passing parents smiling gratefully at her. "He hardly pulls at all now unless there's food coming his way."

"Hmm, I guess. I doubt I'll ever be able to walk him off a lead, though. Well, except for the beach and up the hills, maybe." He looked critically towards the busier streets. "It looks like the town is crammed with tourists today, you're as well heading off while I go and get the shopping. Be back by 5, they could arrive any time from then on, and your mum will be beside herself."

Lana paused briefly at the next junction after saying their goodbyes, debating whether to turn towards the beach or head up the hill. Hoping that the beach and riverside would be less busy later in the afternoon, she turned away uphill and headed off into quiet residential streets, calculating a rough route that should keep them walking for the right amount of time. Todd appreciated the quicker pace Lana set as they headed out of town, walking tidily to heel and looking rather pleased with himself and the admiring glances he garnered.

Ninety minutes or so later, they approached the town centre once more - this time from the far side from home, with its sandy beach and broad esplanade. Lana was glad some friendly locals had left water bowls at their gates; she had forgotten to bring anything for Todd to drink and the afternoon had been hotter than she expected. Lana herself was thirsty and keen to get home. They took an easier pace along the esplanade and past the castle and small harbour, watching children and their parents fishing and crabbing off the pier. A child in a sundress shrieked as her catch raised its sunburned claws defiantly. Families and couples ate ice cream and fish and chips, benches and bins all full to capacity. Lana didn't mind the crowds, and Todd was tired enough to restrain himself as they wound their way past the heady aromas and scraps on the pavements. They met a few friendly faces, but Lana didn't stop to chat for long: Jen would be home soon.

After the initial maelstrom of greetings and happy tears, Lana busied herself helping Cal bring the family's belongings in from their car. "Changed to a larger model, then?" she laughed, as they emptied the cavernous boot of the last few things. Lana spotted a jettisoned dummy and reached under the seat to retrieve it. The car was surprisingly pristine, and Lana wondered when Cal found the time to clean it.

"We had to, even just taking the pram out with us takes up so much space. It's such a short while that we need it before Robbie can fit into a much smaller buggy, but what can we do? Go against all the safety advice for newborns? Anyway, the extra room was certainly useful for this trip! Although Jen still spent the drive worrying about what we might have forgotten." Cal glanced back at the house, some mix of concern and frustration marring his usually open face.

"Ah, if you've forgotten anything, we can always pick up a replacement. Did you really bring all the nappies for a week? You know we have babies here too, right?" she joked, before realising she'd gone too far. "No, don't worry, I know what Jen's like for wanting to be organised. And she does hate spending any of her holiday time doing chores like shopping."

As the family settled into the house, Lana watched Jen with little Robbie. He was seven months old now, a large baby with strong lungs and clenched fists. He had slept for a lot of their journey, and now was hungry and feisty. Lana and her mother had both had a cuddle with him when they first arrived, but now Jen held him protectively, clearly torn between wanting to soothe him herself and the need to get him something to eat.

"We should have visited before we started weaning," she rued. "It would have been easier."

"Now, don't worry, pet," Peter stopped her. "We've got a highchair for your stay, and we've got proper baby plates and cutlery, and we've got a whole choice of things for him. Let's take him through and see what he fancies. What is he eating now?"

As Jen detailed the latest guidance on weaning, Lana spotted a wince crossing her mother's face. She had heard her decry the rigour Jen was showing when it came to sticking to the latest baby rules, "She's just making it all harder for herself, poor girl." Lana knew better than to intervene.

Robbie settled happily into the highchair with some cucumber sticks while Peter quickly scrambled an egg. "Unsalted butter!" he announced proudly. "Tastes awful if you ask me, but if Robbie likes it that's all that matters!" He blew on the egg lightly, hoping it would cool before Robbie bored of the veggies. "Does he like a little cheese?"

Lana could never quite believe the mess and fuss babies created. Here were four adults, all focused entirely on one child eating, she mused. Eggs, cheese and peeled cucumber slices would have scattered the floor if it hadn't been for Todd's attentions; he had only once raised his head to the table and wouldn't risk all the adults reproving him again. Robbie clearly adored the attention, though, giggling and smearing yogurt across his face with his spoon. Feeling a throb of guilt for being so detached, she glanced at her sister. The worried frown had never left her, despite the worst of mealtime being over, and Robbie clearly so happy.

"Jen, you must hardly find time to eat yourself?" she tested.

Jen shrugged it off. "I just make sure Robbie has eaten first and is happy, then we can make our own meals," she explained. "There's plenty time to start proper family mealtimes once he's older, and we still prefer to eat later on once Cal is home." Jen glanced at Cal, who was checking something on his phone, a slow flush spreading across his neck. "He goes away to bed at seven, so sometimes we eat after that."

"Oh! He's not away to bed so early tonight, his first night at Granny's!" exclaimed Lana's mother. "He'll be wide awake after sleeping in the car anyway." Lana thought Jen might prefer some time to herself, but kept quiet; she knew little about parenting, and her older sister had always been somewhat of a conundrum to her. She rarely disagreed with their mother and said nothing now.

After dinner, the two sisters were clearing the kitchen while their parents bathed Robbie. Splashing and giggling gurgled down the hall, and they shared a smile. "The bathroom will be awash," Lana surmised.

"He loves his bath time. We're lucky, bath and his bottle and off he goes to sleep. Most mornings he doesn't wake us until after 6, too. Some of my friend's babies are up all night, but he only fusses if he's unwell. He might be a bit harder work during the day if he's hungry or teething, but at least we get a decent sleep most nights. Those early weeks were horrific."

"How are you getting on with it? I mean, not Robbie, but you. Are you enjoying being at home with him all day?" Lana asked. There was a new brittle tension about her sister, which she'd attributed to tiredness until now. They had discussed Jen's reservations while she was expecting, but Lana had naively thought motherhood came naturally.

Jen dropped the cloth she'd been rinsing and wringing over the tap, and relaxed her arms and shoulders, releasing a long low breath. She stared hard into the garden, then winced. "It's hard, Lana. I didn't expect it to be so hard. I'm tired all the time, and I never feel clean or fresh. I have people I see, but every conversation is about teething, or weaning, or how tired we all are, or controlled bloody crying for god's sake. It's miserable, draining. I do get a break, when he's sleeping, but it's never when I need it. And I get so cranky because of it. I don't get to do anything just for me. I know that sounds selfish, but I'd love to just sleep until I woke one day, and shower and look nice, and it doesn't need to be anything special, maybe just go shopping. Carry a handbag instead of a changing bag," she laughed ruefully before sobering. "I shouldn't complain, I'm lucky to be able to take time off with him, and we have it a lot easier than some people. But knowing that just makes it worse, because I feel like I can't even complain."

Lana was horrified to see tears welling in her sister's eyes; Jen rarely cried. "Would you like to do all that while you're here? We could look after Robbie one day if you show us everything. You could have a soak in the bath and do your hair, you and Cal could go out for a bit? We would love to help, and you're not being selfish at all, a little time to yourself isn't much to ask."

But Jen shook her head. "No, Cal wouldn't like that. He thinks a baby's place is with his parents." Now Jen had a bitter twist to her eyes and mouth. "Fine for him, he only sees him for an hour or two a day most days. No, thanks. I do appreciate it, but best not. If I upset his routine, I'd kick myself."

"Whose routine, Robbie's or Cal's?" Lana wasn't quite joking; she didn't like what she was hearing or how her sister had changed.

"Don't start, Lana, you have no idea what it's like!" her sister snapped back. Jen's eyes were sharp and wide; Lana knew better than to say any more. She raised her hands in mock surrender and turned to stack the leftovers into the fridge. Jen would talk more when she was ready, most likely to their mother.

Chapter 12 – Lana, Tuesday 1st July

The train clattered and clanked its way over the rail bridge and into the Fife countryside, stopping at nearly every town to collect sleepy-eyed commuters. Fields and low wooded hills flashed past, reminding Lana of summer holidays spent in caravans and on farms. She sipped her peppermint tea - only just cool enough to drink twenty minutes after she bought it - and snapped a chocolate finger with a smile. Lind had pulled them from a bag with a flourish, claiming them the breakfast of kings.

"Thanks again for inviting me the other week, Lana," Lind reiterated. "It was so nice to meet your sister and her family, and your dad's barbecue was amazing."

Peter had pulled out all the stops for the occasion. The evening was glorious, the sun still hot in the west facing garden. Groups of tables and chairs were scattered across the large patio behind the kitchen, and bunting hung from the pergola which provided some shade on the hottest days. Fairy lights decked the shrubberies further down the garden, but they wouldn't be noticed until after ten o'clock; at this time of year the evenings were long. The barbecue sat off to one side, near the kitchen. There, Peter had held court, grilling marinated chicken, burgers, sea bass and langoustines. Salads and breads had thronged a side table, and drinks were cooled in an old, galvanised washtub filled with ice.

"I hadn't expected your dad to be such a good cook," Lind confessed from the seat across the table. "That chicken was amazing with the caesar salad."

Lana laughed. "Yeah, my dad loves to cook, and it keeps him busy. I'm glad you enjoyed it; it's not often we get everyone together like that. Jen said she had a great time, too. She loved your boots!" Lind had worn beautifully embroidered cowboy boots, and had threatened Peter with line dancing classes. "Thanks again for offering to come with me today," she added. "I'm still not sure about all this. Dr Cargill seems really nice, but my nerves are giving me hell."

"Ah, I was due a visit to some decent shops anyway, it's no bother. I'll keep you company until they admit you, then have a fantastic day misbehaving on my credit card," Lind confided. "Will you be okay?"

"Yeah, it should be fine. It all sounds quite interesting, really. It just feels like I'm going to be revealing everything about myself to total strangers. I know it will be okay, but... I don't know, it's just hard to tell how it will all go."

Lind nodded sympathetically. "Just think about what you'll treat yourself to afterwards, that's what I would do. Plan a shopping trip, or a nice meal, or even just a huge bag of crisps and a cider for the train home," they laughed. "We could go into town at the weekend, trawl the posh makeup counters and choose overpriced lipsticks or something. I know it sounds frivolous and materialistic and everything, but just focus on good things, instead of worrying. If you can't change it, there's no point fretting over it."

"Lind, you're remarkably wise sometimes, you know that. I'm not taking the mick, I mean it. Thanks." Lana smiled at her friend, pleased she'd accepted the offer of company on her journey this morning. "And let's do that at the weekend. We could have lunch and cocktails and go shopping for nonsense. It'll be nice to let our hair down a bit."

Lana's phone rang just as they were crossing the Forth, the rust diagonals of the bridge splicing the sunlight as they passed through. Lind watched on in interest as Lana held her end of the conversation, asking who it was as soon as it concluded.

A light blush washed Lana's cheeks as she answered, "It was Dr Alexander. He knew it was my appointment today and wanted to wish me well."

"Well! That was very... nice of him," Lind chose their words carefully. "Not many doctors would do that." After a pause, they dismissed their caution. "If you end up pulling a gorgeous doctor when I'm still with Kenny and his ex-obsession, I'll be well and truly jealous."

Lana snatched the opportunity to change the subject. "Oh no, he's not still involved in all that, is he? I thought things were settling down?" she asked. Lind sighed and gazed out across rooftops as they confessed how little was well in the relationship. Lana could see that Lind was unhappy but knew they would have to reach their own conclusions. Mostly, she was glad to have swerved Lind's interest in Munro's call.

As the train pulled into Waverley station, they gathered bags, and crumpled their rubbish ready for the waiting bins. Tannoy echoed in the high arched ceilings, as pigeons fluttered between studded and rusty beams, and crowds commingled on concourses. They would grab a taxi and head to the hospital where Dr Cargill had her clinic: Lana was meeting her there at ten and they had plenty time. She was once again thankful Lind was coming all the way to the clinic; over the next two and a half days, she would see only strangers - an uncomfortable thought. She wondered how anyone could cope in hospital for any longer than that and resolved to visit more often if someone she knew was admitted.

Lind cheerfully took their leave as they exited the taxi, and soon Lana was sitting in a reception waiting room, glad she had brought her e-reader with her. Briefly losing herself in another world full of familiar characters, her tension eased. By the time Dr Cargill arrived to welcome her, she was looking forward to getting the process underway; sooner started, sooner finished, as her grandmother used to say.

"Ms Knight, welcome! Please, call me Bev, I'm not one for formalities. Let's head through and we can get you settled before you meet everyone, and we can start the process."

Ushering her through doors and corridors, Bev Cargill wasn't what Lana had expected. She had an open face, dainty and free of makeup, and a warm smile which lingered long after it had formed. A petite woman, she was dressed in cropped, loose jeans and a pair of walking sandals under a white coat thronged with pens. Her hair was pulled up into a clip, and delicate silver leaf earrings dangled from her ears. Lana liked everything she wore and curiously found herself trusting Dr Cargill a little more in consequence.

As they moved along a walkway and through secure double doors into an older, adjoining building, Lana glimpsed many white coats but few patients. "How many people do you see here each day?" she asked, intrigued to know with whom she would be sharing Bev's time.

"Only one patient at a time, at the moment," Bev surprised Lana. "We're being very careful with both the process and the external stimuli patients experience during it. It's still quite early days, and we're all keen to get it just right for you."

Lana found this more than a little overwhelming, rather than reassuring, but kept her thoughts to herself. She just hoped she wouldn't let anyone down. They entered a room unlike the others, windowless and holding a wardrobe, some tub chairs and a coffee table, a hospital bed and monitors, and a further door into an en-suite shower room. A TV furnished one wall, but the others were bare of decoration.

"So, this will be your home for the next two nights. I need to let you know that there's a camera in this room, to help monitor your sleep, but none in the bathroom, obviously," Bev explained. "Hopefully it will be comfortable. Here you'll have sessions with the therapists, some to talk over how you're doing here and some to get the background info we'll need for the analysis. You can pop your clothes into the wardrobe and make yourself at home. There's bottled water in the bedside table, but no stimulants while you're here, please. Have you had any alcohol or caffeine this week?"

Lana shook her head and put her overnight bag in the wardrobe; nothing she had brought would wrinkle. "When do we get started?" she asked.

Bev smiled. "One of my colleagues will be with us shortly," she replied. "We'll start with a discussion about what brings you here and your life and upbringing, get to know you a little. Then we'll do some brain scans using MRI and our new technologies, as a baseline. You're not claustrophobic, are you? No? Good. It's nothing to worry about, but some people can be affected slightly by such large machinery. After lunch we'll have a more in-depth discussion about some of your issues, and any personal trauma you feel has affected you. We'll also do some further scans, this time as we talk over some of your experiences. After that we'll debrief and run through the plan for tomorrow, then leave you to eat, relax and rest. I won't be present for all the testing, I'm afraid, but I'll be in and out during the process. Feel free to ask any questions and raise any doubts you may have. It's important that you are comfortable with what we're doing, so we can focus on the testing. But first we need to run through the paperwork and get your formal agreement to complete the analysis and any further treatment we recommend."

Lana nodded throughout, pleased to have some clarity of the day ahead but unsure what the scans would really entail. She thought back to Lind's advice and focused on the immediate; this would soon be over and there was little point in worrying. She signed the paperwork where it was marked for her and grabbed a bottle of water before the first session kicked off.

As the morning progressed, Lana relaxed more. The doctors were neither shocked nor dismayed as she described her moods, and why they troubled her so much. They lingered over her family relationships, interested in the closeness between Lana and her father, and Jen and their mother, and asking whether the girls were competitive for their parents' affections. They quizzed Lana over her mother's illness and how it had affected the family as the girls matured and headed off to university. They discussed past relationships and how they had been affected by Lana's moods, as well as how they had ended. Everything was recorded, on paper and electronically, as the doctors worked to better understand her.

The group decamped to another room for the baseline brain scans to be taken. The equipment dominated the room, and Bev explained its workings. "Bizarrely, this was one of the most difficult hurdles in our work, Lana. MRI scanners, metal and devices don't mix, but we wanted to be able to do our scans while patients viewed video. We also needed to add our new scanning technology into the mix so they could all work concurrently. We had to go back to square one and design a new multi-scanner which could incorporate it all. I must admit, I don't know everything about how they achieved it, but the design is now being picked up more widely because video gifts patients a good distraction from an otherwise lengthy and noisy process. Sound and one-way communication from the doctors comes through these special headphones. Don't worry, we'll hear you fine if you just speak loudly. However, unless answering questions, try to wait to talk after the scan has completed." The doctors took their position behind a screen at the rear, and the process began. This time, there was no video to watch, and Lana lay still, astonished by the noise the machine generated, as one of the doctors praised her patience and advised how much longer they would be. When it completed, she was glad to be free of the machine, and happy to take a break.

Lunch was a choice of sandwich and fruit in a little self-serve canteen; one of the doctors dropped her off and arranged to collect her again in half an hour. As part of the process, Lana had agreed to make no phone calls or use any social media. She could read; the doctors took note of the book title and asked her to let them know the chapters she had covered by the end of each day. She was happy to do so, considering it small payment for the benefit of passing time more easily. The scans had proven more mundane than she expected but she wasn't looking forward to repeating them.

The afternoon instilled a sense of déjà vu in Lana, as many of the previous activities were repeated. They reviewed the discussions of the morning, probing with further questions and focusing more on how Lana felt about some of her experiences. Some of the questions were more intrusive, too. Did she feel glad that it was her mother who became unwell rather than her father? Had she felt envious of Jennifer when she headed to university and left her behind? Did she ever use her relationship with her father to make her mother angry or jealous? Lana answered as honestly as she could and kept her sharp retorts to herself; by the end of the session, she was struggling with a strong dislike of the doctors present. It took the warmth and empathy of Dr Cargill over peppermint tea and shortbread to calm her before they returned to the multi-scanner and ran through more questions and answers while they examined her responses once more.

By the time they had finished for the day, Lana was exhausted and emotionally drained, and wanted nothing more than to grab her bag and head home. As she walked back into her stark room, her heart fell further. She had three or so hours of free time, then a nurse would hook her up to some monitors which would measure her brain activity during the night. A journal sat by her bed, to note any dreams she remembered. The doctors had advised her to detail any of her daymares there as well, although Lana suspected she was too fried for that to happen. Bev knocked gently on her door.

"How are you doing?" she asked sympathetically. "I know this process is tough, we did the tests ourselves as part of our trials. It's a lot to reveal, and a lot to bear."

Bev looked genuinely concerned for her, Lana thought. She must look as wan as she felt. "I'm okay, I think. I hope I wasn't rude to any of the doctors... some of the questions were a bit of a shocker."

"No, no, don't worry about them, trust me. It's their job to provoke you; from what I heard and saw you handled it remarkably gracefully. We need to get you something to eat. Would you like some hot food? We can get anything you like from one of the local takeaways. Would you like some company, or would you prefer some peace?"

Bev's face gave nothing away as to whether she would prefer to stay, and Lana hoped she wouldn't mind either way. "If it's okay with you, I'd love to just eat alone. I know it seems rude, but I'm used to time to myself every day, and it's been a bit hectic." Watching Bev closely, she was glad to see the doctor smile understandingly. "Umm. Is there anything you'd recommend for dinner? I'm so washed out I don't really mind what I have."

Bev laughed, "Well, my favourite is the prawn biryani from the Indian just up the road. They even send extra sauce if you ask for it. But we can get you pretty much anything you like."

"No, that sounds wonderful," Lana stopped her as her stomach rumbled loudly. "I really appreciate it. I expected more hospital-type food," she concluded.

"Well, that's the benefit of being such a new service," Bev explained. "They haven't set us up for in-patients yet. I'll let the night staff know what to get for you. Is there anything else you need? There's decaf tea of various sorts as well as the water, if you'd like?" When Lana declined, she took her leave, mentioning that she'd be back in the morning. "The overnight staff are on hand if you need anything and will wake you in the morning. I'll bring in some breakfast with me about eight. Have a good night's rest, Lana."

Abruptly alone, Lana fetched her toiletries from her bag into the bathroom and washed her hands and face. Feeling slightly refreshed, she sat down with some water and her book, and tried not to be impatient for her meal. When it arrived, with crockery and cutlery, it was just as delicious as she'd hoped. The room would smell of spices in the morning, but Lana couldn't bring herself to care as she ate perfect fragrant rice and juicy spiced prawns. The nurse cleared her things a little later, then advised Lana to give her a shout once she was ready for bed. She seemed welcoming, but Lana was beyond pleasantries and simply nodded. She pondered the day. It had felt so much longer than 14 hours since she and Lind had boarded the train. She had disclosed and clarified a lifetime of emotion today, and her real life seemed long ago and far away. She felt lonely, not for the first time, and bit back a rush of homesickness. Only another day and night to go, and she would be done with this, thankfully. She returned to her book and focused intently on the story, strictly not allowing herself to become maudlin.

Later, as she lay in bed, hooked up to monitors and positive she would never be able to relax, she realised that she had won a battle over her depression tonight. She had felt the tide rise but had refused to submit and stepped out of harm's way. With her spirits lifted, she switched off the bedside light and dropped off to sleep.

Chapter 13 – Munro, Tuesday 1st July

Munro hung up the phone, and placed it face down at the far side of his desk, flustered and unsure of the primary emotion he battled. He was embarrassed, he was ashamed; he had been excited to call Lana but now felt foolish. What was he thinking, bothering a patient at such a time? He felt a faint chill of nerves: what would happen if any of the partners found out he had called her with no good reason? What would Bev think if Lana mentioned his call to her? It had been inappropriate, especially when calling from the surgery. Face flushed, breathing rapidly, he put his head in his hands and willed his pulse to slow. It had been a simple act of kindness, that was all. Wishing a patient luck with a procedure was just showing concern, nothing more; he could explain it easily enough if he needed to. All would be well.

There was no fooling himself, though; he knew he had called because he was attracted to his patient. He would have to do the right thing and ensure she saw another doctor in future. The General Medical Council guidance was clear that a professional relationship must be maintained and not abused. Munro shook his head; his behaviour was entirely unlike him, and he would put an end to it.

At lunch, Theresa Clark settled beside Munro and assembled her salad and chicken breast with precisely four splashes of low-fat salad dressing. Munro glanced at his ham and cheddar mayo doorstop sandwich with guilt, then shrugged it off. Food should be enjoyed, he felt. If he ever struggled with his weight, he would rather increase his exercise than make food the enemy.

"I heard your Bryant-Cargill is in being tested today. Do you think there will be anything for us to do? I hope not. I still think we should be compensated for referring early cases, they're benefiting from having patients as guinea pigs." She punctuated her points by repeatedly stabbing her lettuce, and Munro began to wonder if she intended to eat any at all.

"There shouldn't be anything for us, they work directly with the Central Care mental health team," Munro avoided saying anything more about Lana, intensely wary of showing his interest.

"Good. All nonsense, in my opinion. Too much pre-emptive treatment as a result of what they think they might suffer at some point. Hah! There's no telling whether a patient would exhibit symptoms if left alone; telling them they have a problem makes it real. Frankly, I think it's a waste of meds treating people who aren't unwell, no matter what they say about the benefit of catching cases early."

Munro kept quiet; often Theresa didn't need a response but simply liked to talk. He finished his sandwich and watched her toying with her salad, wondering how happy his fellow doctor was - little she said was ever warm or cheerful, and she always left him somewhat dismayed and uncomfortable. He made his excuses and headed back to his room.

Walking home that evening, Munro took a calmer view of his day. No harm had been done, and he would take steps to make sure he wasn't in charge of Lana's treatment again. It felt good to have made the decision, to have asserted some control over the situation. He wondered again what he had hoped to achieve by calling her, and for the first time felt a punch of guilt: Ann. He hadn't felt drawn to another woman since he had met his wife, and if asked he would have emphatically stated he was still grieving her. Was this a significant milestone in his grief? Was he moving on, without recognising it? Not for the first time, Munro wished he had someone nearby to talk to, but his parents were in Glasgow and his friends had dispersed after medical school. Ann and Stuart had become his whole life; after she passed, and her family had moved away, he was left with little support. He could call his parents, but what would that gain? His father had always been distant and would judge him harshly; he always had. His mother would be kind and understanding but would never be entirely honest with him or challenge him - her love was too forgiving.

Looking back, it had always been his friends who had given the clearest of advice. He smiled, remembering it was Bev who had pushed him to invite Ann for a drink when they were first year medical students and she an experienced ward nurse. Bev had spotted how flustered he became whenever she was present for their rounds, but held off for a few weeks before asking bluntly, "So are you going to wait until you've qualified before you ask her out?" Their other friends had been oblivious, but Bev was perceptive. Munro had been certain Ann would refuse, replying, "What would someone like her think of a shabby student asking her out? She's beautiful, and brilliant, she must have a boyfriend already." But Bev had continued to ride him until he found the courage to approach her, and when Ann had married him, she had made a short speech of thanks to their guests, including acknowledging Bev for her efforts.

As his long stride brought him nearer to home, his thoughts turned to Stuart, and his trust and love and certainty that all would be well. It buoyed Munro to have Stuart's supreme faith on his side; he wouldn't let him down, whatever came to pass. He would be careful of his career, and careful of Stuart's fragile happiness. That was his biggest responsibility; he would be there for his son whatever he needed. Resolved, he entered the warm and enveloping comfort of their home and grabbed Stuart in a bear hug. Surprised, his son squealed in excitement and rubbed his jammy face on his dad's shoulder, and the best part of their day began.

Chapter 14 – Wednesday 2nd July

Lana woke to a distant clatter and took a moment to orient herself. She had rolled over in the night but thankfully the snarl of monitor wires still seemed to be in place. Rubbing her face clear of sleep, she was wishing she had asked whether she could unhook herself from the machine, when a tap at the door and a smiling face interrupted her.

"Morning!" The same nurse from last night bustled over. "Let's get you dismantled, then you can grab a shower and get dressed. You've plenty time before Dr C arrives. She called to say she's picking up bacon rolls and doughnuts for everyone and will get here around eight. Do you need anything to eat before then?"

Lana shook her head, though she was surprised to find she was hungry after eating such a large meal the night before. "No, that sounds lovely," she replied, hoping the bacon would be crisp and the roll soft. Bacon was a rare treat, she loved to eat it but disliked the smell lingering in her home so rarely made it herself.

"Cool. There you go, free at last!" the nurse quipped. "Just pop out and join us at the desk when she arrives, we all head to the canteen and start the day there with a wee chat." She wiped down and left the room with a last smile thrown over her shoulder. "See you soon!"

Lana sat up and stretched her neck. She had slept remarkably well, but still would have loved to be heading home this morning instead of the following day. Another day of tests yawned ahead of her, and a further night of monitored sleep. Resigned to her commitments, she sighed before grabbing fresh clothes, and heading to the shower room.

Breakfast was a cheerful affair, the doctors and nurses almost unrecognisable as they chatted about their lives, their faces animated. The canteen was otherwise empty, so they had pulled two tables together and piled the food in the centre. One of the nurses had brought some sachets of sauce, and Lana gratefully grabbed one for her bacon roll. The small, high windows showed the grey drizzle outside, making Lana grateful she hadn't had to travel this morning. Seagulls circled through one pane, and she was startled by nostalgia for her small flat with its expansive views of over the Firth of Tay to Fife. She sat quietly off to one side as the others congratulated one doctor on her son's first steps, quietly eating her roll and marvelling at the warm human side to these people who had seemed so daunting the day before.

"How are you feeling today, Lana?" Dr Cargill was smiling while licking doughnut glaze from her fingers. "How do you feel about today?"

Lana wiped her fingers on her napkin, honesty and nerves battling her innate manners. "Um, I'm not sure. I'm a bit worried about the tests today, to be honest. I'm not really sure what to expect."

"Well, we can help there. It's absolutely nothing to worry about, the only problem is the noise of the MRI in the multi-scanner. It's just a case of watching videos while we scan, and then a quick debrief after each to cover how you felt throughout. You'll get some free time between each session, too − it's important to take a break from the scanners. It's all a lot less intense and personal than what you experienced yesterday." She reached for the donuts and offered Lana one. "You might as well enjoy one now, they'll be gone by lunchtime," she laughed ruefully.

Lana accepted a custard-filled doughnut and sipped more tea. She wasn't sure she could enjoy any more food, although doughnuts had been a favourite since childhood. Clearly, everyone thought today would be a breeze, but they knew exactly what was scheduled, and weren't the target of the assessment. Lana's vivid imagination kept returning to the baseline test scenes in Bladerunner, her father's favourite film. The tortoise question, the replicant's eye being checked for responses. The tension. This sounded similar, and Lana feared what she might be shown; she feared how she might react and what the analysis would conclude. She poked fun at herself: at least she wouldn't be a replicant, she cried far too often.

"Honestly, Lana, it's nothing to worry about. We wouldn't show you anything too traumatic, it may even be things you've seen before," Bev added softly, head lowered and tilted so she could look Lana directly in the eye. Lana blinked twice, discarding the worst of her fears, smiled, and took a bite. The doughnut was delicious; perhaps Bev knew the sugar rush would do her good. The others were discussing someone's pet cat, and Lana turned enthusiastically to the diversion.

Later, the food lurked malevolently in Lana's stomach, mocking her earlier stoicism. Doubts thronged and nerves jangled as she was strapped into the scanner table. She'd been through the process twice yesterday, and the mechanics of it held no fear for her, but she very much wanted this whole process to be over. For the first time, she wished she had someone there with her, and was surprised to find it was her mother she craved. Her no-nonsense attitude and calm practicality would have served Lana well. "Be more Mum," Lana thought to herself. "Think of other things, this will soon be over, tonight you can finish your book and maybe have a nice takeaway again."

The sterile colourless walls and polystyrene-tiled roof gave no distraction. She flexed her shoulders against the table and was glad for the scrubs she was dressed in; hospital gowns were too exposing to be comfortable. The air felt fresh over her bare toes, and she wriggled them tentatively, picturing dipping them into a cold pool. She recalled a glorious May day spent picnicking beside the River Isla, on the land they used for the local Highland Games. It was before her mother's diagnosis and they were all there, her aunt's family and her grandparents, too. They had played games of hide and seek, rounders and dodgeball, and the children fished with nets for tiny freshwater prawns they held in glass jars to show their parents. She and Jen had run feral with their cousins, pretending they were Native American tribes hunting wild buffalo, bows and arrows made from branches and twigs and long grasses. After lunch, the sun had become so hot that they had all rested, the children dangling their feet in the ice-melt river water. Jen had suffered from sunburn that day, sweat and splashing undoing her sunblock. Lana rarely burned, and that evening she had felt sharp jealousy of the attention Jen received, aloe vera and whispered love. A nurse covered her legs and feet with a blanket and squeezed her toes in reassurance: "Not long now."

As the table retracted into the scanner, the disembodied voice of a doctor reassured her that the time would pass more quickly than she expected. The running time, he said, was approximately two hours but wouldn't seem nearly that long. Immediate, irrepressible panic spiked along Lana's back and arms; tingling electrics arcing the backs of her hands.

"Two hours? Wait, they didn't say it would take that long!" she called out.

"Don't worry, if you're not warm enough or anything, just shout. You should have had plenty fluids this morning, but if you need a comfort break, just let us know. It's best to watch this all in one go, though, so please try to make it through the film."

Stomach roiling and unexpected bubbles of anger forming low in her gut, Lana steeled herself for a difficult day. She thought back to Lind smiling and laughing on the train; they had better make good on the promised weekend day trip. The screen before her blinked, commanding her attention, and an introductory screen was briefly displayed. Lana couldn't stay still, despite the many reminders to do so: her jaw dropped open. Twentieth Century Fox? She watched, astonished, as she recognised the opening scenes of a favourite movie.

"Wh... Marley and Me?" she asked. "Seriously? I've been so worried about this!"

The doctor, alarmed, replied immediately. "Was this

not explained to you?" he asked. "Do you need to take a break?"

"No, it's fine, I just... well, I just misunderstood. Sorry. I'll stop speaking now." Feeling foolish, and a little fooled, Lana blinked and focused on the movie, determined not to skew the test results. Returning to repeat this was not an option.

Watching a movie while hooked up to multiple scanners would never become a popular fashion, but Lana was warm and comfortable enough, barring the background noise levels. It was slightly like watching TV in bed while the neighbours had their kitchen refitted, she mused. She let herself become absorbed in the characters and their lives, and time passed quickly. Soon she was coming back out of the scanner, stretching stiff limbs and laughing off her worries about the video content. She could turn this into quite the story for everyone. She was granted an hour-long break over lunch, divided equally between answering questions about how particular scenes had made her feel, and a rest for food and water.

The process was repeated twice during the afternoon and early evening, Lana amused to find herself watching first John Wick and then Cold Pursuit, a film she was not aware of but would recommend to her friends. Both were violent, predicated around loss and vengeance. She wondered about the analysis, if the team chose particular films for each patient, or if everyone watched this same selection. She worried that they had chosen such violent films for her to watch; she enjoyed them as entertainment but didn't condone violence in the real world. Would the scans reflect that; would the doctors understand that distinction?

"Lana, welcome. This will be your last debrief. Tonight, you'll have some free time, and then we will monitor your sleep again just to check for any effects from the day's testing. How are you feeling?"

Lana was back in the canteen, dressed in her own clothes and feeling exhausted but a lot less unnerved. Two doctors sat with her, hot drinks and a plate of biscuits in front of them. "Sorry for the canteen, we wanted to grab a hot drink and it's brighter here than in your room," they concluded.

"I'm fine," Lana started. "Glad to be out of the scanner, that's a lot of time to spend in it. My bones feel like a church bell!" she laughed. "Perhaps it would be better to split it over another day?" she suggested.

"Thanks," the second doctor answered without taking a note. "We'll think about that. We'd like to review how you've felt throughout the two days, if that's okay? We want to make sure you leave us tomorrow without any concerns or lingering effects, for example after some of the sessions we had yesterday discussing your past."

They spent an hour or so covering Lana's time at the clinic, Lana listening and responding, but aware she had disengaged before she arrived for this last meeting. She felt a weariness beyond anything she had experienced before: neither long days hillwalking with heavy packs nor lengthy university exams had instilled this jaded exhaustion she now felt. Nibbling on biscuits to stay her tired eyes, she failed to hide her condition.

"Lana, you look exhausted, I think we have enough.

Would you like something to eat just now, or would you like to rest first?" asked the older doctor.

"Maybe just a little rest," Lana agreed. "I'm not very with it," she smiled. She headed back to her room and lay down under the bedcovers, scratchy hospital linens tangling her hair. The room spun lightly as it did when she'd had too much wine and too little food, and a shushing sounded in her ears, sea on shore echoing the scanner's mechanical bass.

Sometime later, she was woken abruptly, one of the nurses rousing her by the arm. Startled and disoriented, she looked around wildly for a moment. "There, there. Sorry, dear, I didn't mean to frighten you. I need to get this monitor sorted, I'm afraid. Do you need the loo first?"

Stumbling, she changed and prepared for bed. "Sorry, I just conked out. I'm so tired. Oh, and I think I ate all the doctors' biscuits, will you say thank you to them?"

The nurse smiled, gently applying electrode pads and checking connections. "Don't you worry, dear, we all understand. I couldn't do it, all that noise and them expecting you to watch TV all through it. You just rest..." she stopped herself; Lana slept again.

Chapter 15 – Saturday 5th July

Saturday morning dawned grim and drizzly, mist covering the hills in the distance and small dogs wrapped in their raincoats. Lana could see her father and Todd in the distance, Peter trudging through the seaweed disconsolately while Todd chased seagulls up from the tideline. She waited to see if he would turn back towards her, but his head was down, and his peaked hood never revealed his face. The firth was a deep grey this morning, its beauty wilder and more primeval than on most July days; Lana doubted there would be many venturing out on the water today. She turned away from the window, cloth and polish in hand, and continued her chores. She usually chipped away at them during the week, but her time off work and trip to Edinburgh had thrown her routine and she wanted to get the place sorted before she went out to meet Lind. She would be able to relax and enjoy herself more if she knew her to-do list was cleared.

As she pottered here and there, wiping ring marks from her favourite paua shell coasters and clearing dust and fingerprints from surfaces, Lana was looking forward to dressing up a little and heading out, rain or no rain. They had booked a table at one of the more opulent city centre hotels for a late lunch and drinks before trawling the department store makeup counters. Lana thought she might choose a new eyeshadow, but most looked forward to helping Lind choose the more eye-catching shades they wore. Having finished her work for the day, Lana headed off to shower and dress, content.

One of Lana's favourite items of clothing was a lightweight summer coat she had picked up a few years before. Far from the ubiquitous waterproof, raincoat or waxed jacket, it was both stylishly tailored and had a practical loose hood to protect her hair on days such as these. She felt foolish if dressed inappropriately for wet weather, but also hated to ruin an outfit with a dog walking jacket. Today, she had settled on a practical combo of a pleated mid-calf satin skirt and high wedge-heeled ankle boots for the day, paired with a sequined silk top and silver jewellery. As she sat at the table they had booked, she felt she'd balanced daytime shopping and upscale lunch quite well. When Lind arrived, however, she was happily outclassed. Folding a vintage Liberty umbrella, with matching handbag perched over a wrist, Lind was wearing the most fantastic beaded black silk trouser suit, with a plunging neckline full of delicate freshwater pearl strings, and pewter spike heeled sandals.

"Oh Lind," Lana breathed, "you have outdone yourself today."

Lind mocked coy, head turned to one side and long eyelashes fluttering. "Why thank you, my dear!" they played in a deep southern states accent. "I do try!"

Giggling and rearranging coats and bags, they settled into the high-backed velvet banquette to browse the drinks menu, debating the choice of cocktails or wine while Lind's fragrance perfumed the air with spicy wooden notes. A table of ladies at the far side of the room smiled at them both and raised a glass in toast, appreciating the image of youthful and celebratory happiness they evoked. Settling on a bottle of sparkling Crémant de Limoux, they toasted the day ahead.

"So, was this one of your purchases in Edinburgh?" Lana asked, admiring the shot silk of Lind's suit.

"I picked this up in the sales last winter," Lind demurred, "it was a bargain. No, I spent Tuesday shoe shopping, my big feet were needing a pick me up! I got these, and a fantastic pair of rainbow metallic mules, and some spectacular baby pink patent trainers, you'll die of envy! I spent the whole day looking for something to replace my favourite black heels but ended up with everything but that!"

"We could have a look today if you fancy?" Lana offered, but Lind declined, announcing they were done with shoes for the week. Lana was glad, shoes were something more practical for her and watching someone else try on shoes brought on the yawns. "Cool, I'm looking forward to watching you work the counter girls," she laughed. Lind was both brazen and exquisite enough to charm the brand advisors into all sorts of freebies, demos and discounts, while Lana could never haggle for fear of offending.

Sipping their sparkling wine and enjoying the menu, Lind turned to Lana once more. "Should I ask how you got on with the docs? I didn't like to say anything in work, I wasn't sure if anyone knew what you were up to on your days off. Was it all okay?"

"Ugh. I honestly don't know how I feel about it all. It was draining, and they were so nosey about everything, and the testing was just weird, hours and hours spent in scanners. I was exhausted by the end of it - even the next day I was so tired. The train home just seemed surreal. I go back on Wednesday to talk through the results; I can't imagine what they're going to say, what on earth can you tell from observing someone watching films?" Lana explained the whole process, Lind's perfect eyebrows drawing together as they listened.

"It all sounds a bit mad to me. But if it makes you feel a bit happier with yourself, that's the main thing, I guess. I don't see why you've put yourself through all this, though. Everything you've ever mentioned to me seems perfectly normal," Lind maintained sternly.

Lana remembered her high point of the experience. "One really good thing, though: at the end of the first day... I don't know, we'd been talking about all these awful things and my mind was spinning. I was feeling so down and lost, Lind, but I managed to be strict with myself and not get upset. I just concentrated on my book until the worst of the mood had passed. It's the first time I've been able to do that, realise I was in a slump and just... choose not to give in to it. I feel like it's been a bit of a breakthrough, to be honest."

Lind marvelled at Lana; how proud she was of making progress. "I don't think you realise how smart and strong you really are, girl. You can handle whatever you need to, I've seen it. It's about time you realised it yourself." Lind squeezed Lana's forearm gently then topped up their glasses to cover the earnest emotion they both felt.

Their starters arrived, Lind having chosen a goat's cheese and roast beetroot salad, while Lana picked mixed antipasti. The food was presented beautifully, and the lavish décor and quiet gentility of their surroundings made the experience truly special. Lana smiled, quietly acknowledging that Lind had been right; this had been worth looking forward to all week. Enjoying a sociable pause between courses, they gossiped about Lind's work week, and the latest impractical sales targets being set by the bank's head office. Lind was describing multiple attempts to convince an elderly customer to move her savings from the deposit account she had held for over forty years, Lana laughing at Lind's exaggerated impressions, when their main courses arrived.

"Oh wow," said Lind, gesturing at the elegant spiral courgette tart, "now I'd never get away with ordering this with Kenny. He'd be accusing me of being pretentious."

"Really? Is he quite critical, then?" Lana was still to meet Kenny but couldn't help having reservations, given what she heard. "How are things there?"

Lind sighed, and stabbed delicate tenderstems of broccoli. "I don't think we're really suited, to be honest. He's one of those guys who likes everyone to concur with him. About everything. His idea of the perfect partner is a little mini him, I think. Things seem to have settled down with his ex, which is good, but recently he's been a bit... I don't know... squirrely? Secretive. Locking his phone when I turn to him, things like that. And to be brutal, he's not that great company unless he's really trying to impress. Not like your friends, Sanj and them; they're just nice people all the time. Kenny is either dazzling or kind of unpleasant, with no happy medium in between." Lind seemed despondent momentarily but recovered. "I'm not talking about him today, we're here to have a nice time. I can decide what to do about Mr Grumpy another time. Cheers, Lana! Here's to us! You're the boss of your moods, and I'm young and fabulous and have plenty time to find my true soul mate."

They rang glasses again, and Lana smiled, picking up on the one friend Lind had named. Raising an eyebrow, she advised. "Sanj is lovely, yes. But remember he can talk for hours and hours about the DC and Marvel universes. No one is perfect! We just need to find the people for us, who we find perfect. If Kenny isn't the right one, then someone else will be. It'll come." Lana wanted to advise her friend that being alone might be preferrable to being with the wrong person but knew that Lind hated to be single; it felt too much like defeat. Instead, she focused on her delicately scented hake and clams, and revelled in the luxury of fine food, wine and company.

Later, laden with overpackaged fripperies and giddy with their carefree afternoon, they walked together through morose Saturday afternoon shoppers. The stores would be closing shortly, and crowds were tailing each other to car parks and bus stops. "Shall we go for another drink, or call it a day?" Lind asked.

"Or we could head back towards home, dump these bags, then go out?" suggested Lana. "Although I'm taking this new lipstick with me wherever we go," she laughed. "I'm free all evening, and happy either way. Although I'm not the one carrying a week's wages worth of Chanel!"

"True, lets drop these off and grab a chance to spruce

up before we go out. We're perfect, obviously, but I could do with some spray plaster and a change of shoes. Let's head to mine. I have some rather nice bubbly in the fridge, too. Are your friends out tonight? We could meet them, share our magnificence?" Laughing, Lind changed direction towards the taxi rank. "These aren't bus compatible heels," seemed a sufficiently valid explanation as they headed off, carefree and happy.

Chapter 16 – Wednesday 9th July

Lana changed up a final gear and settled into her journey, glad to be out of town and under way at last. She rarely drove, but today she hadn't fancied another train journey and her dad was happy to lend her his car. The lingering aroma of dog shampoo told her that Todd had visited the groomers this week, and Lana smiled, remembering his disgusted but adorably fluffy face on the one occasion she had picked him up from their small premises. The groomers had added a fetching little bow on his collar, which her dad had removed as soon as they got home: "Todd doesn't like these," he had explained, wryly.

The road was quiet as she passed her favourite diner, pleased to see plenty cars and a few motorhomes in their car park. So many businesses had closed over the years; few remained from her childhood like this one, still serving the same menu of sublime breakfasts and calorific lunches. She hadn't visited for years and made a mental note to arrange a date with her dad. It could be her thanks for borrowing the car.

To her right, the Carse of Gowrie rose in farmed and wooded pockets, polytunnels and furrows filled with verdant produce, and fields of cows and bulls rinsed lustrously clean by the overnight rain. A lone cyclist hastened along the path beside the carriageway, then headed up into the hills towards more peaceful roads. Lana found herself enjoying the freedom of another day away from the bank. After taking annual leave the previous week, she had been quizzed about a further mid-week break but had simply answered that she had an appointment and didn't want to have to rush back. Her manager hadn't pried any further, showing unusual solicitude. Now, she enjoyed the drive and the views on such a clear day and magnanimously wished everyone back in the branch a stressless shift.

As Lana approached the hospital entrance from the car park, she felt a bound in her step and realised she was looking forward to their last meeting concluding. This process had been a mistake; she was more than capable of dealing with her problems herself and was wasting everyone's effort by being here. Soon it would be over, and she could focus on her future. She entered the building to a warm welcome from the receptionist and had barely settled in her seat when one of the many doctors came to receive her. Lana recognised her as the proud parent of the toddling baby but was embarrassed to have forgotten her name.

"Lana, welcome back! How have you been? Come through, and we'll run through your results. Would you like a drink or anything? We have an hour today, plenty time."

Lana smiled and suggested a tea; it had been a smooth journey, but the city centre had taken some time to navigate. As they settled into an interview room, Lana finally recalled the introductions from the previous week. "Thank you, Doctor Meziani. What can you tell me? I must admit, I'm fascinated."

Dr Meziani opened a red file and leafed through a thick bundle of printouts with notes. "Let me start by reminding you a little of the process. We started with more traditional, intensive, talking therapy; getting to know your past, your issues, your concerns and any unhealthy behaviour patterns. We then moved on to our scans: first some baselines, then observing patterns of brain activity as we talked through some of what we had learned and re-enacted some of the emotional trigger scenes from your past. We then spent a further day performing scans while we deliberately invoked strong emotional responses: love, loss, anger, frustration, vengeance, violence and so on. We subsequently used our machine learning algorithms to compare all those scans and correlate your own accounts of past events, focusing on your reactions and how you described some of the more difficult times in your life."

Lana nodded, not wanting to be impatient, but tired of hearing generalities. "Yes, we covered that last time. Did you find anything which might explain my depressive moods at all? I've been having some success with trying to avoid them, actually."

The doctor held up a hand, stopping Lana before she could continue. "Lana, please don't worry, but we've found some anomalies in your reactions to events and triggers. That, combined with your own concerns about your self-destructive behaviour, lead us to believe you may be in danger of wider mental health issues. As I said, please don't worry. We've found these problems at a very early stage and can treat them easily. Let me explain."

Lana sat back, staggered and bewildered. How could she not worry? She fought to focus as the doctor described the team's findings. A tendency towards sudden and deep depressions, including a disregard for the welfare of herself and others. Periods of overly high self-confidence. Inappropriate and imbalanced reactions to both events and criticism. Tendency to dark fantasy. Potential for psychotic breaks. Approval of violent revenge themes. A concern for society.

"Sorry, what?" she interrupted. "A concern for society? I'm not a concern, or a bad person, or anything. I've never broken any laws or hurt anyone. Well, apart from maybe speeding once or twice, and that time I got in fight in primary school. But I'm just normal. I'm a decent hard-working, quiet sort of person!"

Once again, Dr Meziani interrupted her. "We understand that Lana, and we can see that you're not a problem to anyone - at the moment. But these are inherent tendencies in your character. Your upbringing has taught you clear moral boundaries, and you are sticking to them. But what we see in you is the capability for that to change quite suddenly and unexpectedly. You could really hurt yourself or someone else if we don't find a way to mitigate those tendencies."

"Surely not," Lana contested hotly. "This is all just supposition. There could have been an error in the tests. Zeroes instead of ones, a malfunction, someone tweeting in the next room when they shouldn't have been. I'm not a danger to anyone!"

"I'm afraid not, Lana. We understand this is a shock. Let me take you through the results. You'll see there are multiple examples, clear patterns. There are no errors. And please, we will absolutely help you deal with this, to make sure nothing bad ever comes of it."

Lana took a steadying breath, entirely unconvinced but prepared to hear and refute the details. "Please, just give me a moment first. I need to process this." Fighting back confused and bitterly hot tears, she stood and walked over to the window, breathing as deeply and regularly as she could until she felt she could focus. Outside, a small courtyard was filled with hardy plants in concrete containers. Sparrows bobbed among the small shrubs, foraging. Lana breathed and braced herself. Returning to her seat, she mustered a polite smile and asked the doctor to continue.

Two hours and considerable soul-searching later, Lana sat in a snug café near the hospital, nursing peppermint tea and a fruit scone. She knew she should call her dad, let him know that she was well and would head home soon, but she couldn't bring herself to speak to him just yet. Revelation and denial warred in her thoughts, as she gradually absorbed and understood all that she had heard. Most of what the doctor had pointed out did make some sense; Lana couldn't refute the truth of what they had identified. But what they had extrapolated from that data: potential for psychotic breaks, Lana was potentially a danger to others? It sat so contrary to everything Lana believed about herself. The doctor had argued that this was a part of the problem; Lana's confidence in her own capabilities meant she underestimated or ignored the risk she presented. She tried to approach the information differently: how would she feel if she heard this news while feeling down? Sighing, she accepted that she couldn't tell; her moods were so variable. As denial waned, she started to tremble, fear rising acerbically in her throat: what might she be capable of if she ignored this warning? She hid a rush of tears by turning towards the cafe wall and raising her line of sight; a poster advertising Miss Saigon at a local theatre, helicopter dramatically twisting towards buildings. The sky was painted as dark and thunderous, the background muted and irrelevant. What might she be capable of, she repeated? Sudden unexpected gratitude flooded her system in a tumultuous swell. Thank God she had come forward for the testing; thank God they had found this before she did any harm. What might she have done?

As she drove home, unnerved but steady, she contemplated the doctor's summary. "We can absolutely level out your moods and stop any adverse overreactions to events, don't worry. We'll write this up into your central record - in the confidential section, of course – and work with Central Care to get you some therapy to level you out a little. Your preferred pharmacy will be in touch once they have your prescription. If you have any questions at all, just get in touch with your GP and they can facilitate."

Lana hadn't imagined medication to be the result of all this; she had expected no real outcome. She had taken very little in the way of medicine since she was a child; she thought of her mother's daily regime of pills and winced. Hopefully this medication wouldn't make her feel the regular nausea her mum experienced. As she pulled into her parents' driveway, she debated how to tell them her news; with the least fuss and alarm, she concluded firmly. No one need worry now.

Chapter 17 – Saturday 12th July

Lana arranged cushions on the bench in her strip of garden and settled with some rich hot chocolate in her favourite mug, dotted with blue Airedale terrier prints. The downstairs flat had been assigned the rear garden, accessing it through their back door, with lawns and borders and a nice patio. Lana's upstairs apartment had the better views, and the loft converted into a spacious bedroom, but her garden was limited to the front strip beside the pavement, and the side path where outside stairs rose to her front door. But she was happy with it; it needed little effort to keep tidy, and her bench by the stairs caught the sun for most of the day and could be moved closer to the street to enjoy the evening light. To the west, the sun was close to setting over the city, gold and bronze and lilac starting to bleed together around darkening wisps of cloud. After such a hot day, it was unusual for the evening to be clear; haar often rolling in from the sea and chilling the air. It would be foolish to waste such an evening indoors.

Lana had started keeping a diary, Ailsa's suggestion.

She thought it might help her track how she felt as she started taking her new medication. She opened the small journal she had bought and paused. She could hear passers-by on the pavement just a few feet away. In front of the building, the hedge was cut lower so as not to block her neighbours view, but just here she kept it higher, thicker and more private. She wrote.

12/7

There was a glass or so left in the bottom of the wine bottle, but I've poured it away. I've got something called a venalink. It holds all these pills together in little bundles for day and night, every day. It's all very clever, I just need to go into the pharmacy once a month and pick up the next 4 weeks of packs. Who knew how organised it all was? The label has big, bold, capitals announcing the death of the "wee glass". I don't mind, it's a small price to pay.

I feel so sorry for Dad, and Mum. They're so unhappy about the diagnosis, or whatever it's called. When I got home on Wed, Dad could barely talk, he was so angry. He's sure there's nothing wrong with me, but he didn't hear the evidence. I just can't take the risk of ignoring what they've found. If I hurt anyone, I'd be... well, I couldn't live with it. The pills have a list of potential side effects as long as Todd's tail, but it's got to be worth it. I'm going to keep this diary, for how I feel, and any consequences.

Not much news today, then - it's my first day of taking them! I saw everyone last night, told them I couldn't drink anything alcoholic, that I was on some new pills. They were all a bit quiet afterwards, hope they don't think I'm only fun when I'm drinking. Sanj said he hoped I didn't become a prozac housewife haha! I think Lind really quite likes Sanj, but he's oblivious and I'm not sure Lind is for him. I hope it all works out okay.

Lana finished her chocolate just as the sun dipped below the horizon, stretching her legs and toes lazily. It would be chilly soon, the onshore breeze stronger than the wind break provided by the hedge and low wall, but for now she enjoyed the last of the warm day. Tomorrow was forecast to be just as nice, and in the morning, she planned to weed the paving at her feet, before the sun was high and hot. Her patch was sparse in the main; there were no borders or flowerbeds. But brightly coloured pots of pansies and patio roses made this corner an oasis of colour, and Lana kept her bench and table tidily painted in a beautiful sage green. Shells and driftwood were piled in a corner, providing a small habitat for bugs, and her neighbour had prolific hanging baskets on either side of their front door, the original entrance when their flats had been a grander house. All in all, it was a pleasant spot, and Lana felt blessed.

As she gathered her things and headed indoors, she heard her phone ringing, and quickened her pace upstairs and into her flat. Recognising Jen's number, she smiled.

"Hello you! How are things? How's my wee nephew doing?"

Jen interrupted, stopping her in her tracks as she turned to lock the door and tidy away her things. "I just heard from Mum; were you never going to tell me? How can you be so selfish, don't you think I deserve to know that you're unwell?"

Lana stood stock still as Jen continued to berate her, adrenaline spiking into her system. "Wait! Wait a minute, what on earth did Mum say? What makes you think I'm not fit to be around Robbie, of all things? How could you think that? Why would you jump to all the worst possible conclusions without talking to me first? It's nothing like that!" Tears again; Lana was so sick of tears but this condemnation from her mum and sister felt just too cruel. "You need to calm the hell down and tell me what Mum has said, before you go too far. Someone has got this completely wrong."

Lana listened in dismay. She had explained everything at length to her parents, deliberately positioning the medication as a preventative measure. She had resolutely avoided using the doctor's inflammatory choice of words. Despite this, it would appear her mum had still overreacted and told her sister she was mentally unwell; her sister had added a level of presumptuous hysteria Lana could barely believe.

"That's enough!" she snapped. "Just stop it and listen to me. I am absolutely not unwell. I am perfectly safe to be around people and children. They found a tiny risk that I might suffer from some mental health issues under certain circumstances in the future, so we're being incredibly cautious and making sure that never happens. Could you say that for sure? Are you so certain you're perfect? I've done entirely the right thing here, getting checked and being as safe as I can be. I can't believe you would think so little of me. What is wrong with you?" Lana's hands were trembling, her legs weak and her stomach seething. She walked through to the lounge and lowered herself into the sofa. There was a hissing silence between them; Lana waited for a reply. "Jen?"

A soft sob. "I'm so sorry, Lana. What Mum said just sounded so serious. I don't know what's wrong with me, these days I'm all upset about nothing." Jen released an unsteady breath, and Lana's anger slowly dissipated and turned to concern.

"Okay, okay, please - don't worry. Jen, what's going on? You didn't seem okay when you were here, either. You can tell us anything, you know, whatever's upsetting you. It's no good for you to be all het up like this." Lana waited, unsure whether they had both gone too far to be able to share.

After a few moments, Jen started to talk, softly and hesitantly at first, as if voicing her thoughts would give them unwarranted power. She was so very unhappy, and so very tired. Alone all day with Robbie, and never a minute to herself. This was a story familiar to so many parents who had dedicated their time to their children. Cal was working long hours, and had so many other commitments, he was hardly home in the evenings. He was a good father, would come home in time for bath time and to see Robbie before bed, Jen stressed. But then he would leave for football, or the pub, or to see his family. When he was home, he was always engrossed in his laptop or his phone, would barely speak to Jen, even when she was upset and desperately needed to talk. He stayed up late every night, well past when Jen was exhausted and needed to go to bed. They had no intimacy at all. Jen hated where they lived, hated being away from her family and home, felt alone and unappreciated and utterly exhausted of all grace.

"I take it you've spoken to Cal about this," Lana ventured.

"Yes. God, so often. He says it's normal, I have a bit of the baby blues. He says he's doing nothing different now than he always has; but that's kind of my point," Jen laughed bitterly. "I've asked him for help, but he says he has to focus on his work, and I have nothing else but Robbie and the house to worry about. I guess he's right, but I just can't do all this alone. His mum once offered to help, but when she comes around, she just sits there waiting to be served hand and foot, criticising how I am with Robbie – he's too warmly dressed, he shouldn't be getting a bit of biscuit, his toys aren't educational enough, we shouldn't have the TV on." Jen sighed. "God, I hate this. I hate that this is my life."

"Oh, Jen. I'm so sorry. What do you want to do? Can I help at all?" Lana asked.

"I just want to come home. That's all I think about. But our work is here, and Cal has always said he wouldn't move to Scotland, says it's too cold and too far from his family. So, what can I do? I'd be taking Robbie away from his dad. But I'm just so sick of it all, and sick of Cal and his selfishness. Sometimes it's like having two children to look after, not a husband. How can you do this to someone you love?" Jen sobbed.

Distance had never felt like such a divide before. Lana wanted to hold her sister, to reassure her, to help in some truly tangible way. "Would you like me to come down for a while? I could help out?"

"No, God, no. Don't worry, you have enough going on in your life just now," Jen asserted. "And I'm probably just tired and making things worse than they are. It'll seem better tomorrow. Robbie sounds like he's asleep, I'm going to pour myself a glass of wine and watch some TV, that'll cheer me up."

Lana was still unsettled when they had said their goodbyes. Her older sister was always organised, always controlled. She'd had her troubles, but she always remained decisive throughout. This self-doubt was a departure, and

Lana resolved to keep an eye on it.

The next morning, Lana was weeding and tidying in the garden, worrying about Jen and pondering adding a small herb garden to her little fiefdom, when she was interrupted by a voice from the street.

"Knock, knock! Don't want to make you jump!" Lana's dad was peering around the hedge, Todd's paws and head over the gate and tongue lolling in welcome. "Looks like you're making good progress!" he gestured at the cleared patio.

"Hello! You coming in? I'm about ready for a break, and I have some shortbread." Lana offered. "Grab a seat and I'll go pop the kettle on."

Drinks made and biscuits perched well out of reach of Todd's nose, Lana told Peter about her call from Jen. "I'm really quite worried, Dad. It was all very not-Jen," she concluded.

Grabbing more shortie, her dad sipped his tea before replying soberly. "Well, we can all check in with her a bit more often. It might just have been a bad week. It's hard to tell when we only ever see them on holidays, but they've seemed happy enough until now. That's disappointing from Cal, though. He's always seemed quite smart; he should know how lucky he is with our Jen." A pause, and a glance at Lana. "You try not to worry about it too much, though. You've had your own hard week; Jen is right about that. And don't bother too much about your mum: she just worries, and she can blow things out of proportion a bit. It's not her fault, she's just not busy enough, she has too much time to think."

"Aye," Lana sighed, "that's true. I wish we could do more to keep her occupied, cheer her up. Which reminds me, I have some books upstairs that she might like. Those Shetland ones I told you about, they're really good." Glancing around once more, she eyed up a sunny stretch alongside a wall and pivoted. "Do you think I could pull up a couple of slabs along here and put in a small herb garden? Would it get enough sun?" Debating the merits of outdoor herbs, the effects of salt winds, and the behaviour of local cats, they whiled away the rest of their morning while Todd dozed contentedly in the cool shade of the bench.

Chapter 18 – Friday 25th July

Lind waved cheerfully from behind the customer service counter as Lana headed out into the hot afternoon sun, pulling her sunglasses from her handbag. Mothers and children thronged the pavements, making their way to and from the park, the beach, or the ice cream shop, the air redolent of sticky sun cream and hot tarmac. Turning away from the stream of families and walking past the jewellers and gift shops, Lana felt grateful to live in such a beautiful area. It may not have a year-round Mediterranean climate, but with easy access to beaches, hills, river and sea, when the sun shone it was perfect. Lana thought of an old school friend, who couldn't expose her skin to the sun without suffering painful rashes, feeling grateful that she could enjoy the warmth without worry.

"Hello you!" A friendly voice roused her from her reverie, and she found herself walking towards Sanj. "Lana," he added, "this is Esme, from my work. We're heading down to the Riverboat to see if they have any outside tables for lunch. Thought if we got there early enough, we might be lucky." Esme smiled freely in welcome. She was pale skinned, with a smattering of freckles across her dainty nose, and wavy strawberry blonde hair covering her shoulders. She wore a bright though feminine floral sundress, which skimmed her curves flatteringly. Sanj was smarter than usual, too, Lana noted with a keen eye, having ironed his jeans and wearing one of his few "going out" t-shirts.

Lana grinned at them both. "Nice to meet you! Are you both off today, then? So lucky, I'll be stuck in work until five. Fingers crossed there's a table free, if not then I heard the hotel has some tables out in their garden. It's a little more out of the way, but it might be quieter. You'll be wanting somewhere nice, I guess," she teased lightly, eyebrow lifted. Sanj coloured lightly, and Esme giggled. Lana liked her so far. "I'd better get going, sorry: I have an appointment. You two have a nice time... Maybe I'll see you again later, Esme? It was nice to meet you!" Lana smiled warmly as she parted from the couple, always buoyed by the prospect of romance for one of her friends. She thought then of Lind and hoped they wouldn't take the news too badly; Lana would avoid telling them anything for now.

As Lana entered the consultation room, she realised she was a little nervous to see Dr Alexander again. He would know about her results, and the new medications she was taking, and that daunted her. While she wasn't ashamed of the findings, Jen's fearful initial reaction had stopped her from telling anyone else. Only her immediate family had heard what the team in Edinburgh had found; her friends knew only that she had medication to take. But as she met his eyes, she saw only warmth and welcome, and felt her tension ease.

"Good morning, Lana, it's good to see you again. How are you?" he asked.

"I'm fine, thank you," she replied automatically, then laughed and shook her head. "Well, obviously not entirely fine, or I wouldn't be here." She paused, deliberating the best starting point. "Umm, have you already seen the results of the factorisation analysis?" she checked.

"I was just reading the details as you came in," he admitted. "They've prescribed for you as well, I see?" he frowned. "Why don't you tell me how it went in your own words, that might be the best thing."

Lana started to talk, first describing her fears for the testing, and surprise at the choice of videos, laughingly explaining how often she had already watched two of the films. As she related the results meeting, and the outlying psychological factors which had concerned the team, she sobered. "So, if I understand it correctly, the problem is that I swing from being very confident, to extremes of depression, and that I tend to disregard risk towards myself and other people. They said I "tended towards dark fantasies" and had the potential to suffer full psychotic breaks under stressful conditions. I can't remember all the exact words... Basically, they said I could end up being a danger to myself or other people; that's the worst-case scenario. It sounds insane, I can't believe I would ever do something like that - but I guess no one sets out to hurt people, do they? I still don't know if I totally believe the tests were okay, but they seem certain. It was such a shock, you know? So unexpected. I went into this looking for answers, but I didn't ever expect anything so serious." Blinking twice, and shaking off her dismay, she continued. "But at the end of it all... I'm just so glad the testing was available; if I ever hurt anyone I'd be horrified. I wish everyone could have this done, to be honest, if it could stop so many people being hurt every year or becoming so unwell. I... well, I wish there was nothing to worry about, but if I have these problems, I'd much rather know. Does that make sense?" Dr Alexander was staring at her intensely, and Lana couldn't discern what he was thinking. "I'm sorry, honestly I'm not a violent or angry person, and I'm definitely not unhinged," she blurted out.

"No, no, please don't apologise. Of course, you're not. I just didn't expect them to find anything to worry about. You seem fine - a very balanced, calm and intelligent person. I'm sure what they've found is merely potential, and they're just being cautious. How do you feel about it all now?" he added.

"I'm still shocked, I think. Disappointed and worried, too, obviously. But overall, I'm so glad I did this, and we know what could happen, and we can control it. The pills, well there's no problem about me taking them; whatever it takes. I haven't told many people - I don't think they'd understand. My sister totally overreacted at first, but she only had half the story at the time." Lana didn't ever want anyone else to respond as Jen had.

"Of course. This analysis is something unprecedented, and until it's commonplace it will be open to misinterpretation. I think that's been a wise decision," he agreed. "And how are you getting on with the medication itself, what's that been now... 2 weeks?"

"Yes, well, that's why I've come in. I checked through the side effects and everything, and I'm sure it's nothing to worry about, but... well, there's been a few little things I've noticed." For the first time, Lana felt flustered. She pressed her palms together and tried to ignore the flush on her cheeks. "Umm, this sounds a bit gross, sorry, but... my urine smells weird, like mostly normal but with a burnt smell. Which it definitely didn't use to have. And I seem to sweat a lot overnight, I wake up and it's like I've been running for miles. And I get a dry mouth all the time, I need to sip water constantly. Sorry, that all sounds like nothing very much, but I thought I should check in with you."

"Absolutely. Let me dig out the side effects, and any contraindications. I'm pretty sure they should settle down as you get used to the regime, but we'll check. How have you been sleeping, fine? Are you otherwise feeling well? No other unusual smells, or changes in your sense of taste?" As Lana nodded or shook her head appropriately, he continued to read. "Yes, it sounds like those are common, and should settle down over the next few weeks. But if it doesn't clear up, or anything else starts troubling you, please just come back in." He stopped momentarily, gazed off to one side then looked down at his hands and drew a breath. "One other thing, if you have a moment?" Looking up to check she agreed, he continued, "It sounded like you were a little uncomfortable telling me about your symptoms. Don't worry, you're not going to offend me. But I think with the medications you're on, and the side effects you're experiencing, you may feel better seeing one of our female doctors? I'd recommend Dr Gillies; she's an excellent clinician and specialises in women's health. Obviously, we're all happy to consult with you at any time, especially in an emergency, but I wondered if you might be more comfortable with her?"

Lana laughed self-deprecatingly, with both relief and embarrassment. "Here was me thinking I was hiding it well! I'm sorry, it's absolutely no criticism, you've been so helpful. I guess I'm just a little old-fashioned, maybe." Lana certainly didn't want to admit that she would prefer to avoid telling a good-looking man the gruesome details of her night sweats. She grabbed the excuse to see another doctor before he could rescind the offer. "I'll do that in future. Hopefully it will all settle down as you say. Thank you, though, for recommending the factorisation testing. It's been difficult, but I do appreciate it."

As Lana left the surgery, she felt an unexpected disappointment that she wouldn't see Dr Alexander again. She didn't know him personally at all, but he was kind and gentle, and certainly attractive. She wouldn't be telling that to Lind, to avoid the inevitable teasing. Stepping out into the beautiful day, she resolved to put any worries behind her. She was naturally optimistic, unless suffering one of her episodes, and knowing that those would be better controlled from now boosted her mood. She was lucky in her life, and from now she would make the most of it.

Munro delayed calling in his next patient, trying to calm his nerves and regain his focus. He simply couldn't believe what he had read in Lana's notes. The prognosis the Bryant-Cargill team had detailed was not at all in accord with what he knew of his patient. The medications especially troubled him: a mix of anti-depressants and anti-psychotics usually prescribed for far more troubled individuals. His initial reaction was to call the team and demand an explanation, but what grounds could he use for that? He had only met with Lana on a few occasions; he had no specialism in mental health. Worse, he had referred her so couldn't now claim he didn't think it was necessary. The truth was, he had been keen to see the new process play out, and that had influenced his decision. He hadn't expected anything but a clean bill of health for his patient. He hadn't sent her for any of the standard therapies first, which probably would have been wise before taking such a drastic step. Steeped in guilt and worried for his patient, he wondered whether his conduct had been appropriate; he would have to seek some advice. He would discuss it with Maria Gillies, under the guise of advising he had recommended Lana see her in future. He just hoped no ill would become Lana as a result of either the analysis or her ongoing treatment. Maria would know what to do.

Chapter 19 – August

4/8.

Deary Diary, here we are again haha!

Today has been a rare day – a compliment from the management! I've been busy last week and today, manually tidying up after a bucketload of errors in the payment processing software. We've managed to get everything sorted for our branch's customers without a single complaint, and they said it was "very much down to my hard work and diligence". Makes a change from them complaining! I was a bit embarrassed, thought the others might take the mick, but they were really good about it. The cakes the boss bought probably helped.

Mouth is still dry, but I think the night sweats have been better the last two nights now. I haven't had any difficult moods since I came back from Edinburgh, so hard to tell if it's the pills or just coincidence, to be honest. But given how busy I was this weekend, and how tired I've been, I'm quite pleased to not have had any odd moments.

Tuesday 5th August

Lana checked her phone one last time as she turned into her parents' street. Since July, she had been messaging Jen more often than usual, checking in with her every day. It wasn't always easy to think of something to say, but she sent some missive anyway. Jen hadn't replied for two days now, and Lana was starting to worry; she would check in with her dad about it. As she crunched up the gravel driveway, Todd started barking from the back garden, so she changed tack and headed for the gate instead of the front door.

"Hi!" she called as she unlatched the gate and raised a knee to fend off the dog's excited welcome. "Todd, down! No, down! And sit... good boy, good Todd, yes you are." Closing the gate with a foot, she stooped to his level and scratched his chest and ears as reward.

"If we ever get burgled, that dog will just roll over for them," her dad complained.

"No, he just knew it was me," Lana interrupted loyally. "How's things?"

"Not bad, I was just about to cut the grass, so you've saved me," Peter grinned triumphantly. "Your mum's on the phone with Jen just now if you want to say hi?"

Lana smiled, relieved. "No, it's okay. I was wondering if she was okay, I hadn't heard from her for a couple of days."

"Oh yeah, I had a quick word with her, she's fine. She'd taken Robbie to the beach and was swearing not to bother again until he's much older. Nappies and sand don't mix, she says," he laughed.

Friday 8th August

Lana sank into her armchair, positioned perfectly to watch the world through her windows. The day had started fair, but the forecast storm had now landed, and gale force winds and rains combined with a high tide to make spectacular conditions. Rain slanted in stinging sheets, baptising all. Huge waves propelled their white stallions up-river, a violent onslaught on an unsuspecting summer land. The turbulent sky was graphite, slate, heather and mercury, wind-ravaged clouds hastening to the distant hills where the sun hid from all. Rollers broke against the sea wall opposite her flat, spray rising well above it and soaking the road. Seaweed already festooned the pavements. Lana was glad she didn't own a car; to see it battered by wave after wave would tarnish her enjoyment of nature's display. Many of her neighbours rightly feared conditions such as these, flooding being a very real possibility, but Lana's flat was safe and the little she kept in the garden storage was hung up high out of the way. She loved to sit and watch the breakers battering the front, the winds whipping trees and shrubs, and walkers and gawkers soaked by the spray, laughing or cursing. A family with children had come to stand exposed in the street, encompassed in waterproofs and screaming with delight at each soaking they received. Lana smiled and hugged her mug of tea. Not many would be enjoying this evening as much as they were. Tomorrow, she was meeting the others at The Bell, and would wrap up and brave the elements, but for now she was snug and glad to spend the time alone in her refuge.

Saturday 9th August

Munro looked back towards his home one last time, waving at Stuart, snug in his pyjamas and onesie. Laurie waved and gave him a cheeky thumbs-up with one hand as she shoo-ed him away with the other; she knew how reluctant he was to leave the house. The wind drove the rain into his hood, and he tightened it unhappily. He was meeting the surgery staff for drinks, and the doctors were expected to attend and buy at least one round each. Munro liked his colleagues, and they liked him, but he would rather be at home with his son, and out of the weather. As he approached the bar, waves of cheerful chat and the clink of glassware reached him, and he looked forward to getting out of his saturated jacket.

"Munro!" called Dr Clegg, waving a list of drinks. "You're in the nick of time, we need another round. Stick yours on the bottom of the list and remember one for the bar!"

Munro dropped his jacket over the last remaining chair at their table and headed to the counter. The girl tending the bar flashed a smile and reached for the list. "Big night out, is it?" she asked.

"A leaving do for our youngest receptionist," Munro explained. "He's off to uni in Aberdeen to become a speech and language therapist." As he waited for the drinks to be poured, he pulled his wallet from his pocket and glanced about the bar. It was quieter than he had expected, probably due to the weather. In the far corner, a couple sat glaring at each other, clearly mid-argument. He was powerfully built and grim-faced, but his partner was holding their own, finger poised in anticipation of the winning point. Munro looked away quickly, not wanting to be caught prying.

Turning to take the drinks back to the table, he nearly

bumped into Lana Knight, who was shrugging off a dripping waterproof, her hair damp around the edges where her hood had been compromised. She quickly moved out of the way of the man from the corner, who was storming out, jacket under his arm.

"Hi!" she said to Munro. "I hope he gets his coat on quickly, it'll blow away otherwise," she laughed, raising her eyebrows to acknowledge his hurry. "Sorry, I didn't make you spill any of your drinks, did I?" she worried, seeing his tray.

"No, no, it's fine," Munro countered. "How are you? Sorry, doctors shouldn't ask that. Are you having a good weekend? Meeting some friends?"

Lana smiled. "Yeah, just catching up, something to get us out of the house in all this weather. I'll not be complaining about being too hot ever again," she laughed. "Have a good night!"

9/8.

The others were a bit stir-crazy today, I think. They drank way more than usual. It's the first time I've noticed them really feeling the effects when I'm still sober, was a bit weird. Plus side, though: I'm feeling fine and won't have a sore head tomorrow – I suspect they all will. Was a shame Kenny couldn't make it; Lind seemed a bit put out, must've been disappointed. I was glad Sanj didn't mention Esme just yet, I'll tell Lind when it's a better time. Dr Alexander looks younger away from the doctors, funnily enough. Can't believe I couldn't think of anything to talk about except the weather, what a berk.

Feeling fine today, no moods despite the dismal day. Sleeping better again, too. Seem to have become teenager again, though, spots cropping up everywhere! Must cut back on piggy food.

Sunday 17th August.

Lana glared at her phone impatiently, as it went to voicemail once more. She had been trying Jen off-and-on all day. She wasn't annoyed by her sister not answering, assuming she was busy with Robbie - but rather because the lack of messages acknowledging the calls meant Jen was also avoiding talking to her. Resolving to try again once Robbie was in bed, Lana set a reminder on her phone and decided to have a soak in the bath to ease muscles stinging from her long run that afternoon. As she added bubble bath and opened the window to let in a fresh breeze, she mentally catalogued her fridge, deciding what to eat for the next few nights. A nice bath and a simple salad tonight, she decided. Then an omelette tomorrow and some pasta Tuesday, which would mean she could delay grocery shopping until at least Wednesday. She was trying to meal plan and shop less often to avoid treats and fattening foods; her weight had increased despite her exercising more and having stopped any alcoholic drinks, which was puzzling. The spots were getting worse, too, she realised. She should visit the doctor if it continued, she didn't want to end up overweight and knew it was easy to ignore the issue until it was hard work to remedy. Lana really hated to diet.

She was just finishing her dinner when her phone rang, and with relief she saw it was Jen. "Hello!" she opened. "Sorry for pestering you earlier, I keep trying to call while I remember otherwise it slips my mind and suddenly it's too late to ring. How are things?"

The sisters swapped light-hearted news; Lana happy to let Jen lead on anything more serious. She didn't want to become someone Jen dreaded speaking to. She told her about the storm and having to brush seaweed from her garden afterwards. They talked about Robbie, and his latest mischief. Jen asked how everyone was, and when the next pub quiz would be.

Lana was letting her silences grow, waiting to see if Jen needed to vent, when her sister blurted out, "Please, Lana, can we forget I ever said anything about Cal? I was just being grumpy, and now I'm frightened to talk about him in case you think the worst. I'm not going to do anything rash; you guys don't need to check up on me all the time."

Lana laughed, then apologised. "Sorry, sorry, that was just such a rush of info. No, I totally get it. We all like Cal, and we understand you guys can have your problems and fix them. We just want to make sure you're okay, Jen. If you do ever need to talk, you can, we won't hold it against either of you forever," she finished, hoping that her sister was reassured.

22/8

Sanj finally brought Esme to the pub tonight. He's been keeping it all very quiet with the others, I think they didn't want to rush anything. It was a good night, Esme seemed comfortable getting to know us all. Ailsa took her under her wing and made sure we weren't boring her too much. Lind was fine about it, thankfully, although a bit moody when we were walking home, and a bit snarky about how girly Esme seemed. Hopefully it won't be a problem, I like Esme and Lind can be sharp sometimes. I'm not sure Sanj would have been the perfect match for Lind, anyway, but seeing him and Esme so happy together might smart, I guess.

Another 2 pounds and 3 spots gained this week, def going to check in with the doc next week.

Chapter 20 – Monday 25th August

Lana stepped out of her manager's office and shut the door calmly behind her despite her disgust. They had complained that she took too many days off; now they were complaining because she was having too many doctor's appointments. It seemed hugely unfair. She'd avoided telling them the full story of the testing and results; had implied that there was a slight issue, and they were adjusting some medication to alleviate it. However, she'd now been asked to ensure that she made up the time she was away from the branch, which no one else had ever been asked to do.

Unable to return to her desk just yet, she headed through draughty back corridors to the refuge of the ladies' room. A peculiar mix of cloakroom and toilets, it had huge, badly fitted frosted windows and a peculiarly misplaced smell of glue. The plumbing rattled alarmingly, and when it was quiet the pigeons on the wall outside could be heard cooing and bobbing on their leathery feet. Lana sat on the hard wooden bench beneath the coat hooks and leaned over her knees, drawing a breath. She would hear anyone coming, the creaky carpentry telling tales. She couldn't risk being caught idle, one of many reportable offences in this office. She felt that she needed time to calm herself, but her absence would be noted. She sighed and headed back to her desk, reluctantly accepting the new rule. Complaining to the human resources department would be futile: the office manager and senior administrators of this branch were a tight and merciless alliance once they had decided someone didn't fit their ideals. Hopefully this would be her last doctor's appointment, she thought, and there would be no more bother.

Later, donning her jacket and heading towards the surgery, she reflected on her past ambitions, and pondered her future. Could she use her accountancy qualifications to find a more rewarding role elsewhere? Should she return to studying, maybe undertake some post-graduate work to start a new career? Or perhaps a complete change in direction would be best, something involving animals or something more creative? She had debated this often, on her own as well as with friends and family. She envied people who had a true vocation in life: how wonderful it must be to know exactly what you want to do for the next forty years. As she walked and thought, she realised that she didn't once consider staying long-term at the bank; that was telling. Perhaps her critics in the branch sensed that within her, her lack of loyalty segregating her from the pack. She would spend some time at the weekend thinking over her strengths and aptitudes, perhaps with more of a focus on what she might enjoy, rather than being restricted by the practicalities of what was considered a "good job". She could surely do better than this.

The surgery was besieged when she arrived, parents and children jostling for space, the elderly offering their seats to expectant mothers and politely being refused. The noise levels were incredible as children fought for attention and harassed adults snapped back. A receptionist was milling through them all, smile a suspended rictus, clipboard and pen in hand. Leaving her to the unenviable task of ordering chaos, Lana found her way to the desk and waited politely.

"Oh, goodness. Sorry, we're in a bit of a state, we're double-booked. We have a mother and baby clinic scheduled with a visiting midwife, as well as an asthma clinic with our own nurse. We've had to start using the staff room for waiting as we've no space free, it's pandemonium. Don't worry, though, the doctors are running reasonably to time; it's just the waiting room which is a problem. Who are you here to see?" the receptionist concluded breathlessly.

"Dr Gillies," Lana replied, trying to be heard above a tantrum. "At 11:40. Don't worry about me, I'm fine standing here so long as you don't mind?" Lana looked around, smiled and shrugged. There was little other standing room available, so her manners were pointless.

When she was called in to Dr Gillies' consultation room, it took a few apologies and excuses to work through the furore. Once she was free of the crowd, Dr Gillies ushered her in, shaking her head and apologising as she closed the door. "The madding crowd," she quoted. "I don't know why some of them can't at least leave their prams outside," she complained. "Thankfully it should be over by one. The staff are a bit overrun since Ben left, someone missed checking the schedule... Anyway, please sit down. Dr Alexander has explained your situation and said that you might be more comfortable seeing me in future. So, I have all the background, no need to explain. What can we do for you today?"

Rather than feeling rushed, Lana breathed out her relief and smiled, grateful to both doctors for being so organised. "Thank you, that makes it much easier. It's a bit of a long story otherwise. I just wanted to check with you again about side effects. It sounds like nothing, but I've been putting on an awful lot of weight suddenly. It's a total of 13 pounds so far, but that's in only 6 weeks. It's piling on," she laughed, embarrassed. "I've cut out all alcoholic drinks in that time because of the meds I'm on, and for the last 4 weeks - since I noticed - I've been exercising more and trying to eat less snacks and cheese and things. I thought maybe it was muscle weight or something, but my clothes aren't fitting now, it's definitely not right. Oh, and I've been getting loads of spots, really nasty ones. I haven't had those since I was young. I've been lucky until now, I guess. This all sounds so vain, but it just doesn't seem right."

Throughout, Dr Gillies had been checking Lana's record, and now interrupted her. "No, it's not vain, it's good that you're careful of your weight. Weight gain and hormonal changes are quite common when you start taking the contraceptive pill, did no one explain that to you?"

Lana rocked back, surprise lightly tingling her nerves. "What contraceptive pills? I don't take those; I don't like messing about with my hormones. My sister tried them and ended up entirely out of sorts. Are you sure?"

Dr Gillies frowned and referred to her screen. "They were prescribed by Central Care at the same time as your other new medications; they'll be included in your venalink." She looked back at Lana questioningly. "This wasn't something you discussed and decided with them?"

As Lana shook her head in dismay, and started to speak, the doctor was already typing and talking. "It must have been an error somewhere while your notes were coded. I'm so sorry. I've stopped the prescription now, don't worry. They'll no longer be added to your monthly supplies. It's not a problem to stop them. You should bleed around two to four weeks after taking your last pill, then gradually return to your normal cycle. However, please ensure you use other protection immediately, as you could become pregnant as soon as you stop. The weight gain and other issues should sort themselves out over time. If not, please come back and see me again. I've added a note explaining all this into your record, so it's clear why we have stopped them. I'll email Central as well, they need to know about this. I can only apologise; it won't have any long-term effect on your fertility or suchlike, so please don't be too concerned."

Still shocked, but mollified by Dr Gillies' prompt action and reassurances, Lana wasn't sure how to react. "Are you sure it will be fine?" she checked. "I'm just... Well, I had no idea. That seems so odd. It's worrying that they could do that."

Dr Gillies smiled kindly, and comforted Lana. "That's understandable, it's a significant mistake for them to have made, but just a mistake. It's all sorted now, and you'll be fine. Is there anything else you need?"

Lana felt rushed but made her farewell. She exited the surgery and left its mass of patients behind, relieved that she had followed her instincts and investigated the changes she had felt in her body. It could have taken months to uncover otherwise. There was a lot to be said for following your gut, she thought. That might be a lesson she should apply to her work at the bank.

Dr Gillies watched Lana hurry out, silently agreeing with her that it was worrying, indeed. She had always had reservations about oversight of patient care being removed from the practice and centralised, and this sort of error compounded her belief. General practice was changing for the worse, she felt; she had started to look forward to retiring but would not yet admit that to another soul. She concluded the consultation with Lana in the system, completing her updates to Lana's record and marking herself as available for her next patient.

As she waited for Mr Brown to make his way through the buggies cluttering her doorway, the updates to Lana's record were synchronised back to the central database. Convoluted logic governed clinical systems: when the contraceptive medication was demoted from being a current repeat therapy to a historical record, the system checked the original prescriber, and a notification was automatically sent to the Central Care team. Later that day, their administrator checked the change and saw that the original prescription was generated following Bryant-Cargill factorisation analysis. The strict protocols clearly stated that only the Central Care team could change these medications, so the contraceptive was re-instated. The system informed neither Lana nor her surgery.

Chapter 21 - Tuesday 26th August

Munro woke early and slowly, watching the lazy dawn light blooming behind his dark curtains. Most days, he was woken by an excited Stuart and had no time for idle introspection. He usually hated the rare mornings when he woke first, as he rediscovered the emptiness of the bed beside him and was afflicted by loneliness and loss. Today he refused to dwell on it, and simply watched the dawn and let his mind wander.

Lana had been to visit Maria yesterday. Munro hadn't raised it with his colleague, and she hadn't volunteered the reason for the visit. When asked if her morning had been interesting, the double-booked clinics were all she discussed. Munro needed to accept this: he shouldn't be prying, shouldn't be interested. Most importantly, he could trust Maria to look after Lana Knight and needed to distance himself from her care. He rose and opened his curtains to the fresh day, mentally reaffirming his decision to put her out of his mind.

As he and Stuart walked to school, Stuart chattering about his new teacher and a new boy who had joined his class, Munro wondered what the future held for his son and his generation. So much had changed since he was young himself, and his parents often spoke of their youth as being far simpler and happier, though hardly idyllic. Life was so hard for so many people. Munro saw that daily in his work: deprivation, depression and despair were sadly commonplace. Would his son manage to find happiness despite the challenges of modern life? Would society become more tolerant, less demanding, allow Stuart's generation to thrive? Munro found himself lacking in optimism. It wasn't like him, a revelation: was he becoming morose? He slowly became aware of his son's impatient attention.

"Sorry, why do you think Miss McKenzie would like a class of just boys?" Munro asked, tuning back into the conversation Stuart had been perpetuating alone.

"Dad!" he complained. "Because: she said all the boys had done a great job of being new friends to Justin, and we'd all done our writing much better than last week, and that Mrs Toner said we'd shared our football well with the other classes at playtime. But she didn't say anything nice about the girls at all," Stuart explained.

"Hmm, I think maybe you shouldn't mention that to her," Munro countered. "It might annoy the girls a bit, and I'm pretty sure Miss McKenzie was just being nice to you boys and didn't realise she was ignoring the girls. And really, nobody would ever want that; a good mix of all sorts of different people makes for the best class."

As Stuart headed into the playground, Munro hoped he'd said enough to divert Stuart from his idea. He didn't want the newest teacher in the school thinking his son approved of segregation, even if it was just an innocent misunderstanding from a young boy. He waved goodbye, marvelling at this confident, happy child who could join any group of children with ease. His heart ached lightly as he imagined the potential disappointments ahead of his son, and the gradual erosion of that childhood confidence which seemed to be an inevitable part of growing up.

So much could hang on a misunderstanding, he thought again, heading off to work. Everyone could struggle to make their point clearly, no matter how eloquent. Were misunderstandings inevitable between people? Some people seemed almost keen to jump to wrong conclusions, but even the wisest people he knew occasionally misunderstood others. Perhaps, he concluded, it was simply too easy to judge based on what you had experienced, instead of finding out what someone had gone through to make them think or act as they were. His subconscious straying obstinately to Lana, he wondered exactly what she had said and done in her interviews and tests to warrant the unexpectedly harsh results from the factorisation team. At heart, he still thought they were wrong - but he also knew Bev and Peter wouldn't have allowed their process to be deployed if they had any doubts as to its efficacy. Munro found it all perplexing. That, and his inability to put Lana out of his mind, was deeply frustrating. He was looking forward to the distraction of a busy day.

"Morning, all!" he called, his long stride powering past reception on his way to his room. He had only a few precious minutes to prepare for his first patient appointment, the price for seeing Stuart to school.

"I've booted up your system for you," the practice manager chased him down the hall in her heels. "Another update this morning; it's finished now, though. This one looks to be okay, thank goodness. Your 8:50 hasn't arrived yet. Maria was looking for you earlier." She dashed back down the hall without waiting for a reply.

"Thanks!" he called as she disappeared into the office. He dropped his things and popped his head around the door of Dr Gillies' consultation room with a light knock. "Do you need me urgently, Maria?"

"Munro, hi. No, nothing urgent – just wanted to update you on Lana Knight, she came to see me yesterday. My patient's waiting, but if you check her notes, you'll see what it was about. It's all a bit strange but shouldn't affect her badly and at least if she makes a complaint, it won't be the surgery's fault." She rose from her seat and moved to welcome her patient.

Intrigued and concerned equally, Munro headed back to his desk and called up Lana's record. As he read the notes, he frowned and shook his head in disbelief at the error. He was glad that Lana had come into the surgery, and Maria had spotted the problem; mistakes like this could have serious repercussions for everyone involved. Glancing across the screen to Lana's current medications, he inhaled sharply as he realised what he was seeing. Microgynon 30 was back in the repeat prescriptions list. Double-checking Maria's notes, they clearly stated that she had removed it. Puzzled, Munro removed the contraceptive from Lana's medications once more, added a further note of explanation, and closed her record. He felt a lingering disconcertedness and made a note to check the system again later.

By the end of the surgery day, the contraceptive had been reinstated and Munro had once again attempted to deactivate it. He fully expected it to be made current again overnight but couldn't quite bring himself to admit defeat and leave it. He suspected GPs were not permitted to change the medications prescribed by Central Care for some reason. This was far from the norm, and worried Munro immensely, but he held off mentioning it to his colleagues – this evening he would research the treatment process following factorisation analysis, then decide how to proceed.

"Hi Mum! How are you doing?" Munro chased Stuart away from the treats cupboard as he made a cheeky lunge while his dad was distracted by the phone. "Yes, he's here, we've not gone up to bed yet. Hang on." Munro handed the phone to Stuart, advising, "It's Granny for a chat."

As his mum and son caught up, Munro continued to tidy the kitchen, waiting for the predictable moment when his son would become bored and drop the phone abruptly in the middle of the conversation, shouting his goodbye and heading to more interesting pursuits.

"Hi Mum! Yeah, sorry, he ran off and now he's rummaging in his schoolbag. How are you and Dad, how's his knee? Uh-huh. Oh, that's good. Yes, we're fine. I know, the holidays seem ages ago already. Stuart's already asking when we can go back to the cottage again. I explained the weather wouldn't be so nice and he wouldn't be able to swim all day, but he has a plan involving hot chocolate," he laughed. "He wanted you both to come down to stay, too, but I explained that it was too small for us all, and it would just be us and we'll pop into yours on the way home to tell all our stories."

Munro's parents had owned a small cottage on the Mull of Galloway, with its own private stretch of stony shore and spectacular views across to the mainland. They preferred warmer holidays now, and didn't enjoy the upkeep of the property, so they had gifted it to their son this year. Munro was incredibly grateful; he loved it there more than anywhere else. The peace and solitude, the views and walks, the wildlife to be seen - they were all wonderful. Thankfully Stuart had always loved being there as well, and it had become their refuge from work and school.

As his mum chatted, and he cleared away dinner plates, Stuart returned, triumphantly bearing a picture from school. He had drawn his family, dad and both sets of grandparents gangling with mismatched limbs and disproportionate faces. Each person's hair was depicted perfectly. The care he had taken with it, and innocent love which imbued it caught at Munro's throat.

"Can we send a picture to Granny, Dad? I want to show it to her!" Stuart shifted from foot to foot proudly and excitedly.

"Of course, we can! Mum, I'll hang up now, we're going to send you a photo of Stuart's family picture from school. I think you'll be pleased! Bye for now!" Capturing the image in the best possible light, Munro was bitterly aware of the small family Stuart had, and that his grandparents were now all quite elderly; there was a lot of grey hair in the drawing. Stuart was happy and loved, though, Munro reassured himself; that was the most important point of all.

Checking in on Stuart before heading to bed, Munro still hadn't reached a conclusion about Lana's situation. His evening's reading had been productive: the team at the

Bryant-Cargill clinic provided their findings and recommendations to the Central Care team, who prescribed for the patient based on a set of principles agreed by a working group of clinicians, social care specialists and the UK government. Therapy prescribed following Bryant-Cargill factorisation could not be amended by general practitioners, only by contacting the central clinic to appeal the results. This was stipulated in the patient's legal agreement to proceed with factorisation; effectively they devolved decision-making to Central Care and the factorisation team. The appeal process had not yet been pursued by any patient.

Reading the high-level process for appeals, Munro knew this would be a lengthy and expensive undertaking involving both clinicians and solicitors. He summarised two possibilities. Assuming the contraceptive was an error, then perhaps Dr Gillies could remedy the situation by negotiating with Central Care. Munro couldn't bring himself to believe the alternative: that the decision had been intentional. However, he still worried that Lana would have to challenge the findings to have it removed from her therapy. Uncomfortable with leaving Lana unaware of the situation, Munro resolved to have Maria investigate with Central Care as soon as possible. The situation still troubled him as he eventually fell asleep.

Chapter 22 – Wednesday 27th August

Juggling a flapping strip of sticky tape, Munro added Stuart's family picture in pride of place on his consultation room wall: a special request from his son. He had shown the rest of the staff on his way in – they all had a soft spot for Stuart, with his sunny disposition and unusually good manners. They were always kind about his improving artwork. He checked the drawing was level and smoothed down the tape before heading up to the kitchen for his break. He had hoped to catch Maria before the morning session but had no time; now he was determined to speak to her. As he turned at the top of the stairs, he was glad to see her already standing at the kettle, chocolate biscuit in hand.

"Maria," he decided against preliminaries, "have you seen that we can't remove the medication from Lana Knight's repeats?" As he explained the situation, and his findings from the night before, his fellow doctors gathered and listened, their expressions first disbelieving, then stern.

"This is ridiculous," Maria finally had to interrupt. "They can't just prescribe and insist that patients continue to take medication, even if the patient has signed some document agreeing to do so. What if they had an adverse reaction or similar? What if we need to prescribe another medication with contraindications? There must be some way for us to override the therapy without having to go through Central?"

Munro quietly explained the details of the process further, wanting to be concise and clear while still ensuring they had all the info they needed. He added that he suspected they would have to contact the Central team directly to remedy the situation, and that there was a small chance Lana would have to appeal the decision if it hadn't been a simple mistake.

Theresa Clarke looked equally horrified and scornful. "How could it not be a mistake? They can't give someone contraceptives without their consent! That's madness, Munro, it must be an error."

As Sheila announced she would take care of things, and the conversation returned to the more familiar ground of the ownership of patient care, Munro stirred his tea uncomfortably. He disagreed with Theresa but knew there was little point in debating the matter. For a female patient with unpredictable moods, he could understand why they might try prescribing the contraceptive pill, no matter how Victorian it sounded: hormonal adjustments could help. Normally this would have been agreed with the patient, but the Bryant-Cargill legal agreements clearly stated that Lana must accept all the treatments suggested. He would have preferred to be as confident of the outcome as Theresa. As he walked back to his room, he couldn't shake the feeling that they should be doing more for Lana.

Munro stood on the pavement overlooking the water, watching a seal bobbing contentedly amongst the waves and cursing his indecision. As a clinician, he had access to all patient information; the onus was on him to use it responsibly and only in the course of his professional duties. He had no right to be standing outside Lana Knight's home, considering ringing her doorbell. He knew Maria had called Central this afternoon and had been asked to complete an online form to initiate a review. She had done this immediately, but the automated response had only promised action within 2 weeks: not quick enough by far. He should leave it to her to handle it all, that was the logical course of action. He wondered why he was here.

"Hello!" Startled, he turned and found himself facing Lana, dressed for a run, ear buds poised. "It's a magnificent view, isn't it?" she added, oblivious to his spiralling panic. "I was heading for a run along the esplanade," she continued, a small frown gradually emerging. "I'm sorry," she closed, "I didn't mean to disturb you, startling you like that. I should go..."

"No! No, it's not that, I... It's a little hard to explain. Umm, I was actually hoping to speak to you. Can we maybe walk a little way before your run?" Munro accepted that he was going to have to explain himself, that the decision was now out of his hands. Thankfully, Lana readily agreed and smiled welcomingly as she turned downriver and started to walk.

"Thank you," he continued. "I should explain myself - I must seem very odd right now. I came here because I was considering talking to you about something. But when it came down to it, I couldn't quite make up my mind to ring your doorbell. As a doctor, I shouldn't be bothering you at your home, uninvited. But, well, I think there's something you should know about. I hope you'll forgive me..."

Lana interrupted him. "Please, Dr Alexander, don't worry. I don't mind you coming here at all. I am a little bit worried about what has you so concerned, though. Whatever has happened?"

Stumbling over the first few words, Munro explained the situation with the prescription, and that at best it might be a few weeks before they could convince Central Care to remove the contraceptives; at worst she may need to make a legal appeal. Lana listened gravely as they walked, keeping a fast pace. As Munro wrapped up, he realised she was slowing her stride as her concern grew. At the last, she stopped and sat down on a bench overlooking the small harbour and ancient keep. She gazed out over the rich mud and dank, weeded stonework for a time, then turned her fiercely intelligent eyes on Munro. She drew a steadying breath.

"So, I didn't read all of the legal agreement, I'm afraid. That's my own fault. I was nervous and just wanted to push through the process and get it over with, go home. I have paper and email copies of it - I'll check later, but I'm sure you're right about what it says. I just don't understand this at all. It was a surprise to hear that I needed any medication at all; Dr Gillies thought the pill had been an error. Do you think it was intentional?" she asked.

Munro quietly explained the link between hormone levels and moods, then posited that they may have hoped a contraceptive would help. He concluded by reiterating his belief that she should never have been prescribed them without her full understanding and approval. He watched as

Lana's face paled in the evening sun.

"I went on my own to the results meeting. I... Well, hearing what they had found - it was all a shock. I'm not sure I fully remember everything they said, to be honest. But I'm pretty damn sure I'd remember any conversation about the pill. It's not something I would have agreed to at all. I do remember them describing the meds I would receive - something about levelling out my moods with a mix of commonly used drugs. But that was all. They put me on the pill without my knowledge." She turned her piercing eyes back to Munro. "I'm sorry - is it just me, or is that really quite messed up? It's such an intrusion, so wrong."

Munro entirely agreed with her and understood her growing dismay and anger. "It's absolutely wrong in my mind, too, no matter what the legal position may be. Dr Gillies is trying to remedy the situation, but sadly it will take time. In the meantime, your venalink meds won't be fixed."

Lana rounded on him, barely containing the anger she felt. "I'm not taking them a day longer; I can tell you that! How can I tell which ones I should avoid? It should be obvious, shouldn't it?"

Munro pulled out his phone and quietly searched for an image of the pill. Showing it to her, he added, "The others will look different; you can just bin these ones. There will only be one per day, three weeks out of four. Shall I send this to you?" he asked. As Lana nodded, he added, flushing, "I don't have your contact details, sorry – I just sneaked a look at your address earlier." He still felt an acute sense of shame at that, but none from informing her of her situation, and was relieved. Lana gave him her details, and he sent the image to her phone. "I'm really so, so sorry that you're going through this. I wish I'd never recommended this testing. I hope you'll forgive me for disturbing you and telling you all this out of the blue."

Lana was hinged over at the waist, elbows on knees, and now breathed out forcefully. "No, don't worry. None of this is your fault, and I appreciate you taking the time to tell me it all. You won't get in trouble for this, will you? This is enough of a mess as it is."

Munro shook his head and advised her not to worry about it. He caught a hint of tears in her bright eyes and reached his hand tentatively towards her shoulder.

Lana shrugged it off, and stood to stretch, ear buds once again raised in both hands. "I'm sorry, I don't mean to be rude, but I just need to process all this; I'm going to go for my run. Thank you again. I'll not take any more of your time." With that she headed off in a steady lope, building up speed as she cleared the last of the benches. Munro watched her until she passed out of sight, hoping he had done the right thing. The other partners would be enraged if they knew what he had done, but more importantly he hoped Lana wasn't worse off for knowing.

As he sat at his computer later that evening, his phone vibrated lightly in his shirt pocket, a message from an unknown contact. He opened it, fully expecting spam. "I was a jerk earlier, sorry. I'm pretty sure you took a risk meeting me, and I was unfair to you in return. None of this is your fault, and I really appreciate you helping me. Hope you're having a good evening with your dinosaur boy! Lana."

His heart rate was raised, and his palms were sweaty; he replied before he could think too long about it. "Dinosaurs abandoned in favour of football tonight, over an hour of it. Stuart somehow still full of beans, I'm sadly exhausted. Should maybe take up running, too! Someone has taught him the term "nutmeg" - whoever it was, they're off my Christmas list. Have a good evening, too - Munro."

Five minutes later, he was rewarded. "Haha, keeping up with kids is hard going! Good luck!" The elation he felt at another message removed any doubts he still held about his interest in her. He knew he was acting out of character; he sat back and wondered at himself, and what Ann would make of his behaviour. She had stated firmly that she wanted Munro to move on after her death: by then the progression of her cancer had been inevitable, and she had been far more pragmatic about her passing than he could ever be. She believed that he and Stuart would both need someone in their lives, though that came with a long list of caveats that could now make Munro smile but at the time were alien and painful. It all condensed to one promise: that he would always put Stuart first, that he would make sure they would both be happy. Whatever happened, he would always keep that vow.

Chapter 23 – Sunday 31st August

Lana hurried out of the shower, drying herself roughly before damply climbing the stairs to her bedroom. Taking the minimum of care, she threw on jeans and the first top which came to hand, grabbing her phone from beside her bed and checking for messages and the time. It had woken her only twelve minutes beforehand, her father uncharacteristically terse. "Jen and Robbie arrived late last night. Breakfast in 30 mins, come around. Back door open x". Not wanting to waste time asking questions she doubted would be answered by messaging, she finger-combed her hair and hurtled downstairs to grab her trainers. As she locked her door and headed out into the day, disquiet raising goosebumps, she couldn't help but catalogue the many reasons for her sister's unexpected arrival. Someone might be ill. She and Cal had fallen out; she may have left him. Something was wrong with Robbie. Something had happened to Cal. Something had happened to their home. As she jogged through the early morning streets, she tried to be firm with herself: stop catastrophising, you'll find out soon enough.

Reaching her parents' house, she was surprised to see no extra car on the driveway or street – they must have flown or taken the train. Why would Jen not drive, Lana wondered. That's how she always came home, once she had passed her driving test. Public transport frustrated her, with too much waiting around and too many roundabout routes. As Lana hurried up the drive and through the back gate, she schooled her face and evened her breathing: arriving in a flap would only unsettle them all.

"Hi," her dad welcomed as she stepped into the kitchen. "In you come, grab a seat. I let Jen know you were coming over for breakfast; she says she'll be down in a minute. Your mum is just minding Robbie while she's in the shower."

"Okay," Lana replied. Her dad had stretched the truth somewhat, but if everyone else was playing "normal and relaxed", then she would join in. "I didn't expect Jen, is everything okay?" She tipped her head lightly to one side and looked her dad in the eye.

"No, neither did we, but that's okay. We're not sure why it was so last-minute. They arrived in a taxi late last night; Jen was exhausted." Peter shrugged and raised his eyebrows back at Lana. "I'm sure we'll find out what's happening after breakfast. Sausages on rolls okay? We've got eggs if you'd rather?" he asked, waving tongs at the frying pan on the stove. The aroma was heavenly; Lana would never refuse such fare.

"Sausages are great, they smell fab. Want me to sort the tea?" She filled the kettle and started assembling mugs and the teapot, biting her cheek lining lightly and knowing she had to be patient. The ritual of warming the pot and measuring out the tea leaves allowed her the time to calm herself, so when Jen entered the room with Robbie in her arms, she was able to smile openly, and head over to hug them both. "This is lovely! Goodness - look how much you've grown already! Are those new teethypegs?" she babied as she chucked Robbie's chin. Lana's mum smiled gratefully at her as she followed them into the room.

"Everyone grab a chair, here's the rolls all ready," her father ushered them into the dining area. "What will Robbie want, Jen? I've kept him a sausage I can cut up, and some bits of roll and butter?"

Jen surprised Lana by allowing her to take Robbie to his highchair and strap him in. "That'll be great, Dad, thank you. Do you have any milk at all? Any kind will do," she admitted. This was certainly more moderate than she had been on their last visit, but Lana suspected it was born of tiredness rather than a change of Robbie's routine. Everyone but Jen sharing glances, they settled down and ate, commenting vaguely on the weather, the sausages, and the bakery rolls. Lana washed down her last mouthful with a swig of tea and grabbed a satsuma.

"Is Robbie allowed some of this?" she asked, separating out some segments. As her sister smiled tiredly and nodded, she decided she could risk further questions. "So how did you guys travel up? I was expecting the car to be outside." Travel was usually a safe option, she thought.

"Oh God, that bloody car," Jen groaned. "We had to sell both of our cars to afford it, and still ended up with a huge loan, all so we could have the same fancy car as Cal's boss. Honestly, it's just stupidly big; I hate driving it. Well, when I get the chance to use it at all. If I want to keep it for the day, I need to have Robbie organised early so I can drive Cal into work for 7:30. And even then, he's not happy about me taking it and grumbles all the way there and back. I mostly just walk everywhere now, with the pram." Jen stared abjectly out the window, Lana's mum reaching across to pat her hand gently.

"Jen," Lana dared gently, "What happened to bring you home yesterday?"

"You're right," Jen muttered. "I'm not starting in the right place, am I? But it's so hard to tell when exactly it all started to go wrong: before Robbie, certainly. He was a surprise, but I thought having him might make us a happy family, rather than an unhappy couple. What a total idiot I was."

The family listened, sympathy and solidarity wrapping Jen in their arms. Lana carefully passed Robbie morsels of food to keep him quietly distracted.

"Do you remember when Cal got that promotion, maybe a couple of years ago? He moved into a management role - the pay is better but there's a lot more stress and he didn't get to do any development work anymore. I've never wanted to do that; I enjoy coding too much. But he made his own decision, and it seemed to be working out at first." They waited quietly for Jen to continue, knowing it was best to let her tell it all in her own time. "But his boss, he's really demanding and very... oh, I don't know, maybe materialistic is the word? It's all about cars and gadgets and holidays and status. Cal started out trying to impress him, but then he became more and more interested in those things, too. We were earning good money, so it wasn't a huge problem. But then... I was asked to join the advanced development team. We work on prototypes, new projects, that sort of thing. I was given a big pay rise, too: it meant I was earning nearly as much as Cal. I thought he would be pleased – but he was so bitter about it. He'd taken on all that stress and responsibility for a "better job" and here was me, doing some really exciting work for the same money. He started being sarcastic about everything we worked on, belittling everything we achieved. He didn't even try to hide his disgust about how much I was paid. He was awful about it all, took all the joy out of it for me."

Jen pushed her plate away, and summarised, "That's probably where it started. We got over that eventually, and when I found out I was pregnant, he was over the moon. I thought everything would be fine. But then he refused to share the parental leave, saying he couldn't leave his job for months as easily as I could. It was the same old bitterness as before. I ended up agreeing with him even though I was disappointed. But since Robbie was born... I don't know, he's just been a completely different man. He's so grumpy. He's hardly ever home - and when he is, he ignores me. He seems to think all our money is his, like we're living in the 1950s or something. It's mad, though, I'm still earning even though I'm on leave! Even so, I try to keep the peace, finding all the best deals for things like nappies and food, but it's never frugal enough for him. He does nothing to help with Robbie or the house. All he cares about is that car and his gadgets and the next TV he wants to buy. He's started spending so much money on stupid things we don't need, but then his favourite excuse for avoiding coming home is that he needs to work so hard to keep us afloat. It's all bollocks, obviously. He just wants to be some fancy lad in flash things instead of being a dad and a husband."

Jen's tears were streaming down her cheeks now, but she barely stopped for breath. "I've tried and tried to talk to him, but he just dismisses everything I say. It's like he thinks he can do what he wants, that I'm stuck with him now that we've had a baby. But I'm sick of it all, Mum. I'm sick of him, and living down there, and I'm sick of our stupid big loveless house and all the stupid things. I just want to come home."

Now she paused for breath, wiping her face and gathering courage for what was to come. "So, I told him. On Friday night, I told him that I wanted to come home, that I didn't want to be with him anymore. And he looked at me like I was dirt, and all he said was "Well, don't think you're taking my car." That was it, for all the years together, and our beautiful boy..." Suddenly, Jen had run out of strength, and covered her face with her hands, breath juddering in her chest as her tears flowed.

Mundane actions provide the scaffold for the traumatic times in our lives; we rarely notice or remember them afterwards. Lana wiped Robbie's hands, and lifted him from his chair, settling him on her lap to play with soft blocks, his innocent happiness a gift to the room at this time. Peter poured more tea and let Todd out into the garden while Lana's mum sat holding Jen's hand, uttering the familiar soft reassurances of their childhood. Time ticked, unrecognised and irrelevant while Jen wept for herself and her son. Lana ached for her sister as she grieved for her marriage. Eventually, Jen looked up at Robbie happily playing, and grated, "He deserves better. I deserve better." She looked at her mum, then her dad. "Can we stay? We'll sort something out for..."

"Of course," her dad interrupted firmly. "Don't worry about what needs sorting out. This is your home, there's no rush for any big decisions. Just try and get your breath back for now, that's the priority. We've got you." As fresh tears rose in her eyes, Jen's dad leaned over and kissed the top of her head. "The man's an idiot," was his last word.

Later that afternoon, Lana took a sleeping Robbie out in his pram with Todd, to allow the others to rest after their late night. It felt good to stretch her muscles and take some of her tension out on the pavement. Todd walked well with the pram, eyeing Lana regularly to make sure she was noticing. She kept to the streets within twenty minutes of home, walking past houses, churches and small businesses, careful of Robbie waking and needing his mother. As the steady rhythm of her steps soothed her nerves, Jen's truths turned constantly in her mind, and Lana alternated between anger at Cal and sadness for her sister. As she had headed out, her father had caught her on the path, anxiety clear across his features.

"She should come and see you at the bank tomorrow, get herself her own account. God knows what he's doing with their money. The solicitors will sort out everything in the separation, but in the meantime, she needs her salary in her own account, so she has something at least," he had urged.

Lana agreed, although she wasn't sure what Jen's maternity pay would be, or what would happen if she wasn't returning to work there. She was sure Jen could find a good job locally - there were plenty software jobs in the area – but would she be happy to leave Robbie with someone else every day? Even if she didn't have any other bills, she would need to find legal representation if she wanted to separate formally. It was a tangle they could tackle as a family, and she was glad Jen hadn't started to worry about it too much just yet.

As she turned down past the primary school, she felt her phone vibrate in her back pocket. Wary of whether stopping the pram might wake the baby, she juggled pram, dog lead and phone for a second, then gave up and slowed gently to a halt. She smiled as she saw it was a message from Munro: "Hi - hope you're having a good weekend after all the fuss last week! Hopefully see you soon." Surprised at the lift the simple message gave her, Lana returned her phone to her pocket; she would answer later when she didn't have her hands quite so full.

31/8

Livid with Cal, but can't let Jen see that, they may well patch things up and it will be difficult enough as it is. I can't believe he's been so juvenile and selfish. Wee Robbie is a sweetpea, he was no bother today at all. I'll get more auntie duties now they're here, can't wait!

Still can't get over what's happening with these meds. Hope docs can sort it all out. Dr A was very sweet, hope he hasn't taken a risk by meeting me and telling me about it all.

Still the same weight, but doc did say it would take a while. Might try and stretch my runs a bit further, see if that will help.

Chapter 24 – Thursday 4th September

Lana smiled as she opened her door and greeted her sister. "It seems odd now to see you without Robbie in your arms," she teased.

"Oh, don't," Jen laughed, "it feels so odd to have left him behind, even if he is just going to bed and only a few streets away. I can't decide if I feel liberated or terrified," she admitted. Her parents had offered to look after Robbie for the evening, to let the sisters spend some time together. "But I must admit it will be nice to be able to talk about things without worrying about whether he'll sense me getting upset or angry. I feel like I'm on tenterhooks the entire time. He's so little, but I swear he senses when something is wrong. I've brought elderflower fizzy stuff, Dad reminded me that you weren't drinking anything alcoholic."

"Thanks," Lana smiled, "I've made that spicy beef you liked before, hope that's okay? It'll be a half hour yet, so we can sit down. What happened with Cal's parents? You were on the phone when I left..." she prompted.

"Oh jeez, it's such a mess. Cal just isn't interested, it's awful: how can he not care about his wife and son leaving, Lana, honestly? He isn't even bothered about arranging visits with Robbie or anything. His mum and dad are livid. At first, they thought I must be overreacting, you could tell they thought I needed to come home and sort things out. But I didn't hold back, I told them what it had been like, and that I was totally sure our marriage was over. Whatever Cal said to them after that, they're totally disgusted with him. They want to be able to see Robbie, obviously; I've said that's great and that we can sort things out. We'll visit them together every so often, until he's old enough to maybe holiday with them or something. I think they're hoping that by then Cal will want to see him, too - but for now he's determined that he wants nothing to do with us. He keeps using the words "your baby", Lan. Like he wasn't ever his dad. He still expects me to keep paying the mortgage and everything, though; he's happy to take my money!"

Lana knew how difficult it could be for couples to separate financially, and how long it could take - especially when the person who stayed in the house didn't want to have to take sole financial responsibility for it. Delaying tactics could drag proceedings out to years. "Be careful, Jen. If he wants to keep the house, he'll have to buy you out - but that could take months and months. In the meantime, you still share responsibility for it."

"Oh! That's the other thing they said, I nearly forgot. They said they don't want me and Robbie to be stuck for money, so they've offered to work with Cal's solicitor to make sure things go through quickly. They've agreed to buy my half of the house because Cal couldn't afford it on his own: he's keeping that car, but wants the house as well, apparently. Ugh, he's welcome to it. I've got an appointment with my solicitor on Monday, but they seem to think that this will stop Cal dragging things out. We'll see." Jen looked dubious about it, but Lana thought it was a positive sign: Cal's parents obviously wanted to keep Jen in their family as much as possible and were therefore willing to help her. Jen shook herself. "Enough about that, I'm sick of thinking and talking about it. How are things with you?"

Lana had told no one about the problems with her prescriptions, or about her growing friendship with Munro. She was desperately tempted to share it all with Jen but didn't want to burden her with any more worries; plus, anything shared with Jen would then be reported back to her mum. She found herself keeping quiet about both, choosing to talk about the bank and how she wanted to find a new career.

"I guess that's something I should be grateful I don't need to do," ventured Jen. "I told my manager what I'd decided, and that I wouldn't be going back to work in Brighton, and she was amazing about it. She talked to HR and they totally understand that I would want to stay here now. They've offered that I can return to work from home here. They're going to send up my things from my desk once my maternity leave is over. I'll maybe need to go down once or twice a year for big company meetings, but everything else is online anyway. It'll still be awkward working for the same company as Cal, but we won't have much to do with each other most of the time."

"That's fantastic news, Jen!" Lana beamed. "I thought you might need to leave, what a relief for you. They're obviously a smart bunch and know how good you are. Will it be weird for you to work from home? What will you do with Robbie?"

"Mum and Dad have offered to look after him some of the time, but I think I'll try and get him into a nursery once we're into more of a routine," Jen explained. "It'll be good for him to be around other kids, and it would be a lot of work for Dad. He'll be less spoiled there, too," she laughed.

"Oh Jen, things are going to work out fine, wait and see," Lana insisted. "I know none of this is what you really want, but you're getting back on your feet already. Oh, I wish we could celebrate with some proper bubbly, but let's crack open the elderflower," she added, heading through to the kitchen to grab glasses. "It's going to be amazing having you and Robbie here, you know. I know it's for a sad reason, but we're all going to be so much closer. It's selfish of me, but I'm so looking forward to being his cool auntie. I can help with looking after him at weekends, and evenings, too. Maybe more depending on whatever I end up doing career-wise. Let's get something to eat, then we can watch a movie or something."

As Lana served up portions of the meal, Jen stood at the kitchen window admiring the garden below. "Your neighbours do a lovely job with their garden," she approved. "I didn't know what to do with mine, it was just all grass. Maybe it would be easier if it was already established. I'll have to get someplace once we have the money sorted out, I can't impose on Mum and Dad forever. Maybe someplace with some room outside for Robbie to play when he's older," she mused. "At least house prices here are a bit more sensible, I should be able to get a mortgage."

"Once you're ready, I could get one of our mortgages experts to help," Lana offered. "I got staff rates when I bought this place, but the deals would still be competitive. Or you could rent for a while until you're sure you've found the right place." They sat and started to assemble heaped tacos from Mexican spiced beef, vegetable rice and salads. "No need to worry about table manners with family," Lana laughed, tucking into hers. "I'm glad you're feeling so positive about it all, I'd be a wreck," she returned to Jen.

"I don't have much choice," Jen answered pragmatically. "I have Robbie to worry about. It totally changes your priorities, being a parent. Everyone says it, but I didn't understand until now. I want to get us settled. I want him to grow up happy, and loved, and never missing his dad. I can cope with a bit of turmoil just now to ensure that it works out for us in the future. This is delicious," she added, helping herself to more rice. "Who is Munro?" she asked suddenly, distracted by Lana's phone notification.

Lana felt herself start to flush, and hid her face behind her taco, raising a hand to apologise while she carefully finished her mouthful and thought briskly. "Oh, he's someone I just met. We started chatting after we bumped into each other at The Bell one night. We're getting on quite well, but I'm not sure what might come of it, it's just been a few messages so far. He's a doctor, has a little boy - Lind says he's a widower, his wife died of cancer." She held back on telling the whole truth of how they met, still wary of worrying her family.

Jen was grinning very knowingly. "I was beginning to think you'd sworn off men," she laughed. "A doctor is promising; he must be clever enough anyway. We haven't been able to have a decent boy chat for years! What's he like?"

Lana paused, taking the question seriously. "I haven't really had a chance to get to know him yet. He's incredibly close to his son, that's obvious: almost everything he does is with Stuart. He has a pretty dry sense of humour. He seems to spend most of his own time catching up with his work, or watching movies – he's into westerns, of all things," she laughed. Jen revolved her hand at the wrist, urging her on. "Okay, okay. He's quite tall, maybe six-two? Broad shoulders, long legs. Light blond-brown hair, not too short and a little shaggy. Brown eyes. He has an intense expression sometimes but it's still a kind face, if that makes sense. Lind says he looks like a hunky lumberjack, I think they'd be a bit jealous if they knew we were chatting. We haven't spent much time together, just a quick hello a couple of times, and we bumped into each other once and walked for a bit."

Jen had been watching Lana carefully as she spoke, noting the wistfulness as her sister considered this new man in her life. "You really like him, don't you?" she asked. "What are you going to do about it?"

Lana twisted her mouth indecisively and shrugged. "I don't know. With his wife dying, and him having a son – I don't want to be too forward. He might not be sure about seeing someone. It's a big leap from a few polite messages to a date or anything. We'll see how it goes; I don't want to rush things."

Jen nodded, approving of her plan. "Sounds wise – you don't want to get into something and then he's not ready to move on. But hopefully he is, it would be lovely to see you happy with someone." Jen looked wistfully out of the window before turning back to the table. "I'm having more, I hope you didn't want leftovers for tomorrow," she giggled.

4/9

Intrusions

It felt odd to tell Jen about Munro. Too early days. She seemed steadier, though, a good thing. She might complain about being with Robbie all the time, but she was clockwatching the whole evening and headed off as soon as she could, haha! She's a great mum, I hope she sees it.

First pound off this week!

Chapter 25 – Tuesday 16th September

Munro was conflicted. For over two weeks now, he and Lana had been sending messages, sharing the details of their days and slowly getting to know each other. He was certain they liked each other, certain they would get on well, but he just couldn't bring himself to take the next step. He worried about disrupting his life with Stuart: bringing another woman into their lives, and the effect any gossip may have on him. He worried what the partners might say at the surgery – he would have to tell them. He worried about his part in her problems with the Bryant-Cargill analysis and her medications, too wary to admit that he knew the lead clinician and that might be why she was seen so quickly. Every time he carefully worded a message suggesting they meet, those doubts overwhelmed him, and he discarded the text. It left him feeling torn and cowardly. He wondered if he was focused on these concerns to avoid thinking about his feelings for Ann; would he feel guilty every time he met Lana? Could she ever accept that he still loved Ann and missed her, and probably always would? Was that a fair thing to ask of anyone?

He poured his morning coffee and waited for his toast; Stuart was tucking into a bowl of cornflakes. "When will it be pancake day, Dad?" he asked.

Munro blinked. "Oh, well, not for ages, it's in February – months and months off. We've got October holidays, then Halloween, then Christmas, then New Year, then Valentine's Day before then." Stuart's face had fallen. "Why?" Munro asked.

"I quite liked having pancakes for breakfast," he explained. "The bananas and sauce and cream were lovely."

Munro laughed. "Well, we can have pancakes on days other than Pancake Day, you know. Although maybe best a weekend day so we can take time and get the batter right. We could do that on Saturday, if you like?" Seeing Stuart's face light up, Munro was struck by how literal his son could be, and how he rarely asked for treats. "You know, if you fancy anything like that – to eat, or something to do – you can always ask. It's not like in school where we do whatever the teachers organise."

Stuart puzzled at Munro. "Mrs Meachan said that those that ask don't get," he objected.

"Mrs Meachan was a bit too grumpy for her own good," Munro admitted quietly. "You can suggest things just as easily as I can," he elaborated. "When I suggest we go to the park, or for a walk, you have a choice. Not with everything, obviously, but with suggestions. So, if you asked to go to the beach, or the cinema or to a friend's house, then we might not go immediately – or I might even say no – but it's definitely okay to ask."

"I'll have a think about what else I fancy at the

weekend, then!" Stuart beamed. "Thanks, Dad!" He came over and hugged Munro about the waist, surprising him all over again. Munro hoped his son never lost this innocent happiness, knowing that was an impossible wish.

Lana felt nervous as she approached the surgery. It had been over two weeks since she had seen Munro, and they had shared so much about themselves in that time. When she saw him next, she didn't want it to be at the clinic, awkward and professional. She was here for her first medical review, two months on from her factorisation testing. It should be a simple visit to the practice nurse, to note any side effects and take samples to test for any problems raised by the medications. After this, they would be every 3 months for the first year, then every 6 months thereafter. Partly, she hoped she could slip in and out of the building without seeing Munro. Partly she would love to bump into him; she had made sure she was looking good, and her stomach was lightly knotted.

The practice nurse called Lana into her room. She was young, a recent hire, and she was bubbly and friendly as Lana entered. Lana warmed to her immediately and smiled broadly when she spotted a Pokémon keyring dangling from her lanyard. The nurse gestured and offered Lana a chair.

"Please, grab a seat, I won't be a minute. This is my first BC factorisation review. I know it's just taking bloods and completing the form, but I want to double-check I have everything right. I'm quite excited to be doing something new, to be honest!" she admitted.

Lana grinned. "I'm the same at the bank with new procedures, even if they're almost identical to the old ones.

For me, it's just not worth the risk of messing it up and having to re-do things!" Lana agreed readily.

"Oh, yes. It's not worth landing in hot water for, for sure! Did you bring the urine sample with you? Perfect. Right, I'll just get your blood pressure, then take a blood sample, then we can do the questionnaire. Is that okay? I think it's great that you've been for the testing, you're so brave to try it out early. I'd love to give it a go, but I need a good reason, apparently," she laughed. "You'll have to tell me all about it on one of your visits."

As the nurse worked her way through the review, Lana briefly heard Munro talking in the hall, and struggled to curb her instinctive smile. Suddenly, it felt odd to be so close by without saying hello; she would message him tonight, let him know she had been in, but he had been busy. She didn't want to look like she was avoiding him.

When Lana arrived back at the bank, the tellers were up in arms, and the office manager stood amid them all, placating and pleading. "Please, please, everyone will get a break - we just need to make sure we cover the counters. One of you may need to go a little later than usual, that's all. Here's Lana back, perhaps she can help. Lana, would you be able to cover a counter over lunch? Lind left the office early and hasn't returned, isn't answering calls. Do you know what's happened at all?"

Taken aback by the unexpected fuss, Lana stuttered, "Yes, of course. Well, of course I can help. I can help on the counter. I haven't heard from Lind, no. Would you like me to try and get in touch, or get straight onto a till?"

"No, I'll deal with Lind," he declared forebodingly. "You get onto a till, and then only two of you to lunch at a time, please." He frowned around the room and stalked off. Lana could only hope Lind had a good excuse for disappearing; she didn't think the management would be particularly understanding of it unless there was a genuine emergency.

Lana welcomed her first customer and started working her way through the bank's busiest spell of the day, worrying incessantly about Lind. Thankfully the time passed quickly and uneventfully, and soon all the tellers, bar Lind, were back in service. Lana hurried to her desk and spent the rest of the afternoon fretting and unsuccessfully trying to track down her friend. By the time they were all heading home for the day, there was a range of theories for Lind leaving unexpectedly, from a lottery win, to illness, to an arrest. Lana despised the vicious gossip and struggled to stay calm when she spoke up: "For goodness' sake, it's Lind. Something must have happened; someone must be hurt or something. Try not to start any mad rumours," she finally snapped as she stormed away from the crowd.

Munro was last to leave the surgery, shutting down systems and running through the security checklist before activating the alarm and locking up the doors. He stood for a minute or two, as he always did, waiting for the alarm to fully activate and mentally shedding the workday before he headed home. The leaves on the trees in the garden had started to redden, and he looked forward to seeing the autumn colours in full. He could ask Lana to join him for a walk through one of the nearby woods, he thought. It could be a friendly thing, give them both time to get to know one another without making any major decisions about it.

Perhaps he was overthinking the whole situation, he realised. As he walked towards home, he resolved to suggest it that evening, then see if Laurie could do something with Stuart. He could downplay it for just now, until he had a chance to think about the future.

Lana stood at the entrance to Lind's street, suddenly uncertain about imposing on her friend. Lind may not be home, may be in the middle of something, may not welcome the intrusion. But if Lind was hurt or unwell, or needed anything, Lana would never forgive herself for abandoning her friend. She steeled herself, prepared for any outcome, and headed onwards. Lind's neighbours' houses were quiet as she passed, as was Lind's. Lana rang and rang the bell dispiritedly, knowing her friend wasn't going to answer but with no other idea of what to do. She could see no movement inside but rang again one last time before dejectedly heading back towards home.

Munro closed his laptop decisively and sat back. He had tucked Stuart into bed roughly a half hour ago, tired out after an evening of football and homework. Munro couldn't quite believe how much homework such young children were being given each week; Stuart insisted on getting it done as soon as possible; spreading it over two evenings was all Munro could convince him to do. He hadn't heard from Lana this evening but had promised himself that once he had finished work, he would invite her to meet him for a walk at the weekend. Now he sat, pondering how best to word it. He didn't want to presume too much and scare her off, nor did he want to make it sound like too serious a thing. He sighed; he had no confidence that he would achieve the right tone, so decided to go for simple and sincere.

"Hi there!" he wrote. "How's your day been? I noticed the leaves have started to turn, and thought maybe we could head somewhere for a walk to see the woods this weekend? Laurie said she would be able to take Stuart on either Saturday or Sunday, so either day is good for me. Let me know if you fancy it, M."

He headed to the kitchen, swithering between making a cup of tea or opening a beer, and grabbing his phone before he went through – just in case it rang. He shook his head in amusement at himself, wondering yet again what Ann would make of his inexperienced attempts to impress.

Lana was in her favourite chair, book forgotten in her lap, gazing out her windows and over the water. She startled as her phone chirped, then again as her doorbell rang. As she made her way to the door, she heard a soft sob, and rushed to open it. Lind stood outside, as naked as Lana had ever seen. Dressed in loose trousers and a baggy jumper, hair tucked behind ears and only faint traces of makeup left on their tear-streaked face, Lind crumpled into Lana's hug and choked, "I didn't know where else to go. I'm so sorry, I know you're busy with Jen just now. But I just couldn't be on my own anymore."

"Oh, Lind," Lana breathed. "Come in, don't worry. I was looking for you earlier. Whatever has happened?"

Lana moved into the kitchen and settled Lind into a chair before filling the kettle and grabbing some chocolate biscuits from the cupboard. "No emergency cake, I'm afraid, but I always have a KitKat." When Lind didn't respond, sitting blankly with their arms wrapped tight around their middle, Lana lowered herself into the next chair, and stared into her friend's eyes. "Lind, you're worrying me. What's happened?"

Fresh tears flowing, Lind focused on Lana and took a deep breath. "I know I'm acting like an idiot. But I'm just so angry, so very angry. It's Kenny, he's been… God. Honestly, I didn't even think we were that right for each other, but I was trying so hard to make things work. I couldn't face another round of "Lind has lost another one" from my family and the snarky gits at the bank. So, all this time, I've been making so much effort, and while I've been dealing with his idiot ex, and loads of hassle from his ex's friends and family… Lana, he's been off seeing someone else. Some butter-wouldn't-melt girl - from a farm, believe it or not. He's been cheating on me all this time, while I've been dealing with all his bother. And now he's got her pregnant, Lana, and he says he can't see me anymore in case she finds out. It's like he's chosen her for the one thing I can never give anyone. I feel like such a fool, Lan."

Despair was welling vividly in Lind's eyes, and Lana felt swamped by the raw emotion she saw there as she imagined her friend's pain. But she would endure it all for Lind. She knew no advice would help; knew that she could only listen, sympathise and support. At heart, she was glad things with Kenny had ended: Lana had suspected the relationship wasn't proving healthy for Lind. But she felt so badly for her friend, that it had ended so cruelly. "I'll make some tea, and you can tell me everything that's happened. Take your time."

Two pots of tea and a lot of chocolate later, Lana settled Lind on her sofa with a spare duvet and pillows, pulling the curtains closed for the first time in months. "Don't worry, no one will bother you here, and tomorrow morning I'll get you home. Take the day off sick - just tell work you had a migraine, and your phone was on silent. They can't complain about that. Try to sleep, you must be exhausted. We'll sort everything out, and you'll come through this stronger, wait and see. We're all here for you, Lind." Lightly squeezing and releasing the fingers of the hand she'd been holding, Lana grabbed her phone and headed off to her own bed, drained and exhausted herself. Lind had poured out heart and soul, and Lana felt like she'd lived every moment with them.

As she laid her phone on her bedside table, Lana spotted the message she'd received hours earlier, and swore. It was from Munro, asking her to meet him at the weekend, and she'd ignored it! He would understand, but at this point it must seem so rude. It was after midnight, but she sent a message anyway, unable to leave him hanging any longer; if he was asleep, it wouldn't wake him. "Would love to!" she replied. "Saturday is good for me, where should we meet? Sorry didn't reply earlier, my friend was here and needed some help. Will tell all later. See you soon, L."

When she rose the next morning, Lind was showered and dressed in the clothes Lana had laid out, sitting in the window seat. The bedcovers were carefully folded, and Lana could smell fresh coffee brewing in the kitchen. "Have you been up long? Did you manage to get some rest?" she asked.

"I did. I didn't think I would be able to sleep, but I must have been past worrying. I thought I might make breakfast as a thank you, but I wasn't sure what you'd like," they explained. "You were so kind last night, Lana. I don't think I've ever been able to tell anyone most of what we spoke about last night. You might believe those idiot doctors when they say you have problems - but to me you're amazing, Lan. You remember that."

Lana was touched. She always viewed her emotional side as a nuisance and forgot that it was often appreciated by others. Even if she found her life more difficult because of her empathy and tendency to over-thinking, she was glad it meant she could help her friends. She smiled and opened the fridge. "Ooft, the cupboards are bare. I meant to shop last night but didn't get around to it. Is toast okay?" As they breakfasted, they chatted lightly about trivial topics, neither wanting to spoil a peaceful mood that was a balm to their frayed nerves.

Chapter 26 – Saturday 20th September

Munro found a space in the busy village street and checked the cars parked around him – he couldn't see Lana but wasn't sure what type of car she was bringing. On the road, he had felt peculiarly conspicuous and over-aware of his driving; any car could be Lana and he didn't want to make a bad impression. They had agreed to travel separately, Lana bringing her father's dog in his car. It was a beautiful morning, the sun warm and bright, but the previous week's rain would make it wet underfoot amongst the trees; Lana said it would be too muddy for the dog to come with Munro in his car. Munro felt as nervous as a kid on a first date: he had spent hours debating what to wear and whether to take a jacket. In the end, he had compromised, putting both a hoody and a waterproof in the car until he saw what Lana had brought. He smiled ruefully, aware that he was behaving oddly but unable to remedy it.

Looking up, he saw Lana approaching, a cheery wave through her windscreen as she passed, scanning for a free space. As she parked further down the road, he locked up his car and walked down to meet her, reaching her just as she fetched the dog from the boot.

"Hi!" she called. "Won't be a min. This is Todd," she smiled, gesturing at a big, friendly-looking black dog. "Hope you haven't been waiting too long?" As Munro shook his head, Todd wagged his tail in welcome as he waited patiently for Lana to attach his lead. "Do you think we might need a jacket?" Lana surprised Munro. "The forecast is to stay dry, so I think we'll be okay - but I couldn't decide." She would never know what a relief this was to Munro; that this had become a small obsession for him today was something he wouldn't dare admit. Lana was busy checking her pockets before she locked the car, so Munro busied himself saying hello to Todd. "I think he likes you," she concluded, turning towards the route uphill to the woodland walk.

They passed quiet and tidy streets, then turned into a pretty square of homes overlooked by an imposing church. "Years ago, I had an elderly aunt who lived in this house here," Lana gestured at one of a terrace of houses. "We used to visit with our grandparents and walk uphill collecting brambles to make jelly. I've always loved it here. As a kid, I used to dream of living in the village when I was older, but I hardly ever come now. This is lovely."

Munro had found the walk on a website and was surprised and pleased to find Lana knew it so well. "I've never been, actually, but I had heard it was particularly nice in autumn," he replied. "At least you'll know where we're going," he laughed. They were passing the church grounds now, taking a narrow footpath which headed away from the village and up into the hills behind. Autumn hedgerows flanked them, full of dwindling wildflowers and the rambling bramble bushes laden with their dark fruits. Lana let Todd off his leash, and he nosed ahead, scenting where other dogs had left their territorial messages.

"Sorry, it won't be a fast-paced workout with Todd in tow," Lana advised. "He's a sniffer. I might need to put him on his lead if we see too many other dogs, too – he can get a bit over excited sometimes. He's still young, he's getting there," she added, a little defensively. "If you're not used to dogs, he can be a handful, though," she finally allowed.

Munro immediately worried why she felt the need to justify the dog's behaviour; he liked animals and hadn't meant to show any criticism. "No, he seems great. I'm not much for yomping full-out on a walk, anyway; it seems a shame to rush past everything," he gestured at the views they were starting to glimpse through trees and hedges. "I like dogs, I just work too much to have a pet at home," he explained. "Stuart would love one. He says he wants a dog that will play football with him, ever since he saw a boy and his wee Scottie dog on the beach one day."

Lana smiled at this, and they walked companionably up the hill, stopping every now and then to let other walkers pass, or to let Todd catch up from one of his distractions. Summer lingered lightly in the air, the scent of fields and trees invigorating as flies danced in the lee of the wind. They had climbed hard uphill for a while, and now turned to look back over the small town, with its central medieval tower and quaint old streets surrounded by more modern housing and fields. In the distance, hills rolled contentedly in the autumn sunshine, stands of trees bright red and gold flags on the green and brown quilted background of the land.

"It's lovely, isn't it?" breathed Lana. "It puts everything into perspective, a day like this. In years to come all our current worries will be forgotten, but this view will still be here."

Munro glanced sideways at Lana's thoughtful face, and asked, "You never did tell me what happened this week; is everything okay?" He watched her as she appreciated the view, indulging in the beauty of her profile while she was distracted. Her smile was sheepish as she turned back towards him.

"I shouldn't complain, really: it's not me that's been upset or anything. My friend Lind – have I ever told you about them?" As Munro shook his head, she turned back to the path and continued, clicking her fingers to grab Todd's attention. "Lind is my friend from the bank. My dad used to work with Lind's dad, so we apparently met when we were younger, but neither of us remember it," she shrugged. "He prefers to be called "they" now," she pre-empted. "So, they were one of four kids, born a year before the littlest, a sister. Lind grew up much closer to her than the two older brothers, who were quite nasty even when they were all young. When Lind was older, they found they were attracted to people of both sexes. For a while, they thought they might prefer to be female, but that didn't fit any better than being a boy. By the time Lind turned eighteen, they were working at the bank, and had rented a room in a shared house which was a lot less stifling than being at home. They asked to be called "they" from then on, and I think that was when Lind really found their feet," she mused. "But then the sister died in a car accident when Lind was around twenty. It was horrendous for the whole family, but Lind had lost their closest friend, and the rest of the family closed ranks. Some pretty awful things were said. Lind's grandmother always defended Lind, but she was elderly and mostly housebound by then. So, Lind walked away from the family and has barely spoken to them since. Despite all this, when I joined the bank, Lind was confident and outgoing, strong-minded and spirited. They have the most amazing sense of style: mostly androgynous stuff – suits, tailoring –

but with all the glamourous things Lind and their sister both loved: makeup, accessories, jewellery, shoes. They date whoever they please, and don't take any criticism. But with that came years of harassment and vilification from family, some old friends, total strangers. It hasn't been an easy life for them." Lana glanced at Munro and laughed. "I am getting to this week, honestly."

"Romantically, Lind hasn't had an easy time either, although they hide the hurt well. And it's such a small town, they know that their family hear about everything and often the brothers make a point of coming into the bank and being cruel. This year, Lind's been seeing a guy called Kenny." As Lana explained the tumultuous relationship and its sudden demise, they circled the top of one hill and headed further away from town towards a second peak. Here the trees had petered out, replaced by bracken and sheep grazing. Smallholdings and houses dotted the scene. Lana put Todd on his lead as they neared the farm animals. "So, it's been yet another blow to Lind, but this time it's even more cruel: Kenny leaving for a very "normal" family situation is such a rejection of everything Lind stands for. I've spent most of this week just being there for them. I can't complain, but it's made for an emotional and draining week. This," she gestured at the view, "this is lovely, to get away from home and recharge a bit. Thank you for suggesting it."

Munro had quietly listened, absorbing Lana's story. He was struck deeply by her compassion and selflessness, her concern for her friend and her innate understanding of the problems in Lind's life. He wondered if she realised how rare that was, what a gift.

"I see a lot of patients who collapse under the strain of much less than Lind sounds like they've suffered," he responded. "They sound very brave, and lucky to have you around. Not many people would give so much of their time to a friend." As Lana started to argue, he insisted, "Trust me, you're kinder than most. And you've had other worries, too: your sister, your work."

Lana shrugged. "I guess so. Lind was really kind at one point, said how much I had helped by being there and listening – they said I'm fine as I am and shouldn't be trying to change," she laughed. "Sometimes I forget that there's a good side to being me."

They chatted lightly, filling in the details of the sparse messages they had sent over the previous weeks, getting to know each other a little better. Munro discovered that Lana had described him as a friend when she asked to borrow her dad's car; she didn't want her parents jumping to conclusions. He laughed, admitting that he'd used the same wording when asking Laurie to look after Stuart.

"I wasn't sure whether we were just friends, really," he admitted. "I didn't want to assume you would consider going on a date with someone who had been your doctor, and who had a young son, and…well, was me."

Lana laughed and tapped his arm lightly in reproach. "No, that doesn't bother me at all. But - while we're being honest…" She slowed to a stop and turned to face Munro. "I wasn't sure whether it was okay for you to get to know a patient. And… Well, I had heard how you lost your wife, and I wasn't sure if you were just being friendly. I didn't want to offend you by assuming today was a date or anything."

Munro didn't want to mislead Lana in any way, but neither was he sure he could bare his whole soul just yet. He told her what he felt he could. "I'll be honest, too: if you had asked me a few months ago, I would have said I would never be ready to meet someone else. Meeting you - and wanting to get to know you - it's been so unexpected. Ann talked to me a lot before she died, saying she wanted me to move on and have a good life with someone else, but it hasn't seemed even vaguely possible until recently. Stuart and I, we still miss her all the time. And I need to be careful of his feelings." He had been watching Lana's reactions all along but paused now to see if she wanted to respond. When she waited for him to continue, sympathy deep in her eyes, he surprised himself by adding quietly, "I think I might always love Ann, and that would be hard for anyone else to accept. But now I wonder if I could love someone else, as well. Fall in love again. It's a lot to ask of anyone, though."

Lana tilted her head to one side, intently reading Munro's expression. "We would just need to wait and see how we get on, I guess," she countered, softly. "But I think that's what everyone goes through when they first meet, isn't it? You're just being more honest and transparent about the risks than most people are. Everyone has their past, their problems, other people in their lives. At least I'll know that it's Stuart or your feelings for Ann that you need to consider. And there's no rush; we can take it slowly. You may hate the way I sneeze," she joked, "or despise my cooking, or find that my house smells of paint all the time, or that you can't deal with my family. There are a hundred ways for a new relationship to fail, and it probably won't be what we expect," she laughed.

They both smiled, each relieved to be honest with each other, each excited to look to a possible future together. The breeze shifted past them and downhill, bringing green scents and cooling the sun's warmth. Munro knew it would be the perfect time to kiss her and reached up to gently tease loose strands of hair from her face. He tracked the revealed curve of her cheek, from brow to jaw, tarrying as he searched for certainty and courage.

Lana suddenly grinned and rocked onto her toes, pecking him on the cheek and breaking the spell. "No rush," she explained semi-seriously. "You really shouldn't look worried about kissing someone," she elaborated.

Munro was mortified, before realising she was right, and laughing it off. "You must think I'm a right twit," he confessed, hoping she would contradict him.

"No, just a bit of one," she ribbed, eyebrow raised and eyes sparkling. She elbowed him gently and turned to continue their path. "Actually, it's very nice to meet someone who takes these things seriously and doesn't go around snogging any old body." She looked him in the eye earnestly. "Let's try not to worry so much, and just see how we get on. If you aren't a total disaster, I may even buy you a scone and tea in the tearoom back in the village. No walk is complete without tea and cake."

Chapter 27 – Monday 22nd September

Lana slid past the occupied chairs in the staff room and refilled the kettle before dipping down into the cupboard to find mugs for herself and Lind. They had finagled a break together, a rare event, and were celebrating; Lind was fetching cakes from the baker's and Lana was on tea duties. As the others finished their drinks and tidied away their things, Lana listened half-heartedly to their discussion about the planned night out on Halloween, which fell on a Friday this year. It was to be fancy-dress, they'd already reserved tables in the pub.

"Will you be coming, Lana?" asked one of the other tellers.

"I think so," she agreed. "No idea what I'll wear, though. Are you all making the effort or is it just a witch's hat and green eyeshadow kind of thing?" she asked, half seriously. There was a mix of responses, which seemed to surprise everyone, and Lana noted to check again before making too much effort. She secretly thought she might give it a miss; bank nights out were often quite fractious.

As she removed the teabags and added milk, Lind arrived brandishing the baker's box. "I went for an éclair in the end, they didn't have a meringue. Probably just as well, I always make a right mess with it. Your fudge doughnut must be the size of my fist, you know." They plated up their treats and settled in for what remained of their twenty-minute break. As they grinned and bit into their pastries, they relaxed, enjoying having the break room to themselves.

"I wish we could take our break together more often," Lana complained. "I always seem to get stuck with Robert and his bunion problems. I do feel sorry for him, but it's just not good chat." Knowing she was whining, Lana changed topic. "How are you feeling today?"

"D'you know," Lind replied. "I think I'm fine. It was just a bit of a shock, and a knock, you know? But I think I'll be okay. I might take a bit of a break from dating for a while, try and have a calmer time of it. I'm tired of the melodrama."

Lana jokingly berated her friend, "That'll last a week or two before you're bored, wait and see. Hopefully you'll meet someone without any drama." They started creating an imaginary partner for Lind, balancing positive features with a drama-free history. "You never know," Lana added, "he or she could be just around the corner, and you'd never know."

"That's why my gran always told me to wear good knickers," Lind giggled. "You'll be taking up crochet next, you old woman!"

Later that day, as Lana carried shopping bags home after work, she wondered if Lind had a point: was she old before her time? She was practical and pragmatic, a worrier and planner rather than carefree and spontaneous. She wouldn't change that, though, she decided; she was happy in her ways. She was a romantic soul but would rather be alone than with the wrong person, something she had noticed seemed unusual in the other young women she knew. Was that a bad thing? That might all change with Munro, she thought with a smile. As she rounded the corner, she spotted her dad and waved. His face brightened when he saw her.

"I was just at yours, dropping off some herbs and cuttings I've propagated. They'll keep in pots over the winter if you don't get around to planting them this year," he explained. "I'll come in with you if you've time for a cuppa?" he asked hopefully.

Lana laughed, unable to refuse her dad and happy to postpone the run she had planned. "Grab that post for me, will you?" she asked as she juggled keys and groceries. "Let me pop these away and I'll stick the kettle on."

"This one looks serious," her dad commented, waving a dull brown envelope. "It's from the NHS," he explained as he offered it to her and binned the junk mail.

Lana perched her full bags on the kitchen counter and turned to take the letter. Her frown lines deepened as she opened it and started to read, then she turned pale and slumped into a chair. "Oh my god," she started, then stopped and looked at her dad in alarm. "Hang on, I need to double-check this." She re-read the letter as her dad looked on, increasingly concerned.

"It's from Central Care," she explained weakly. "Last week I had my first medical review after the factorisation testing. I... The samples have shown that I'm not taking all my medication." She quickly summarised the situation with the unexpected contraceptives. "So, my doctor is in touch with them about it, to have them removed, and in the meantime, I've just been binning those particular pills. But the samples must have shown that, because now they're saying that I need to take all the medication they prescribe. They're saying that I signed up to do that in the legal agreement; there's a whole list of potential consequences if I don't. I have to go for more regular testing to ensure I'm conforming, this says."

Her dad took the letter from her hand and read through it, becoming agitated. "This is insane, Lana! They can't do any of this. They don't have the right to force you to take things, surely. And all these threats? Flagging your medical and social records to show you're a dangerous individual refusing your controlling medication? Notifying anyone who accesses your records, including employers and reference checks? That's the sort of thing Orwell worried about!" he exclaimed.

Lana was shaking her head, "No, no it won't come to that. I'm taking the other pills they wanted for the issues; it's just the contraceptive pill I've stopped. Dr Gillies will sort it out, surely? They need to sort it out!" Lana felt a rising panic, and tears filled her eyes. "Oh God, what have I done, signing up to all this? What have I done, Dad?"

Peter pulled her into a hug, holding her protectively as he fought the anger he felt; Lana needed him to be calm. "It'll be okay, wait and see. Get straight into the doctor's tomorrow morning, make them sort this out. It'll be fine, just some bureaucratic nonsense, I'm sure. They'll sort it all out for you." He wished he felt as sure as he sounded.

Later that night, Lana soaked in her bath, trying to unwind taut muscles and tangled thoughts. After her father had left, she had run far further than she intended, pounding her fears and frustrations into the coastal path, unable to bear the thought of turning back towards home and an evening alone. By the time she returned she was exhausted, legs weak and stomach cramping. She had showered and eaten a light meal before calling Munro, timing it for when Stuart would be safely in bed for the night. She'd sent him a photo of the letter, worried he would think she was overreacting. He had been horrified by the contents, unaware that Central Care had so much control over a patient's government-held records. It was the first time either of them had realised the full extent of the medical and social care reforms, and the additional authority the Bryant-Cargill factorisation agreement had given them. Munro agreed that she should see Maria the next morning and let the surgery resolve the issue for her. They had talked for over an hour, Lana initially pacing her living room then gradually relaxing as their chat moved on to more pleasant thoughts. They both wanted to return to the tearoom they had visited; the scones had been perfect and the home-made blackcurrant jam delicious. They planned to meet for another walk at the weekend while Stuart was at a friend's birthday party, this time at the beach. Munro asked her to bring Todd along again, he had enjoyed having the excitable overgrown pup with them. When they finally said their goodbyes, Lana was happier and looking forward to her week — she still felt drained and achy but was reassured that Dr Gillies would be able to help. She shifted in the hot and bubbly bathwater, enjoying the scent of lavender and eucalyptus, certain she would be sore the next morning but pleased by her new record distance.

22/9

I think I overreacted to that letter, I'm sure it will all get sorted out. Feeling a bit sheepish about it now — ah well, it'll be a story to laugh about in a few years. I've messaged Dad to try and stop him worrying, but he's all up in arms about government control, says we should go to our MSP. I doubt that would help much; politicians are all the same. The scrambled eggs I had earlier were amazing, can't stop thinking about having more, so off to bed.

Chapter 28 – Autumn

Friday 26th September

Lana considered her half-full glass and shook her head. "No thanks, Sanj, there's only so much lemonade I can sink," she grimaced. The others were ready for another round, though, so Sanj headed to the bar, claiming he was being treated like a lackey. Lind had twisted an ankle on the way to The Bell and was enjoying using it as an excuse to order him about.

"It'll do him good to do what he's told," Esme joked. "He's been offered a management spot at work and it's going to his head."

"I'm not taking it, though," Sanj added from the bar. "Working outdoors, walking all the time – that's what I like about the job."

"You shouldn't be complaining about a trip to the bar, then," quipped Lind.

As Sanj delivered the drinks, Ailsa and Colin made room for Jen, who had just arrived. "Robbie is finally asleep. I don't like leaving Mum and Dad to do everything," she explained. "It'll be bad enough next week when I start work again. It's just two days a week at first, thankfully, then a gradual ramp-up to full time in December. Robbie starts nursery then. I'm not sure they know what they've let themselves in for in the meantime," she laughed.

27/9

Poor Munro hadn't expected a howling gale when he suggested the beach! It certainly wasn't romantic, but it was a giggle. He seems to really like Todd; they had a great time throwing sticks and seaweed about. He says Dr G is chasing about appealing my prescriptions and has made a formal complaint about the letter I got. Fingers crossed, diary!

All my other symptoms seem to have calmed down, except the night sweats. I might just need to get used to those. My weight is coming down again, and my skin seems to have cleared up. Jen appears to be looking forward to work. I need to think about what I want to do, but I never seem to get time. Maybe next week!

Monday 29th September

Munro waved at Stuart, who was already fighting his way out of his coat and running to join the other kids with their football. The scout leaders were smart and always let them run loose for the first ten minutes, knowing that they'd focus on their activities better if they'd had a chance to bond and burn energy. He smiled and waved at the scout leader, a teacher from Stuart's school. He didn't know how she found the time for everything she committed to do, knowing she also had kids of her own and still found time for karate lessons and a running club. He admired people who juggled so much, while all he did was work and look after Stuart. He should do more in the community, he thought, but knew he had intended that for years without success.

As he walked towards Lana's flat, he felt a chill of excitement. This was the first time he'd been to her home, even if it was just for the short time while Stuart was occupied. As he entered her garden, he saw a throng of potted plants running along the garden wall, labelled in clear, strong handwriting. He wondered if she was a keen gardener, briefly ashamed of the professional he employed to keep his own plot tidy. As he rang the doorbell, he belatedly ran a hand through his hair and straightened his coat.

"Hi!" Lana welcomed. "Come in. Don't mind the mess, I've got a project on the go. I'm sprucing up this chair for my dad's birthday, he's always fancied one." Her large hall was dominated by the deep blue rocking chair, protective sheets covering the wooden floor and paint pots stacked to one side. "I've finished the blue coats, I just need to add a white stencil on the seat to match the tiles in their conservatory before I lacquer it," she explained.

"Something smells amazing," Munro sniffed.

Lana smiled and blushed lightly. "I made oatmeal and raisin cookies; I hope you like them. There's shortbread if you don't. Tea or coffee? Or there's peppermint tea, hot chocolate or lemon, if you like?"

Settling with their drinks and the plate of cookies, Munro admired Lana's kitchen. "Have you done all this yourself?" he asked, gesturing at the refurbished vintage sideboard and table and chairs, and the carefully chosen pieces decorating the room. "These are beautiful," he added, pulling out another chair to see the detailing and feel the quality of the finish.

"The trick is to use lots of thin coats of paint, or varnish, or oil," Lana replied modestly. "It's trickiest on drawers, too many coats and they tend to stick rather than running smoothly. I just think it's such a shame that everyone gets rid of such good quality furniture and replaces it with flatpack things. I'd much rather take something solidly made and make it right for the room."

"You have a real skill here," Munro countered. "People would pay good money for furniture like this. And these cookies are amazing, thank you."

Lana laughed. "You should take some home for Stuart, otherwise I'll end up eating them all," she admitted. "I hardly ever bake because I can't resist it."

Munro watched Lana as she sipped her peppermint tea, drinking in her lively features and strong hands. She downplayed so much of what she did, he observed, or possibly just didn't realise how remarkable she was. He had a hundred questions he would love to ask her, and no idea where to start.

The time passed too quickly; soon he had to leave to collect Stuart from the church hall. Lana bagged up the cookies and handed them to him at the door. She stood, smiling, eyes twinkling as he shrugged into his jacket. He stilled; thanked her. "This has been really lovely, to see each other instead of being on the phone. I'm getting an over-developed thumb from all the typing," he exaggerated.

Lana shook her head lightly. "No problem. You can pop around any time. I'll not bake for every visit, though, it wouldn't be healthy," she added, patting her stomach and smiling. She stepped forward to open the door, and stopped to look him in the eye, one eyebrow minutely raised.

He smiled, stepped forward, and kissed her lightly, catching a hint of her peppermint tea. He lingered a little, lost in her eyes, before reluctantly stepping back. "I'd better go," he rued. "I'll see you soon?"

"Definitely," she smiled.

30/9

Jen's first day at work seems to have gone well. She must have been nervous, especially with separating from Cal, but she said everyone was lovely. She's starting on some new project, was quite excited. Dad and Mum were in fine form, they seem to have coped with Robbie while Jen was upstairs at her desk. I got my stencilling of Dad's chair done tonight, quite pleased with the effect - it's not too bold and should tie in nicely with the rest of the room. Saw a goldfinch in the garden tonight! Told M, he was polite but obviously now thinks I'm a bird nerd. Just as well I didn't tell him about the binoculars I have on hand for when I see something exciting, hah. Bizarrely, I'm becoming obsessed with planning menus for him – not often I get to show off my cooking to someone new.

Fat day jeans are fitting better again, can't wait to get back into the others, though. No bad side effects. Still no word from doc that situation resolved, must be patient.

Intrusions

Chapter 29 – Thursday 16th October

Lana woke before her alarm, burrowing into the covers and enjoying the quiet peace. The night had been windy and wet, and she'd slept fitfully through the rain reverberating on her bedroom skylight windows. She shifted to a cool patch of pillow and fantasised that it was still the small hours, and she could go back to sleep. She sighed, knowing this wasn't to be as the growing light seeped past her blinds. She wondered how Munro and Stuart were doing on their holidays: the schools were off, and they had headed to a cottage someplace for the week. Munro had messaged her every evening, detailing days of rock-pooling, walks and board games, and visits to gardens and lighthouses. She was surprised by how much she missed him; they didn't see each other often, but during a normal week the hope of bumping into him buoyed her day.

Before her alarm could spoil the serenity, Lana rose and prepared for the day, treating herself to a poached egg on toast with tea and some fruit in the extra twenty minutes she had gained. As she donned her shoes and raincoat and stepped out into the morning, she looked forward to delivering the rocking chair to her dad this evening; Jen had promised to help her carry it through the streets. She had picked a deep red velvet ribbon to tie across the spindles and had made a gift tag printed with a similar chair. Peter's birthday wasn't until Monday, but she wanted to give it to him early. He had said he planned to spend this weekend with his feet up and a new book: a birthday gift to himself.

Her morning passed quickly; the branch busier than usual due to an audit scheduled for the following week, everyone performing random sample checks to ensure protocols had been followed since the last inspection. Soon it was time to rush along to the surgery for her extra follow-up review, as requested in the letter. It felt odd to be visiting the surgery when Munro was away; despite being as busy as usual it felt somehow emptier without him. As she sat in the waiting room, she wondered what the father and son would be doing, picturing them sitting together at a rustic table, enjoying their lunch and planning their afternoon. She started from her daydream when the nurse called her name, then smiled brightly in recognition.

"Hi there! What a busy morning I've had!" she volunteered. "How are you doing this week?"

The young nurse looked at her askance, and tentatively replied, "Umm, fine, thanks. Sit down and we'll get started."

Surprised at the cooler reception, Lana removed her coat and sat. "I've brought the urine sample," she mentioned, placing it on the table. "It feels so weird to be carrying that about all day, I'm glad to drop it off!"

The nurse barely met her eyes, taking the specimen and checking the label. "Thanks. It's the same routine as last time, blood pressure then blood sample. Do you have any change to how you're feeling?"

As Lana replied in the negative, and sat quietly during the blood pressure reading, she wondered at the change in the nurse's demeanour. Perhaps she wasn't feeling great or had been through a tough morning. She seemed almost timid, wary of Lana. "I'm sorry but is everything okay?" she finally asked. "You seem a bit quieter than last month."

The nurse looked mildly alarmed at this, stammering, "No, no, nothing's wrong. Just a busy morning. I'll send these off like last time." She ushered Lana out and called her next patient.

Lana was perplexed but tried to be strict with herself about not over-worrying. Yes, there was a small chance the nurse had somehow heard about her relationship with Munro, but they were doing nothing wrong. If anyone disapproved, that was their problem, she resolved. She put it out of her mind and headed off to pick up some lunch, rubbing absent-mindedly at the sticky bandage covering her inside elbow.

Later that evening, she and Jen were carrying the rocking chair down Lana's stairs and out into the street. "Thanks for the hand, Jen," Lana mentioned. "It's not that it's heavy, it's just a bit awkward and I don't want to bash into a lamppost or anything. The lacquer coating is pretty resilient, but I still wouldn't want to risk it," she admitted, as they carefully negotiated past an expensive-looking car parked on the pavement.

Jen laughed. "And you think you're less likely to bash it

if I'm here?" she asked. "I'm as clumsy as they come. Cal insisted on using a removals firm when we moved to the new house because he said I would damage everything." She shook her head at the memory. "He always had a bit of a side to him, didn't he? Anyway, I'll certainly be careful tonight! Dad will love this, it's beautiful. He always used to talk about the one in his gran's house, do you remember? He wasn't allowed to play in it, the noise annoyed her, he said." They both grinned, recollecting their dad's indignant tone whenever he told the story. "I was a bit stumped for ideas this year; I've gone for a gift voucher for the new restaurant down by the beach. I'm hoping Mum will go with him, I thought using a voucher might be enough to convince her."

"That was a great idea," Lana approved. "She needs a push to go out sometimes; she always enjoys herself once she's there, it's just the thought of being in the public eye that puts her off. Dad will love it; he's always trying to talk her into lunches and the like."

They had arrived at their parents' house and cut up the path to the front door. They set the chair down on the paving and Jen rang the bell. "It'll be more of a surprise for him," she explained. Just then, there was a loud crash from inside, and Robbie started crying. "Oh no," Jen exclaimed, and burst through the door just as her father opened it.

"What on earth!" her dad cried out as she rushed past, and he hurried after her, leaving Lana alone outside with the chair. She quickly pulled it into the hall and followed the rest of her family.

"He just made a sudden grab at it, and it toppled," her mum was explaining, as Jen held Robbie, rubbing his back and soothing him. A vase full of fresh flowers was in pieces on the hearth, water and petals spreading. "He just got such a fright when it went over," she continued. "He's not hurt or anything, thank goodness." Peter went to fetch a cloth and dustpan and brush, while a flustered Jen apologised for her son.

"Don't worry about it," he called as he went. "It wasn't important or expensive. We need to do a better job of toddler-proofing."

"No," Jen disagreed. "You and Mum shouldn't have to change everything, especially as Mum needs to be able to reach things easily. We're just a burden," Jen fretted. "If we had our own place, it would be fine."

Lana's mum looked worried at this. "Jenny sweet - don't be daft. This kind of thing happens sometimes, even if you were just visiting. You can't do everything on your own. Your dad and I love having you here, it's no bother."

Jen sighed, and gently wiped the tears from Robbie's cheeks. "I know, Mum. But I still wish I had someplace of our own. The separation is taking so long, it feels like I'll be here bothering you for years." Jen looked dejected, while her mum bit her lip, uncertain of what to say.

"Oh!"

Everyone spun towards Peter's exclamation, nerves still on edge. "Oh Lana!" he continued. "Did you do this for me?"

Lana's mum looked puzzled, and started to move towards the hall, but Lana and Jen grinned in relief.

"Yep," Lana confirmed. "Happy birthday, Dad!" Peter

brought the chair into the living room and set it where his wife could see. He grabbed Lana into a bear hug, squeezing her so tight she heard the breath whoosh softly from her lungs.

"It's perfect," he said. "It's going in the sunny spot in the sunroom. It won't fade, will it?" he suddenly worried. Seeing Lana shake her head, he looked back at the chair and spotted the stencil detailing. "Oh, that's why you were taking a picture of the floor in there!" he laughed. "I thought you'd found ants or something!" They followed him as he carried the chair through to the conservatory, and set it in place, easing himself into its curves and gently rocking. "Oh yes," he said. "One of you put the kettle on and this will be perfect."

Lana took her time walking home, happy with her efforts and her dad's reaction. He had sat in his chair all evening, occasionally swatting Todd's tail out the path of the rockers when it came too close. Lana worried that it might not be safe, not having considered Todd when choosing it. Her father had laughed this off, advising that Todd would learn to steer clear, and in any case, he usually sat looking out through the windows when they were in that room. Throughout the evening, there had been a subtle tension between her sister and their parents, and Lana wondered if Jen was right to want to move out sooner than expected. Perhaps she should consider renting someplace nearby while she waited for the financial settlement. Lana's family had always been close, and she knew they would sort things out if living together became too difficult for them, but she didn't like to see them uncomfortable with each other. As she approached her own flat, windows gleaming darkly in the moonlight, she felt a familiar welling of gratitude for the privacy of her beautiful home.

As she tidied her hall, clearing away the paints, brushes and covers and mopping her cleared floors, she was messaging Munro. She told him about her evening; he described an afternoon collecting driftwood and creating dinosaur sculptures. She mentioned her visit to the surgery and suggested that the staff might have heard they were seeing each other; he said it was unlikely, but he would try to find out discreetly. They agreed that it wouldn't be a problem if everyone knew they were seeing each other – they were happy together, she was Maria's patient, and Munro had done the right thing as early as possible. Feeling content and optimistic, Lana headed for bed.

Chapter 30 – Mon 20th Oct to Wed 22nd Oct

Monday 20th October

Lana was checking the back offices were tidy for the coming audit, when her phone vibrated silently in her pocket. Checking no one was around to see her take a private call, she was surprised to see it was Munro calling: he should be with patients at this time of day. Carefully, she shut herself into a storeroom to avoid being overheard.

"Hi!" she answered. "Is everything okay?"

"Lana, do you have a minute? I know you're busy at work…" he started. Immediately as she started to agree, he interrupted her. "I'm sorry. I don't know quite how to tell you this. After you mentioned that Siobhan was a bit off with you, I thought maybe she'd seen you and I on the beach, or something. I thought I'd see how she was with me this morning: she was totally fine. I also meant to speak to Maria to see how she was getting on with your appeal, but she was already with a patient. So, I decided to check your record for any notes. Lana, there's a warning flag system that we use on all records, for violent or difficult patients. It's a traffic light system. Yours has been marked amber, a warning level. It's only usually used if patients could turn nasty. They must have increased it from green to amber after they sent your letter, goodness knows why when they should know it's all under appeal. Siobhan would have seen it when she was doing your check-up and been wary - she wouldn't have known that we were questioning their decision. I'm so sorry. I'll talk to Maria as soon as she's free, to try and get this sorted. And we'll make sure all the staff know that it's an error, just as a precaution. I'm sorry this is such a mess, Lana. Are you okay?"

Lana had barely moved since Munro started talking, fingers of her free hand gripping the desktop so tightly her nailbeds and knuckles were white. "I thought that was just a threat in the letter. For all they knew I could have started taking the pills again. I thought I was okay to keep throwing them out; Dr Gillies said she was going to sort all this!"

Munro understood her frustration. "I know, and she is, but it's taking time. In the meantime, they've set this flag. It will take time to get it all cleared up, I'm sorry."

Lana interrupted him, "But what about the samples from last week? Now they'll know I'm still not taking the pills. What if this gets worse? They said they could tell the bank."

"Don't worry, I'm sure they would give you more warnings first. It's all just bureaucracy, and they know the appeal is under way. And if somehow, they do change the flag again, then I doubt any employer would be checking these systems anyway. As a worst-case scenario, if the bank does get wind of this flag and try to hold it against you, then

Maria can call them and explain that you changed your medications based on our advice, explain this whole mess."

Lana breathed deeply, trying to calm the panic she had started to feel, relying on Munro to understand the situation better than she did. The whole system seemed so chaotic, and she felt she had no way of clarifying her situation alone. She felt dizzy and nauseous, and it took all her effort to calm herself.

Munro just hoped that he was right, and it would be remedied soon.

Lana reached home, relieved that the day was over, and she could shut herself into her own comfortable bolthole for the evening. She had barely been able to concentrate for the rest of the day, wanting to trust in Munro and the other doctors, but unnerved by the control the Central Care team were able to enforce on her life. She knew the bank would take any warnings about her seriously; she was in close contact with the public, and they were responsible for anything that happened in their branch. This left her jittery and prone to catastrophising; after 6 hours of it she was exhausted. Each step towards her front door was a labour, and as she turned the key in the lock, she let loose a deep breath saturated with tension and anxiety.

She stepped over the post on her doormat, seeing a familiar brown envelope amongst the leaflets and special offers. Suddenly enraged, she grabbed it and tore it open, not caring if she damaged the contents. This, she expected, would be Central Care finally advising they'd put a warning on her record. How dare they? she raged. She walked into her kitchen, taking a deep breath and switching on the lights so she could read it clearly and calmly. She sat at her table, smoothed the crumpled paper, and read, rage giving her a simmering clarity.

But she was wrong, this was not the notification she had expected. This was worse. They had tested the samples she had submitted last week, it said, and they had determined that she continued to avoid taking the full complement of medications she had been prescribed. Her health and social care records had, as a result, been marked with a red alert indicating she was a potentially dangerous individual who was currently refusing medical treatment. It included a copy of another letter which had been sent to her employer, advising them of her new status. It declared that she would be treated as a potential danger to the public and herself, and that she now had two weeks in which to start taking all her medication, or she would be at risk of being issued a Compulsory Treatment Order. This could include detention in a mental health facility.

The room pulsed and swayed around her. She felt sick, her neck felt too weak to hold her head up. Rushes of heat ran from her extremities to her face, followed by chills. The colour slowly leached from the room, darkening to black.

Somewhere, a ringing - then blissful silence. Confusion first, then the sharp smell of cleaning fluid. Pain throbbed down her side and arm, and her head felt woolly. Lana blinked, but she couldn't focus, couldn't resolve what she saw. She shut her eyes and pressed her face into the cool surface below her: the floor. Realising where she was, she tried to rise but could only manage a small movement before her head spun, and she stopped and leaned against her sideboard. Her bag was nearby, and her phone was ringing again. She fumbled for it, just answered in time, her voice stumbling.

"Lana, it's Dad. Have you been sleeping?"

She shook her head, tried to focus. "Yeah, sorry, I must have dosed off," she lied. "Bit of a sore head." The details were starting to come back to her now: the letter and the horror and confusion it brought. She couldn't bear to tell her dad any of it. "Dad, I'm going to have to lie down, sorry. Did you want anything?"

"No, no, it's fine. We just wondered where you were, but no worries. Give us a call when you're feeling better." He rang off, and Lana levered herself off the floor using her good arm. She sat at the table, distraught and in need of help but equally unwilling to burden her family, and unable to face explaining the mess she had gotten herself into. She touched her temple and found sticky blood, gasping with the pain and unfairness of it all. She reached for the only thing which made any sense and called Munro.

Munro packed the first aid away, as Lana sipped on the orange juice which he had poured for her. He had taken her to the sofa before cleaning her grazed forehead with gentle, cool hands. Her colour had improved a little, and he was relieved to see her eyes seemed more focused.

"Do you think you could manage to eat anything?" he asked. "Did you eat at lunchtime?"

Lana nodded, wincing as her head throbbed. "I did. I didn't feel like it, but I get a bit sicky if I don't eat enough," she explained. "I don't think I could face anything just yet."

Munro nodded, deciding to give her a half hour before making some toast. He re-read the letter she had been sent, unable to imagine the alarm of being the one to receive it. She had started to tremble again, so he took the glass from her hand and pulled her into his arms.

"I'm so sorry," he breathed. "We had no idea any of this was possible. I can't imagine how you're feeling right now."

"I can't seem to think straight," she admitted. "I just keep coming back to those words. What does it all mean, Munro? I think I'll lose my job; I won't be able to pay my mortgage. Can they really force me into some hospital?"

Munro couldn't bear to worry her, but also couldn't bring himself to lie. "Clinicians do have the right to take people into care if they are a danger to themselves or others; that's been true for years. There's a process they follow, a mental health tribunal and the like. What I struggle with is them continuing to pursue this when they know we're appealing against the prescription. I can't believe they would take it any further... but to be honest, I can't believe they've gone this far." He could see he was making things worse, but he just couldn't lie to her. "I'm so sorry. Maria can contact the bank, we can chase the appeal, we can represent you – but that all depends on Central interacting with us. In the meantime, they have control over your care."

Lana buried her face in his shoulder, and confessed, "I don't think I can bear it, Munro. I don't care about my job, but I can't lose my home and I couldn't bear to be locked away. What's going to happen?"

Munro did the only thing he could. "We won't let that happen. You're not alone, Lana. We'll do what we can about the bank, but whatever happens we'll make sure you don't lose this place. The surgery will fight any treatment orders or other madness. Try not to worry; you need to rest. I'm going to make you something to eat, then you should try and sleep. You don't seem to have a concussion or anything," he added. "Tomorrow we'll start fighting this and make some contingency plans for the meantime. I would stay home tomorrow, if I were you. You've had a fright and a nasty fall. I'll need to go home soon for Stuart, but you can call me any time. We'll be fine, I promise."

Lana trembled. "I'm so sorry. We've only just met, and I'm dragging you into all this mess," she whispered. "This is the last thing you need."

"No." He tipped her chin until she met his eyes. "I wouldn't want to be anywhere else but with you, fixing this. Don't ever apologise for it." He kissed her forehead gently. "I'll get you some toast."

Munro watched over Lana as she ate and took some painkillers before getting ready for bed. He helped her upstairs and was amazed when she somehow found the strength to smile at him.

"You're tucking two people into bed tonight," she said as she pulled her duvet up to her chin.

"Call me whenever you need me, and I'll be here as soon as I can." He turned off her bedside light and slipped from the room, lingering at the doorway to check that she was calmer. As he locked her door and posted the key through the letterbox, he hoped she would manage to get some sleep; he knew he wouldn't rest tonight. Guilt for his part in her predicament was gnawing at him: if Lana ever found out that he had agreed for her to skip the factorisation waiting list and be seen immediately she would never forgive him.

Tuesday 21st October

Lana woke with the sun; she had forgotten to close her blinds last night, and her phone was downstairs. As she remembered everything from the day before, she grimaced, wincing at the tug of pain from her cut forehead. Nothing had changed this morning, but she felt better for a night's rest: less panicky, less desperate. She knew she owed this to Munro: he had given her more reassurance than she had expected anyone could. She rose and padded downstairs, too thirsty to linger in bed. As she gulped cold fresh water, she checked her phone and found two messages, from her dad and Jen, both checking if she was okay. As she read, she realised what her worries yesterday had caused her to forget: she had been due at her parents for her dad's birthday tea. Horrified, she rang him immediately to apologise. She held back from telling him about her predicament; until she found out how the bank might react. She didn't want to worry him. As they said their goodbyes, Lana promising to spend the day resting, she realised she had no idea what she could achieve herself that day. Everything was in someone else's hands. Munro and Dr Gillies were pursuing her appeal, the bank was a complete unknown: it could be weeks before she heard anything from them, or they may not react at all. This left Lana feeling useless, her life in the hands of paperwork. She sighed and resigned herself to a day fretting indoors.

Wednesday 22nd October

When the call came just before 8:30, Lana was walking into work, having decided she couldn't hide at home forever. She stopped and sat on a bench on the waterfront, looking out over a group of swans.

"Hello Lana, this is Kim Evans, from head office HR. Do you have a moment?"

Lana breathed deeply; at heart she had been expecting this call. "Yes, of course," she agreed. "How can I help you?"

"We wanted to catch you before you got into the branch this morning. I'm afraid I have some difficult news. We've received a letter from your clinicians, I believe you have a copy?" When Lana agreed, she continued. "I'm afraid the bank cannot continue to employ you in your role; under the circumstances your position is untenable, and we will need to terminate your employment. We realise this is difficult for you, but we cannot continue to have you in the branch. Your notice period will start from today, for three months. This will be paid at your full salary, but we ask that you remain at home on gardening leave for the duration. This is all covered by your contract of employment. You should return your security pass and any keys and bank property to head office by post as soon as possible. You should not approach the branch except, if necessary, as a customer. After your notice period completes, any staff accounts and rates of interest will revert to standard, and you'll be issued with new account details. Do you understand?"

Lana looked skywards to avoid the tears swimming at her lower lids. "Yes, of course. The thing is, though, it's all a misunderstanding. My doctors are trying to sort it all out, they're appealing the decision. I shouldn't have been taking the medications they prescribed in the first place. Can my doctors get in touch with you to explain?" Lana knew she was grasping at straws, that the bank wouldn't take such a risk for any single employee, but she had to try.

"I see," Kim replied. "Unfortunately, we have no visibility of any appeals or similar, we can only go by what we've been advised. We cannot continue to have you in a position working with the public and their confidential information. Your termination letter should be with you tomorrow, it will detail how you can have a solicitor pursue a challenge to the decision." Here the professional's voice softened somewhat. "On a purely personal note, good luck for the future."

As Kim hung up, Lana felt an unexpected sense of calm acceptance. She had spent the last 36 hours preparing for this eventuality; now it had arrived she could at least move on. She stood and turned back towards her home, looking down at her work uniform and realising that this would be the last time that she wore it. She couldn't keep this secret; she would have to tell her family. But first she was going home to change, and to think.

Chapter 31 – Thursday 23rd October

Lana shook her head and confirmed, "No, it's okay Dr Gillies. I really appreciate it, but I've honestly been thinking of finding something else for a while. This has given me the push I needed. I'm not worried about my job, I'm just worried about getting the flag removed and ensuring they don't take any further steps. The treatment order thing really worries me." Lana and Munro had agreed that everything should continue to be done through the surgery; their relationship would only complicate matters in the appeal, so they would continue to keep it quiet for now.

Dr Gillies re-confirmed that she was now working with Central Care and had submitted a request for either the appeal to be expedited or for the current situation to be resolved in the interim. She hoped to hear more soon.

"I realise that, Dr Gillies, but that hasn't stopped them so far. It's really unnerving," Lana admitted. As they finished their discussion, Lana turned into her parents' street and steeled herself. The night before, she had spoken to them and Jen, explaining the full situation. Their disbelief, fear and anger had been understandable, and their support was invaluable, but the conversation had gone on late into the evening and was exhausting to process.

As she entered their kitchen, her dad rose from the table and came to hug her. "Oh, Lana. I'm still so worried for you. I just wish there was something we could do," he fretted.

"I know, Dad. I'm in the same boat, to be honest. But we just need to leave it to Dr Gillies to sort out." The futility of it all grated heavily on Lana, but she needed to be patient. Somehow, she had to find a way to keep busy and calm while the process continued. "I was hoping to speak to Jen quickly," she surprised her dad. "I'll be back in a min."

As she headed upstairs, she waved a quick hello to her mum; Robbie was sleeping in her arms. Lana smiled to herself – Jen would disapprove, she knew. She poked her head around the door of Jen's bedroom, and saw her sitting with headphones on, typing at speed in front of three screens. She stepped into the room and tapped her shoulder, miming dropping headphones in case she was on a call.

"Lana! In you come," Jen said. "It's just music, don't worry. Robbie was crying earlier, it's so hard to concentrate when I can hear him," she explained.

"Don't worry," Lana reassured her. "He's sound asleep in Mum's arms now."

As predicted, Jen reacted badly, but restrained herself. "I wish she wouldn't do that. He gets used to it so quickly and then he won't sleep alone. I can't really complain though, when they're looking after him for me. Roll on

December when he goes to nursery, and we all get some time back. It wouldn't be so bad if it was just the days I'm working, but she'll barely let me look after him on the days I can," she complained. "I know I shouldn't moan - other mums would kill for support like this – but by then it will take so long to sort out his bad habits."

"Actually," Lana interrupted. "That's kind of what I wanted to talk to you about." She took a deep breath. "I know this sounds a bit mad, but hear me out and give it some thought, okay? I'm sure I will find a way to make some money before my three months' notice is out; it's not about that really. But in the meantime, I'm going to be sitting in my flat bored witless and worrying about paying my bills. Meanwhile, you're here, desperate for some space and privacy, and can afford someplace, but don't want to commit to anything when you're not sure when your financial settlement will arrive to let you buy your own place."

Jen was frowning and looking to interrupt, but Lana stalled her. "Just wait, please. I've had an idea. How about we swap houses for a while? You could move into mine, cover the mortgage and all the bills. It would be space for you and Robbie to yourselves, and let you try out living with him alone without being totally committed to it. It would get you out of feeling like you're with Mum and Dad all the time, too: I know that can't be easy. You can stay there until you move into your own place – or come back here if it's too hard being on your own. I can move back in here, but I'll be out a lot of the time so Mum and Dad will get a lot of their privacy back. Well, some," she laughed. "And while I'm not working for anyone, I can help them with the two days they look after Robbie. And we can do it here, so you can focus on your work those days. It'll help you both get a bit more used to being separated before he starts nursery, too."

"Lana, that's an amazing offer, and I really appreciate it," Jen replied, grabbing Lana's hand. "But what about you? You'd be back living with Mum and Dad, and I honestly don't know how long my money will take to sort out," she repeated. "It could be months and months, maybe years. And what would you do all day? You can't hang around here, you'd go mad," she finally whispered, checking her parents weren't in earshot.

Lana smiled. "I hope I'll hardly be here. I'll be trying to find a job, or maybe setting up my own business. Once this red flag nonsense is sorted out, I could at least volunteer someplace or something while I get organised. I don't intend sitting about for long, and most evenings I'll be out for a run or something. It's only a little bit of bother for me, and things will be much easier for you and Mum and Dad."

Jen still wasn't convinced. "You love your flat. You love having your own space. I remember when you used to stay here after university finished and you were desperate for someplace."

"Yes," Lana agreed, nodding. "But this will only be for a short while, and my home will be waiting for me at the end of it. This will save me worrying about paying the mortgage, I don't have much savings," she admitted. "Honestly, Jen, I'll be happy to have that worry taken off me and it will help everyone else. Let me do this for you."

The sisters talked it over for a while, Lana sticking to her position and Jen slowly coming around. "All you would need to buy are a couple of stairgates," Lana finally argued.

Jen laughed and raised her hands in defeat. "Okay, okay, you win. God, you've really thought about this, haven't you? I... It would be amazing to have someplace for Robbie and me, I would love it. Your flat is perfect. Are you totally sure?"

Lana hugged her in agreement. "Come on, let's go tell the olds. Don't let them talk you out of it, or you'll eventually need a SWAT team to kidnap Robbie for you," she laughed.

The evening sun was just setting as Munro arrived at Lana's door, and she surprised him by opening it with her coat and shoes on. "Come on, let's walk for a bit. Do you need a drink or anything first?" she checked. "I've been in the house all afternoon; I could do with the air."

Munro smiled and agreed, kissing her quickly and turning to head back down the steps to the street. "You seem happier!" he said in surprise. "How are you doing?"

Lana laughed at his puzzled expression. "I know, I must seem so contrary. But actually... today I feel like I've made some progress. I have a list of options I'm going to consider, career-wise. And I've convinced Jen to move into my flat until she has her separation sorted out. That leaves me mostly commitment-free for the next few months, so I don't have to discard the riskier options."

Munro looked taken aback by this, so Lana explained her reasoning behind the agreement to let Jen move in. "I know this means I'll be back living with my parents, it's not ideal. But it helps in a bunch of other ways."

"A bunch of other ways that help everyone else," Munro marvelled. "That's an incredibly selfless thing to do, Lana."

"Not really," she disagreed. "It frees me from money worries for a while, so I can focus on what I want to do next. And that will stop me constantly worrying about this situation," she sighed. "Do you know, the bank told everyone at the branch that it was a mutually agreed solution to my health problems!" she exclaimed. "Can you imagine? Lind was raging, was saying they wanted to leave as well, except they need the money. I'm hoping it doesn't come to that; Lind loves that job, bizarrely. I'm just kind of relieved to be out of it," she admitted. "My only worry is if the factorisation people take this all further."

Munro nodded, understanding. "Maria is on it. She's demanded a direct contact to pursue this with, so fingers crossed that will help."

Lana crossed her fingers and grimaced. She stopped to lean on a railing looking out over the river and the city. "Look at that sky," she exclaimed. "That's just the perfect shade of blue." She checked they were alone and took Munro's hand, smiling. "One of the things I'm thinking about is setting up my own business. I've got no experience whatsoever, but if I could spend my day creating furniture, or doing interior design, that would be pretty cool. This is my chance to change direction completely, you know?" She spotted Munro glancing at his watch. "When do you need to head back?" she asked.

"Soon," Munro admitted. "Laurie is so kind, but I don't like to take advantage by keeping her late too often. Stuart will need to eat soon." He looked into her eyes. "Maybe later I could give you a call, you can run me through your list," he suggested. "Sorry. I hate to have to dash off, but I wanted to see how you were for myself."

"Don't worry, I totally understand," Lana waved off

his apology. "The last thing I want is to be totally dependent on you to keep me distracted. I need to be able to deal with this myself, so I don't feel completely useless," she laughed.

Chapter 32 - Saturday 25th October

Munro stood on the doorstep, unnerved and unsure if he was ready to take this huge step in their lives. Stuart was beside him, dressed in his favourite things and ogling the house on tiptoes, trying to peek through windows for a glimpse inside. Munro ruffled his hair fondly, using the opportunity of a half-hug to pull his son back towards him on the doorstep.

"Best not to be too nosey," he advised, "you'll see inside soon enough."

A clatter inside cut off Stuart's response, and a call of "Be right there!" had them both grinning nervously at each other.

"You sure you're ready for this?" Munro whispered. Stuart nodded energetically as the door opened.

"Hi Munro! Stuart, lovely to see you. Come on in, Justin is upstairs in his room, just head up!" Justin's mother beamed at them both, clearly very comfortable with having guests. "Just bring in his things," she added to Munro. "Come in, please!"

Munro brought Stuart's overnight things and sleeping bag into the modern hallway and placed them on the bottom step of the stairs. "Are you sure this is no bother?" he asked. "Stuart's never been for a sleepover before: he seems fine and he usually sleeps no problem, but just call if he's any trouble at all."

Justin's mum grinned. "Oh, don't worry. We have three boys; another one is no bother. But if he misses you or anything I have your number. Justin has been so excited to have him come to stay. Is there anything particular which he likes for breakfast? We're having pizzas and chicken and salads tonight."

"That all sounds great; he eats almost anything, don't worry."

As Munro thanked her again and made his goodbyes, Stuart rushed downstairs and hugged him quickly. "Thanks, Dad! Justin has loads of cool things! See you tomorrow!" The two parents looked at each other and laughed, Munro realising his worries were unfounded.

As he walked back towards town, he struggled to pinpoint how he was feeling about Stuart's first sleepover. This was the first time they had ever been apart overnight, and it left Munro feeling bizarrely untethered. It wasn't painful, nor was it an enjoyable sense of freedom, but it left him feeling purposeless, directionless. He was glad he wasn't going home to be alone.

He crossed the main street and entered the small

supermarket. He had wanted to pick Lana some flowers from the florist but couldn't imagine taking them to Justin's house without giving them to his mother; it just seemed too rude. He compromised by picking the most lavish of the ready-made flower arrangements available and headed towards Lana's flat. Tonight, it would be her last night staying there, and when she had heard he had the evening free she had insisted on cooking for him, claiming she wouldn't get a chance to cook for anyone again for months. As he reached her door, he could smell tomatoes and garlic, and his stomach rumbled anticipatively.

"It's open!" Lana called from inside, so Munro entered the hall and hung his coat on the hook behind the door. As he turned into the kitchen, Lana was loading a casserole into the oven, the fan gently shifting her hair in its heat. As she turned to him, her smile broadened as she saw his gift. "Oh, I'll be taking these with me," she said, happily. "I'm all organised for tomorrow," she added. "I've even put up the stairgates. Grab a seat and I'll pour some wine. I'm going to risk one small glass, just tonight," she admitted. "Unless you'll worry?" she checked.

Munro knew her prescriptions would allow a small amount with a meal, so he laughed it off. He was glad he had chosen a nice shirt for the evening: Lana was spectacular in a burgundy wrap dress, her hair falling in waves across one shoulder and her makeup delicate but elegant. He could just smell her perfume as she moved across the kitchen.

"Tonight, we're not talking about my records, by the way. This is a proper date; we're sticking to cheerful topics." She raised an eyebrow in challenge. "Any transgressions and there's no chocolate mousse for either of us," she joked. "And I made it myself, so I know that's a serious penalty!"

They sat and shared their stories, stopping every so often to eat. There were buttery-flavoured nocellara olives with the wine, and Lana had prepared roast asparagus wrapped in parma ham with a hollandaise sauce to start. Munro hadn't appreciated how good a cook she was; the chicken cacciatore was the best he'd ever eaten. By the time he was lost in the chocolate mousse and delicate shortbread, he knew he was outclassed in the kitchen.

"I think you might be disappointed when I return the favour," he confessed. "This has all been wonderful. I have no idea how you've fitted it in with packing."

They stayed at the table, listening to music and talking through the evening. Munro hadn't realised how much of their time had been spent in the present, anxious; tonight, he learned so much more of Lana from stories of her past and her hopes for the future. He felt he would never tire of being there with her. He didn't want to spoil the evening, but there was something he had to share with her.

"Lana," he started. "I know we said that we wouldn't talk about your situation, but there's something I feel I have to say." She tilted her head slightly to one side, frowning slightly but nodding encouragement. He continued, "Recently, we've been so caught up in worrying about your prescriptions and the actions Central are taking. But I think there's something more intrinsic that we need to talk about. Lana, I honestly don't believe you need any of the medications. I never have. When I first met you, you sounded like a very self-aware, intelligent woman who was just very empathetic and prone to overthinking. Sometimes, people just need a little time to learn how to cope with these things: I think that's what you've needed. When I saw those results from the factorisation team, I was stunned. And now that I know you better... well, I know I'm biased, but I just think they're wrong. There is nothing wrong with you that I can see. You're... amazing." Munro shrugged, unable to relate how much he admired about her.

Lana had listened carefully but was now shaking her head. "No, you don't know what I can be like. I can overreact to things so badly; I can get so down. I was shocked, too – but they must know what they're doing. I could have a turn for the worse at any time."

Munro stopped her there. "No, please listen. It's normal to overreact sometimes when things go badly; it's normal to get down. It takes experience to realise that what seems like a huge problem is instead something fixable. Everyone learns that at their own pace. And particularly sunny people always take things harder, in my experience. I don't believe for a minute that you're going to suddenly turn violently angry, or suicidal, or have a psychotic break. Look at you just now, these last few weeks. You're under immense stress, and you're coping amazingly well. Your resilience is astounding. The pills won't have taken full effect yet, they don't get the credit. You're not the problem they think you are. Something has gone very wrong with their analysis." Munro stopped there, knowing he was pushing her hard, but desperate for her to understand. He watched Lana think over what he had said.

She raised her eyes and countered carefully, "It's so difficult when you doubt yourself. It becomes impossible to know the real root cause of anything. Am I feeling ropey because I'm depressed? Or am I feeling sad and weepy because I'm coming down with a virus? And this factorisation has made it all worse: am I going to have a breakdown if I don't take these meds? Am I feeling well just now because of them or despite them? Who knows? When you can't be certain of yourself, it undermines everything.

But who else's opinion do I take? These experts? They don't know me. My friends, my family, you? All biased, surely. That's what appealed about the factorisation in the first place: having a definitive answer as to whether I'm okay or not. But it's just been yet another opinion, except this time they have control over my future." Lana sighed and rubbed the tension in the back of her neck. "I don't feel like any of this is necessary, either. But look how hard it's been to appeal something as simple as the contraceptives; God knows what it would be like if I wasn't taking the other medication."

Munro had never suffered such doubts himself but had heard similar feelings from patients with chronic depression or pain conditions. His heart ached that such a competent woman could doubt herself so much, but he knew that she would need to learn her capabilities for herself – confidence based on other people's opinions was temporary. "I think you should seriously consider appealing the whole analysis, but there's no rush. Once Maria sorts the issue with the contraceptive you can take your time to decide. I'm sorry for bringing it up. Over the last few weeks, I've just become more and more certain that they're wrong, and I couldn't leave it unsaid. Would you like to take a walk for a bit, to put this behind us? It's a lovely clear night if we wrap up."

They walked along the shoreline, eyes drawn to the abundance of bright stars above them and the reflection of the waxing crescent moon on the water, a comfortable and accepting silence between them. Seaweed crackled beneath their feet, gaining them a stern look from a heron dozing at the edge of the lifeboat pier. In the distance, pub doors opened: they could briefly hear the camaraderie within before they swung closed once more. Munro wondered if he should offer Lana a drink, but she was already shaking her head as he turned to her.

"No," she smiled. "Thanks, but I think I'd like to walk for a bit longer, then head home. I don't want to be among other people tonight, if that's okay." Munro agreed readily, happy to continue enjoying the quiet privacy of the moonlight.

"I love this area," Lana continued. "I've been to other places, and they're nice - but we're so lucky here. The river, the countryside, the sea nearby, beaches, forests, hills, the city. Everything is so close to hand, and most of it is just beautiful. It always amazes me how many people spend their time indoors with the curtains closed, ignoring all this." She looked around at the gleaming monochrome view before them, an oil painting waiting to be crafted. "I've spent years acting like a spoiled child: having everything I could want, all the opportunities I could ask for; and I haven't made the most of them at all. I've worried, and complained, and been indecisive, procrastinated. I've wasted the last few years. When I think that I could lose all this, that I could be taken away to some hospital and all those possibilities taken away from me: what a fool I've been."

"We won't let that happen. Whatever they try, I won't let that happen," Munro promised, gathering her into his arms. "We'll do whatever it takes." He wished that he had the courage to do the one thing that might solve the problem, but instead was left hoping they could resolve everything without ever letting her know of his friendships with both Bryant and Cargill.

Chapter 33 – Monday 27th October

"Munro, Theresa, we'll get started." Maria was chairing the partners meeting and had no patience for the niceties the others were exchanging. "Before we start with our usual agenda, I have an important update. This may affect us all. I've heard back from Central Care about the Lana Knight appeal."

Munro sat forward and listened carefully while Maria summarised the situation for the others, endeavouring to keep his face calm and interested but neither worried nor invested.

"Unfortunately, the appeal about her contraceptive medication has been refused," Maria continued. "On medical grounds, which isn't terribly informative. I've discussed it with my contact there, and they say she can now appeal the overall factorisation diagnosis, but that will require a court action on her part. It would be the first of its kind, and I suspect lengthy and expensive. I'll have to inform the patient today; I suspect the practice will be dragged into the legal proceedings," she added with distaste. "The immediate question is how we advise Ms Knight. To date, we have said she can refuse to take the contraceptives. However, if she continues to do so, Central may continue to advance their threat of a Compulsory Treatment Order, which in her case is complete overkill. My contact says that as soon as they are aware of a legal challenge, they will stop pursuing such an order – but we all know how long these things can take. What are your thoughts? Munro, you have seen her in the past?"

Munro was overwhelmed by the news and struggled to retain his professional veneer, instinctively choosing to continue hiding his relationship with Lana. "I only consulted with Ms Knight a couple of times, but I didn't see anything that concerned me or that would warrant this level of..." he shook his head, struggling to choose a word to summarise the situation. "... persecution," he finally managed. "I'm appalled at the way they're handling this. She might be better to start taking the full suite of meds just to keep them happy while she pursues a legal challenge - but that's a lot to ask of her and it shouldn't be needed. From our perspective, we would be advising a course of treatment we don't agree with or think necessary, which is most definitely wrong even if we aren't the prescribing organisation."

Maria nodded, agreeing with Munro but looking to the others for their input. "Mark, Theresa, what are your thoughts?"

Mark Clegg shook his head in disgust. "This just seems one giant dysfunctional debacle," he summarised. "I agree with Munro, no woman should have to take contraceptives against her will, and we should not be advising her to. We would have to accept the risk that they might pursue her for refusing, though. We would need to be entirely transparent about that risk - and let her decide. Make sure that's done in writing to ensure we're covered legally, Maria. It's a good thing she gets the venalink directly, so we're left in a purely advisory position. In general, I find it unacceptable that they can deal with her like this. I think we should consider taking a complaint to the medical association, possibly even to the Scottish parliament. We can consider that another time, though."

Munro watched the others nodding, knowing that from their perspective, protecting the practice was paramount. He was surprised to realise how little he cared about that himself. He turned to Theresa, who was lengthily agreeing with Mark, but could barely concentrate on her words. With both senior partners in agreement, little she said mattered. Lana would have to decide for herself whether to restart the contraceptives. More worryingly, she would have to pursue legal action to regain control of her life. He was desperate to go to her but would need to wait until his workday was over.

The late afternoon session overran, and by the time Munro was able to leave the surgery his nerves were frayed from trying to appear calm. He locked away the valuables in his consultation room, gave his desk a perfunctory tidy, and hustled out the door. He knew Maria had called Lana that afternoon and sent out the letter per Mark's advice. He also knew Lana hadn't told her parents about him, but his need to see her was foremost in his mind. His long stride carried him past gardens full of leaves and houses decorated for Halloween, reminding him that he had promised Stuart he would carve their pumpkin that night. He checked his watch and picked up the pace.

Munro had never met Lana's father but recognised her features in the man who opened their door. Peter looked drawn and pale, and Munro guessed Lana had brought them up to speed.

"Mr Knight, I'm sorry to bother you. I'm Munro – I'm a friend of Lana's; sorry we haven't met. May I possibly see her?" he asked, knowing that anything short of being polite may be enough to trigger a parent's protectiveness. Even so, he could see that Peter was apprehensive about agreeing until Lana appeared behind him.

"Munro, I'm so glad you've come!" she welcomed him, then slipped past her father and into his arms, surprising both men. "Dad, sorry, I haven't told you much about Munro," she added, turning back into the hall. "Come in, everyone knows what's happening. We need to work out what to do," she added, shrugging helplessly.

Lana led the way into the family kitchen, where her mother and sister were playing with a toddler. She introduced Munro to the adults, and he added, "And this must be Robbie!" with a smile. "Lana's told me all about you!" The child giggled at Munro's attentions and offered him a soft book full of furry animal tails. Lana smiled sadly at Munro, and he stood up once more, briefly rubbing Todd's ears in welcome.

"I'm sorry for coming unannounced. I... when I heard the news, I came as soon as I could," he added, uncertain of how much to say.

Lana waved at the kitchen table, faintly smiling her understanding. "Grab a seat." She turned to her dad. "I think we'd better explain everything from the start." She sat down beside Munro and explained how they had met and why they hadn't been open about their relationship.

"Will you have difficulty at work because you're seeing Lana? Can you help her?" Peter asked bluntly.

Munro shook his head. "I think my partners may disapprove, but I did the right thing and passed Lana to another doctor as soon as I realised that I wouldn't be able to treat her objectively," he answered honestly. "However, these are unusual circumstances because we're involved in Lana's appeals and because of the actions Central are taking. I've kept it quiet for that reason, and I think now that's been a good thing." He turned to Lana. "Did Dr Gillies explain everything to you?"

Lana nodded uncertainly. "I think I understand everything. I just don't know what it takes to pursue a court case. I'll need to find a solicitor."

Munro elaborated. "The appeal Dr Gillies made as your primary care clinician has failed. Central, or perhaps the Bryant-Cargill team, are insisting that the Microgynon is part of your necessary treatment, and that you must take it. That leaves you needing to pursue a court case to have their entire analysis, prognosis and treatment plan overruled, and to have responsibility for your care returned to the practice. The arguments could be twofold – firstly, that their analysis is incorrect, secondly that you signed the legal agreement unaware of the types of treatment they could try to enforce. A court case like this tends to take a long time, though, and it will be expensive. Try not to worry too much about the money, for the moment. You'll need a small deposit to engage the solicitor, but I can help with that if you need it. In the long run, you may be eligible for legal aid, and winning the case could mean you could pursue your fees from them."

Here, Munro took Lana's hand gently, feeling the pressure of her family's eyes. "The immediate decision you have to make is about the treatment they've prescribed. If you don't conform to their demands, they could legally take their precautionary countermeasures, having already warned you in the last letter. Dr Gillies has spoken to her contact at Central, and they say they would step back from enforcing those as soon as they were notified that you were pursuing a court case – but that could take some time." Munro stopped to make sure Lana was paying full attention. "I don't have much faith in them, either – they haven't acted promptly or behaved sympathetically so far."

Seeing tears welling in Lana's eyes, he apologised. "I'm so sorry. I know it's frustrating. This whole situation has appalled everyone at the surgery. They're considering making a formal complaint to try and get the powers at Central revised – but that's not going to help you right now."

Munro had thought carefully about his next suggestion. "One thing that does strike me, though." All eyes turned to him once more. "I still don't believe there's anything wrong with you at all. If they're going to pursue maximum penalties just because you won't take the contraceptive, there's nothing to stop you coming off the whole suite of meds they've prescribed. It's something to think about," he concluded, leaving the decisions to Lana.

Lana's mum broke her silence, anger and determination quietly evident in her voice. "I agree with you. I think it's mad that they've got her taking all these things. I say we get a solicitor involved, and you stop taking everything. Munro could tell you how to wean yourself off them if that's needed. And if anyone comes here trying to threaten you, they'll have to deal with us!" she finished fiercely. Lana's father was nodding, Munro was glad to see.

"It's all just so much to take in," Lana contributed miserably, looking around at her family. "I have no idea what I should do. I'm just so tired from worrying about it all this time."

Munro rubbed his thumb across the back of her hand. "There's no rush. You know where you stand now, you can take your time to decide. Although I'd advise seeing a solicitor as soon as possible, getting the legal appeal started is the most urgent thing."

Lana nodded. "I'm becoming worried that men in white coats are going to turn up at the door one day," she said bitterly. "Every time, I hope things will be sorted out soon; then they get worse. It's hard not to imagine a disaster now. I feel like I'm on edge all the time, it's just horrible." She shuddered, and Munro realised for the first time how exhausted she looked.

"You have to be able to relax, Lan," her dad advised. "This is no good for you. You're going to need your energy to fight this."

Munro watched them all, the concern and love in the family resonating deeply. Everyone was on Lana's side, believed in her and were ready to help; he was glad they were all together, and there were no secrets between them anymore. He caught that thought, realising he still hadn't been wholly honest, and felt a deep shame.

Jen spoke for the first time. "My solicitor has been happy to do everything by phone and video call, Lana. Once you've got things started, why don't you think about getting away for a few days, get a break and some rest? Go see one of your uni friends, or something?"

"What, and have them harassed when these people realise that I'm not picking up my prescriptions from the pharmacy or attending the nurse reviews?" Lana countered. "Who knows how far they're willing to go. I don't have much time: they were talking about only having two weeks to comply, and that was a week ago already!"

Munro looked at Lana, surprised she hadn't outright turned down the suggestion to leave the area for a while. "Lana - would you like to get away someplace, though?" he asked gently, not wanting to be parted from her but seeing a way he could help.

"I don't know... I don't know if it's just adrenaline, or the stress... but yes. Every bone in my body is screaming that I should get away from all of this, get some peace. I just really, really need some quiet, some time out, you know? I'm sorry." Lana's eyes were pleading, and Munro grasped that she understood how he felt, and didn't want to be apart. But she sounded desperate for some space, and that was something Munro could easily give her.

"Actually, I might have the perfect thing," he replied.

Chapter 34 – Wednesday 29th October

Peter reversed into Munro's driveway, parking behind a large dark Irish yew which needed a good tidy. Stuart was already at school, and Munro had called in sick to the surgery, the first time he had ever done such a thing.

"Thanks for coming," he welcomed Peter. "The less I drive about town the less likely I am to be caught pulling a sicky," he rued, embarrassed. Lana slipped out of the passenger seat, looking emotional but resolved. "Are you sure about this?" Munro checked.

"Yep," she confirmed. "I feel a bit daft, like I'm overreacting and running away – but the idea of being able to relax for a while is just too tempting. Sorry, Dad, I've only just moved in and now I'm leaving," she joked. Peter gave her a brief hug and moved to unload her things.

"She's brought enough for a month," he joked, enjoying the cliché and using it to hide his concern for his daughter. As he loaded Lana's bags into the boot of Munro's car, he saw that the back seat was already stacked high with bags.

"Food, drinks, some bits and pieces I've been meaning to take down there," Munro explained. "There's a local store a couple of miles away from the cottage, but I wanted to make sure Lana had plenty supplies."

Peter nodded approvingly. "Good plan. She eats a lot, you know."

Lana thumped him lightly on the arm in reprimand. "We need to get going, Dad. Munro needs to be back for teatime, so no one realises he's been away. I'll give you a call this evening."

As they said their farewells, Munro opened the passenger door for Lana, a habit picked up from his dad. She raised an eyebrow at him, acknowledging the outdated courtesy with humour. They waved off Peter, then set off on their own journey.

"So, when did you get a cottage? Tell me all about it, I'm quite excited to see it," she asked.

Munro described the small house and its position, explaining where they were headed and what she could expect. "There are a lot of tourists in the area for most of the year, so you shouldn't attract too much attention if you pop into the shop or get the bus into Stranraer," he advised. "But in the main it will be you, and the seals, gulls and otters. If it gets too much for you, just shout and I'll come and get you. There's a landline, and wifi and a TV with streaming services all set up, so you hopefully won't get too bored. Did you leave your mobile behind like you planned?"

Lana nodded. "I know you think that's overkill, but I really want to get away from it all. I have a note of everyone's numbers; I can use the cottage phone to stay in touch. If I took my mobile with me, I'd be checking email and worrying just the same as at home. The solicitor knows to contact me by phone, I've explained I'm going away for a week, and I've given him the cottage's number. He's sending anything important to my dad's. He doesn't think he'll need me to sign anything else for now, though. I should be fine to go radio-silent for a while." She laughed dispiritedly. "I still can't believe it will take months to sort this all out, but if I get a bit of a break over the next few days, I think I can face it all."

Munro was always impressed with Lana's optimism and resilience; she took such an accepting and pragmatic view on what would frustrate and anger most other people. "Okay. Promise you'll call at any time if you need anything, though." Lana nodded, smiling. They were travelling on main roads now, traffic light and the day fair. "It'll take just over three hours from here if we're lucky. Do you want to stop someplace for lunch, or just eat when we get there?"

They planned their day, opting to get the journey done as quickly as possible so Munro could return home promptly. He was painfully aware of their coming separation but didn't want to burden Lana with his selfish concerns. He kept the conversation light and easy, trying to take her mind off her troubles. As they left the areas she knew, and travelled down through Ayrshire, Lana regularly asked about the sights she spotted from the car. As they passed Ailsa Craig, she admitted she loved to see lighthouses, and related a story she had been told as a child about the lighthouse keepers on another island. Munro was captivated by her animation as she spoke, and happy to tell her of the lighthouse within twenty miles of the cottage, which had a visitor centre and award-winning café, promising they would visit it when he came back to collect her. As they passed Stranraer and headed south into the Mull of Galloway, they talked through his childhood holidays in the area, and he pointed out anything of interest which he thought she might enjoy. As the route wound alongside the shore, Munro slowed and pulled off the road onto a broad driveway.

"We share this part of the road with the camp site down the coast," he explained. "They maintain it, we're lucky. You'll not see many visitors at this time of year, but there may be a few cars." The drive carried on down the coast and out of sight, but Munro took a left turn onto a rougher, narrower route. "From here, the drive is ours. On the right there," he gestured at a path through the bracken, "heads down to the public footpath along the coast. It's a nice way to get to the towns on either side. There's a map in one of the kitchen drawers." They continued to drive slowly for a few minutes, their bags jostling behind them. As they cleared a stand of trees on either side, Lana got her first sight of the cottage and the sea beyond. Munro heard her gasp softly.

"Oh Munro, it's so beautiful here."

Munro stopped the car, taking in the familiar scene with fresh eyes. The cottage was small and square, single storey and painted white to contrast with the dark slate roof. Flanked by twin chimneys, the wall currently facing them held two small-paned windows, gleaming in the late autumn sun. To the cottage's left, the drive curved around to the front door, the land rising beyond it towards the main road, broken intermittently by stands of trees. To the right was the wide expanse of shoreline and beach, the views out across the water incomparable in Munro's opinion. Behind the cottage, to the North and West, there was an old outbuilding which stored clutter, gardening gear and tools, and a woodshed which Munro always kept fully stocked, enjoying the monotonous repetition of cutting the logs. Beyond that was a larger wood, dense and dark, which covered the lower slopes right up to the main road and then continued uphill for some way.

"There's a path up through the wood, too," he pointed. "If you cut up through there and cross the road there's a lovely walk up into the hills. The views from up there are spectacular." Munro wished he could stay with her and share his love of the area, but he knew this was for the best. He put the car back into gear and continued around to the parking area.

As he unlocked the front door and entered the cottage, Munro relaxed. He preferred the privacy gained by maintaining the building himself, but always worried that there might have been a leak or structural problem while no one was home. Today, the air was chill and slightly stale, but that was the only sign that it had stood empty since his last visit with Stuart. He ushered Lana into the main room, a rectangular living room and kitchen with a cast iron stove in one corner and a large black open-fire range at the far side.

"The modern stove is the easiest to use and keep clean," he advised. "But if it gets very cold, the fireplace in the range works as well. I wouldn't try it for cooking on, it hasn't been used for decades," he joked. "But my mum always loved the look of the thing, even if it takes up so much space."

There was a small sofa and two comfortable armchairs as well as a small dining table and chairs in the kitchen area. There was a TV on a unit filled with boardgames and books, and a small, rickety coffee table. A door to their left led into a compact but cheerful double bedroom, with a window facing out onto the parking area. Another door off the kitchen revealed a small but modern shower room, and by the back door there was a set of coat hooks and a bench for shoes.

"It's lovely," Lana approved. "But where did you sleep when you were here with your parents?" she puzzled.

Munro grimaced. "A camp-bed. Don't laugh, it creaked something awful. I didn't even get to sleep out here where it was cosy, either: they laid it along the bottom of their own bed. Stuart is lucky, he gets a nice modern sofa bed here by the stove. I go to bed and read when he gets tired. It's the most rest I ever get," he laughed. "I'll get the stove lit once we've unpacked the car. You bring in your things and I'll fetch the groceries."

They shuttled companionably back and forth, Munro filling the kitchen cupboards and the fridge-freezer and stacking some boxes by the back door. He was just making a pot of tea when Lana emerged from the bedroom.

"That's me filled your wardrobe and drawers, maybe I did bring too much," she wondered. "How much food did you bring?" she exclaimed, catching sight of the full fridge.

Munro could feel himself begin to blush, knowing he had been over-enthusiastic. "Well, I wanted to make sure you had plenty choice. There's room in the freezer for some of the meat and fish, depending on what you fancy over the next couple of days. Umm, the cupboards have lots of staples, too."

As Lana rummaged through the small kitchen, he

worried he had been too extravagant. "There's enough here to feed a whole family for a month!" she laughed. "Thank you. When you said you would organise the groceries, I was expecting a couple of days' worth as a maximum, and then I'd go to the shops. I could have dinner parties if there was anyone around to invite," she joked, holding up a box of spices and raising her eyebrows. "What would you like for lunch?" she asked. "Thank goodness we didn't decide to eat out!"

As they tucked into ham salad sandwiches and enjoyed their tea, Munro realised he didn't want to leave; he wanted to spend the week with Lana, exploring and relaxing. He smiled quietly, realising that could easily be part of their future together. Lana gently asked him what was making him smile, and he explained, "I was just thinking that if things go well, and once you've got to know Stuart, maybe we could all come down for a break. It would be amazing to spend some time here together."

Lana's eyes were shining when he looked across; she reached for his hand across the table. "I would love that," she agreed. "And I'd love to meet Stuart and get to know him. That's something to look forward to when this is all sorted."

Munro glanced at the old clock on the mantelpiece; he had set the time and wound it when they arrived, enjoying the reassuring baritone of its tick. "I should go, sorry. Will you be alright?"

Lana laughed this off. "Oh, yes. This is perfection, Munro. I have everything I need and more." She caught his worried expression. "I have my list of phone numbers. I have your directions for weaning myself off all those pills. I have all my toiletries and clothes and loads of good books.

I have way more than enough food. Honestly, I'll be fine. I'll be more worried about you driving all the way home again on your own."

Munro collected his things, and lingeringly kissed her goodbye. "I'm going to miss you," he braved. "And I'm jealous," he added mischievously.

Lana smiled, looking him in the eyes with her familiar unconscious tilt of her head. "I'll miss you too. I appreciate this so much; I appreciate you, more than you know. I'll see you soon; call me tonight once Stuart is settled."

As Munro pulled onto the main road and headed back northwards, he spotted Lana standing at the cottage door, waving. He recollected her parting words and smiled through a rush of emotion. "I love you," he murmured.

Chapter 35 – Thurs 30th to Wed 5th November

Thursday 30th October

Lana lingered in bed the next morning, deliciously aware of her empty schedule. The room was chilly, the warmth from the stove long departed, but the duvet was thick and comforting. A voluminous fleece dressing gown hung beside the bed; grabbing it would be the first thing she did when she rose. For now, she snuggled into the covers, warm and content, and pondered the day before.

After Munro had left, she had phoned her dad to let him know she was safely settled, then gone exploring. She had walked down the coast, past the empty caravan park and along stony coves and huddled cottages. When the wind picked up from the north, she had turned back to head home to the warmth and comfort of the cottage. She had giggled as it came into sight, recollecting the comic strips of her childhood: the "but 'n' ben", they would have called it. She had passed the path to the drive and continued north on the beach until she stood directly in front of the cottage, relishing the luxury of having such magnificence to herself for a time.

Seagulls had swaggered through the wind, enjoying their freedom; oystercatchers peeping disconsolately from amongst the rockpools. Some way offshore, a dark shape had bobbed: perhaps either a seal or a cormorant, but Lana couldn't determine which. She had wondered idly if there were binoculars at the cottage, and smiled, suspecting there were. Munro was an organised sort of person. When she arrived back at the cottage, she had checked through the various cupboards, finding all manner of useful things for a shoreside break: wellies, waterproofs, waders, fishing gear, a camera and, thankfully, binoculars. Now they hung on a hook at the back door, ready to hand.

Later that evening, Munro had called, checking she was finding everything she needed. "Have you looked in the old outbuilding yet?" he had asked. "There are a few things in there you might like – something to keep you busy if you get bored. Help yourself to anything that takes your fancy." It had been too late and too dark to explore at the time; but now as she lazed, her curiosity bettered her. She rose and scrambled into the previous day's clothes, slipping on her boots and out the back door, remembering to grab the old iron key from its hook.

The aged wooden doors creaked open argumentatively, letting in the morning sunlight. Lana's eyes widened, and she clapped her hands to her face, laughing with joy; this was a treasure trove to her. Old wooden and cast-iron furniture and crofting implements were stacked to the ceiling. She could see chairs and bedframes, cupboards and drawers, an old sewing table, a large wardrobe, and ancient freestanding kitchen units. Turning and running back to the cottage, she tore open the boxes Munro had stacked up out of the way.

White spirit, cloths, sandpaper, brushes and paints and lacquers and oils of all varieties were inside. "Oh Munro, you marvellous man," she breathed.

She returned to the store after a quick breakfast, deciding to shower after she had braved the dust and spiders. Reluctant to dismantle the precarious pile of items, she walked around the outside, picking out the shapes and features within. An ornately carved pine blanket box sat at one edge of the pile, reasonably accessible. She uncovered it and pulled it out into the daylight, amazed to find it dirty, stained and scratched but mostly undamaged. Delighted with her find, she cleared the area where the light from the doors was brightest, and pulled some of the covers onto the floor, creating a temporary mini workshop. She spent the rest of the morning gently cleaning the wood and debating an overhaul versus restoration. As her stomach started to rumble, she was amazed to discover it was well after two in the afternoon; she still hadn't had a shower, so she called it a day and went to clean up before getting something to eat.

Later, she returned to the blanket box, standing back with a mug of tea, considering the warm tones of the wood, and the odd rough edges where it had been knocked over the years. Ring marks persisted on the lid, marring the intricate carving of interwoven celtic knots, but she would be able to fix those. She wondered again why such a beautiful piece had been relegated to the store; the pine would fit in with the rest of the furnishings in the cottage living room. She resolved to enhance its natural colour rather than painting it: the wood was too beautiful, and if Munro didn't want the box for the cottage, then they could find it another home.

She spent some more time eyeing the aggregated clutter in the store, finding a pile of smaller pieces towards the back of the building. An array of picture frames, mirrors, and glass leaned against a wall, and Lana pulled one frame out speculatively, running a finger lightly over its edges to check for rough or sharp points. Finishing her tea, she got back to work. She had just over a week in which to tinker, but she wanted to make sure she had this finished; the perfect thank you.

As the light started to fade, she rose from her knees, stretching and rubbing her cold joints. She thought longingly of her deep bath at home in her flat but shrugged it off; such a beautiful setting was well worth it, and a glass of wine on the sofa in front of the stove would ease the chill. She headed indoors and rekindled the stove before cataloguing the fridge contents, separating multipacks of meat and freezing the excess portions. She chose a selection of meals for the week, prioritising the most perishable items Munro had chosen; Lana hated to waste good food. With an excess of fresh vegetables, she opted to make a pot of soup; a warming lunch would be perfect each day after a chilly morning in the outbuilding. Once the soup was simmering at the back of the hob, she checked in with her dad, excited to tell someone about her finds in the garage. She realised he was the first person she had spoken to all day and felt a wonder at not having missed human contact at all.

"I bumped into Colin today," he mentioned. "He was asking if we were going to come along to the quiz night, next weekend. I mentioned you were away on a break and wouldn't be back until the Saturday, was that alright?"

Lana felt guilty for having worried her dad further. "Yes, of course. That's the truth; they don't need to know why I wanted to get away. I haven't told anyone else what has been happening, it would be such a long story now! It's my fault, I didn't think to let them all know I was going away; I told Lind but I'm not sure if they'll have met up."

They chatted about their days, Lana exaggerating the stacks of food Munro had brought to make her dad laugh. She described her meal plan for the week, Peter rubbishing her choice of roast vegetable couscous for with lamb, then envying her favourite smoked haddock omelette recipe. By the time she hung up, she was ravenous, and headed back to the stove to prepare her pan-fried sea bass and salad. She opened a bottle of crisp sauvignon blanc, knowing she was still taking her medication but throwing caution to the floor: tonight, she deserved a treat.

By now it was nearly full dark outside her windows, the sky to the east a velvet black and glimmering with early stars, and a magnificent indigo wash over the hills to the west. At home, her ex-colleagues from the bank would be preparing for tomorrow's Halloween night out. Lana sat to eat, content.

Tuesday 4th November

The storm seethed outside the cottage, gorging itself on leaves and branches stripped from the stands of bent trees, spewing them out to slap darkly against the white-washed walls and misted windows. The rain bass-drummed in waves across the slate roof and beat on the windowpanes in rapid staccatos. The sea was barely differentiated from the shore, shades of grey piling up and tumbling down, tides and rollers carved apart by the onslaught of the intense south-westerly gale. Lana stretched her feet towards the stove and relished the warmth on the soles of her thick socks. She had ventured out first thing, briefly standing on the beach and marvelling at the awesome forces at play, but the day was too brutal to be outside for long and she had no intention of leaving the house again today. She sipped her peppermint tea and snuggled further into the sofa cushions, contrarily happy for her plans to be ruined. She returned to her book, intent on losing track of time and troubles in the lamp-lit cosiness.

"Hi! Yeah, it's wild down here!" Lana laughed. "I'm so glad this place is solidly built; I went out for a bit and nearly lost my woolly hat! I shut the curtains just after 3 and I've ignored the outside ever since."

Munro had heard the background noise as soon she answered the phone, derailing the usual hellos. "How are you all?" Lana asked.

"Poor Stuart isn't feeling great," Munro answered. "He's been listless since he and Laurie got home; he says that eating hurts his throat. Hopefully he'll be better in the morning. Laurie said she'll come over if he needs to stay home, bless her. I bumped into Jen and Robbie after work, too. They were asking how you were, I said I'd ask you to give them a call."

Lana felt an unexpected slither of jealousy deep in her stomach and was startled to realise she didn't know who she was envious of; she missed her family and Munro equally. Certainly, she didn't mind Munro having stopped to chat with Jen, but she deeply wished she could be at home with them, or perhaps that they were all here with her. Pushing the confused morass of emotions aside, she agreed to phone Jen later.

They finished their call more quickly than usual, Stuart needing his dad's attention. Lana poured herself a glass of wine and sat down, thoughtful. She had only been here a week, was it normal to miss her family and Munro so much already? She had been fine until Munro mentioned meeting Jen, was it simple jealousy? Refusing to countenance that possibility, Lana chalked her feelings up to the amount of stress she'd been under; a week of rest didn't remedy months of worry. She refused to spend her time here moping. She had been given the perfect opportunity to relax and be creative, and she was going to continue making the most of it. She would call Jen now, then watch a cheesy vampire movie.

Wednesday 5th November

The storm had passed at some point during the night; now scattered clouds speckled a bleached blue sky and only a light breeze stirred the detritus scattering the grass and driveway. Lana walked down the drive, checking for sizeable branches and kicking them into the verge with her walking boots, startling two roe deer. She called after them, apologising, then laughed to herself: "Talking to the animals, Lana! Do you think you're Snow White?" As she came out onto the main driveway, she could see clearly to the main road and was relieved that no trees had fallen to block the way. She turned back towards the shore, hoping to finish most of the remaining work on the blanket box this morning; she wanted it ready for Saturday.

Later that afternoon, arm muscles aching pleasantly from the polishing she'd been perfecting, she returned to the cottage to find a bedraggled wood pigeon huddled in the doorway. As she approached, it hopped away from her, clearly reluctant to take flight. She watched with concern as it stretched both wings, flapped limply then slowed to a walk, watching her warily.

"Poor thing, you must be exhausted. Your wings seem fine, anyway." She went indoors and returned with two bowls, one of clean water and one of mixed seeds. "You're lucky Munro seems to think I'm a health nut," she muttered as she lowered them to the ground halfway to the pigeon. She retreated to the house and stood watching as the bird inspected her with one eye then another, before waddling over to the bowls. It drank first, scattering drops like jewels onto the paving. It finally ate, flicking seeds out of the bowl and choosing its favourites. "Ah well, I'm sure someone will enjoy the rest of them," she smiled. She kept an eye on the bird while the daylight lasted, uncertain what predators might pass by. She could only hope that it could fly in a genuine emergency.

As she pottered inside, preparing her meal and tidying afterwards, she thought over her week here. She was surprised to find that she wasn't terribly missing most of her old life, only certain people: her family, Munro, her few close friends. The hubbub of working in the bank, her routine at the gym, visiting shops and going out – these things she hadn't missed at all. She remembered her dad's concern about her urge for a quieter life and realised he was wrong: she probably would be quite happy to have quieter days and evenings, so long as she still saw the people who she loved every so often. Her reverie was halted by the phone ringing, and she turned the oven off before answering, wary of burning her casserole.

"Munro, hi! How is Stuart doing today?" she asked

immediately. "Oh no. Has he had tonsillitis before? Oh, the poor kid, he must feel miserable. No, no, I totally understand, you can't leave him when he's poorly and you can't trek him all this way. Is it okay if I just stay here a little longer? That will save my dad the journey. No, it's no problem. No, the solicitor hasn't been in touch but neither have Central Care, so that's a good thing. No, don't worry at all. You can come down once Stuart is better, if you like, or if I do need to get home urgently, I can always go up to Stranraer and get the train. Some extra time here will be great, and I have everything I need. So long as you're okay with it! I know... I miss you too. Give me a call later if you get the chance but don't worry if Stuart needs you, he's the priority. Bye!"

Lana looked around the cottage, a smile slowly gathering on her face. She was sorry for Stuart, and missing Munro, but she was suddenly glad her countdown to reality had been postponed; she was really very happy here.

Friday 7th November

Lana checked out her window for Cheeky and Fussy, the wood pigeons. They seemed to be a mated pair, and with the original visitor having smaller neck patches and a paler breast, Lana had decided that Fussy was the female. Cheeky had joined Fussy at the back door last night, letting his mate do the work of scattering the seeds, and nibbling on her discards; he gave Lana an impertinent glare every so often as if daring her to approach. They were absent, so Lana refilled their bowls while she could do so without disturbing them. She had phoned Lind last night, full of chat about this wonderful spot and the wildlife, much to her friend's entertained bemusement. "Don't stay too long," Lind had advised. "You're going native, and I miss my night out buddy. The bank is rubbish without you. You should've seen them all last week in the pub, acting like they'd never seen someone dressed as Cruella DeVille. Only Robert made any effort, he came as "In the Red", all dressed in red and covered in overdue bills. They were all appalled because they were photocopies of real bills he'd received," Lind laughed. Lana had left the call cheered and thankful for their friendship.

Now she turned towards the store, keen to see the blanket box in daylight and decide whether it needed more work. It would need a tray or coasters to protect it, but she thought it would make a good coffee table, replacing the damaged one beside the sofa. She would mend that next, but it was so badly scarred that she thought it would be best filled and sanded then painted. As she laid covers over the grass and brought the box into the light, she exclaimed in pleasure. Her work repairing the small chips and scratches, smoothing off the rough edges on the carving, cleaning and waxing and polishing was all worth it. The box gleamed in the sun; natural aged pine hues augmented by the finish. She would swap them over today and start work on the coffee table tomorrow, she decided. Today, she was making a tea tray from one of the old picture frames and some spare wood; it would sit on the blanket box to hold mugs perfectly.

Chapter 36 – Monday 10th November

Laurie had messaged just before lunch to let Munro know that Stuart was doing okay, saving him from having to call her on his break. He smiled in fond appreciation of the woman who had become so important in their lives after Ann had died. He could leave Stuart with her confident that he would be looked after - possibly better than he might manage himself, he admitted ruefully. He headed upstairs to the kitchen, lunch in hand, wondering if he would be able to travel down to the cottage this weekend to collect Lana; even if Stuart was better, he didn't want to impose too much on Laurie.

As he sat to eat with two of the reception staff, he let their chatter wash over him. It had been a hectic morning of house calls and he was left in need of respite. He treated himself to a soft drink from the fridge; the sugar rush might do him good. He was still sitting, staring absently out the window, when the practice manager rushed in.

"Munro, Maria needs you. She's in her room; the police

are with her." She shrugged when Munro asked what had happened. "I've no idea, they said it was confidential and asked to speak to one of the senior partners directly, but she's also asked for you. You'd better go down."

Munro knocked on the consultation room door, and waited to hear Maria invite him in. Two policemen were with her, both young and both looking slightly abashed.

"Thanks for joining us, Munro, I hope you don't mind," she started. "Officers, this is my colleague, Dr Alexander. He has also consulted with Ms Knight in the past." Introductions done, she briefed Munro on the matter at hand. "These gentlemen are here enquiring about the whereabouts of Ms Knight. They say a Compulsory Treatment Order has been declared for her, but I fail to see how that can possibly be the case - there certainly hasn't been a tribunal and there is nothing further added to her medical record. As far as I'm aware Ms Knight is continuing to appeal against her diagnosis. A process I have explained at some length." At this, she glanced disparagingly at the two officers. "Apparently, she no longer stays at the address we have for her, and her parents say she is away on a break. The police are checking with anyone who may have contact with her. They have been asked to escort Ms Knight to the Mental Health Unit. They have the relevant paperwork."

Munro was frozen, terrified of reacting in any way. He locked eyes with Maria, knowing she would recognise any falsehood from him but unable to betray Lana. "I only consulted with her twice," he reiterated, sticking to the few truths he could tell. "The only home address I would have access to is the one on the system, and perhaps her parents': I believe they are also patients here. I'm afraid I can't help you," he turned to advise the policemen.

To his relief, they accepted this readily, and thanked Maria before making their exit. Munro let out a shaky breath and raised his gaze to meet his colleague's eyes. "I can't believe they have a CTO. She should have been given a named representative and invited to a tribunal with a legal representative; due process has to be followed."

Maria nodded. "I agree. But worryingly, they did have the appropriate paperwork. I'll call my contact at Central immediately. Why did you react so badly, Munro? Do you know something?" Maria's eyes were always sharp, but now they were penetrating.

Munro knew he couldn't lie outright and sighed. "I know Lana quite well, now. We met at the pub recently, chatted, became friendly. It was after I handed her care over to you. I know that all the advice is to avoid any previous patients when it comes to relationships, but it was happening before I realised it. We just became so close so quickly." Maria was rigidly still, giving no reaction, so Munro continued. "I wanted to tell you but didn't want to worry you - or disappoint you." Maria was now looking stern and disapproving, but he moved on to his highest priority. "Anyway, you're right, her solicitor is appealing everything; she's headed off for a break to try and get some rest, she was exhausted by it all. I don't know the solicitor's details, though. Her family would know more, but frankly I'm wary of helping the police find her. How have Central managed to agree to an enforced CTO without a tribunal? That shouldn't be possible, it's a terrifying precedent to set."

Maria was uncharacteristically biting a nail. "I know, I'll talk to the others and some of the other practices, maybe try and get hold of someone at the GP Committee. We need to get to the bottom of this; they can't change policy by the back door." She lowered her hand from her face. "I wouldn't have asked you to join us if I'd known you did have any information, Munro. They asked if anyone else might know anything and I thought that hearing it from you as well would shut them up and move them on. You didn't lie to them?" As Munro shook his head, she sighed. Munro couldn't tell if it was weariness or relief. "Good. You ought to be okay. But someone needs to get word to Lana Knight that she's now in some considerable bother. If you do have a way of reaching her, you may want to let her know. It would be best for her to stay out of the way until we can see if there's anything else we can do for her. Perhaps we could meet with her solicitor, if we got her permission," she mused. Munro nodded, understanding. He would warn Lana immediately and get permission for the practice to start working with her solicitor.

That afternoon, Munro found himself obsessing about the simplest of his decisions: whether to visit Lana's parents first, or phone her immediately. It was tempting to go and see them, compare notes and call Lana together – but what if the police were there when he stopped by? Should he call them instead? Or go straight to Lana? He knew it was a subconscious distraction from his real worries but didn't fight it; this latest development could have been avoided if he'd had the courage to do the right thing and call Bev to sort things earlier. Now he was close to being overwhelmed by guilt and fear, and he knew it. When he finished his last consultation of the day, he stopped by Maria's room. She was on the phone but waved him in when she spotted him. She completed her call shortly after, Munro unable to ascertain who she was talking with.

"Hi. What an afternoon. I used my break and two DNAs to try and get some info. Central are due to return my call, they have my mobile as well as the number here. No one I've spoken to has heard of any changes to the mental health policies, and the website for the Act hasn't been updated. So: whatever has happened is either very new, or dodgy. That won't deter the police from pursuing the enforcement order, though – they won't take the risk of being blamed if anything went wrong." Seeing Munro's dismay, she changed tack. "Don't worry, I'll continue pursuing it. I've notified Mark and Theresa, as well as the staff. I still think we should talk to the solicitor; we need to be on the same page if we're to help Lana. What will you do?"

Munro shrugged unhappily. "I wondered about stopping in to see her parents, check what the police told them and compare notes on how best to handle Lana. They might need some reassurance, too. But I was worried that the police might see me visiting them somehow; it sounds paranoid, I know. Otherwise, I was just going to call her and let her know what's happened... try to reassure her that we'll work with her solicitor to resolve it all. I think she's best staying away for now, as you said; hopefully she can. I'm worried about putting her under this much pressure when she's alone. She's resilient, but this is an incredible ordeal to go through."

Maria was nodding. "Yes, you're right. But she's better where the police can't find her and forcibly admit her. You realise our innocence hangs on the fact that we don't know where she is?" she stressed. As Munro nodded his lie and stared at his hands, she sighed. "What a mess; this will take some untangling. In the meantime, I've agreed with the others that I'll skip an appointment every hour, so I have time for phone calls and the like. They're being supportive; they don't want to get involved so they're happy for me to shoulder it. Go and talk to her – we should check in as often as possible to keep up to date. As soon as we can see her solicitor, we should involve him. I'm not letting my health service be subverted in this way, and we're not letting that girl be railroaded into inpatient care she doesn't need."

Munro registered the steely determination on Maria's face, relieved to have her on their side.

Munro walked down to the beach and found an empty bench. He had chosen to call Lana immediately, rather than visit her family first: he could call them afterwards if Lana was concerned for them. He shivered, but despite the chill, he preferred to talk here, where he could focus. In the distance, a mother and son were walking along the beach with their small dog, laughing and playing. The father wandered along far behind them, absorbed in something on his phone, missing the moments that should be the best of his day. Munro shook his head, realising he was being judgemental and knowing he himself should be with Stuart right now, but still appalled at how often people didn't appreciate what they had until it was gone. He hated that he couldn't be with Lana, had to abandon her at such a difficult time. But he had Stuart to look after, and he could help Lana better from here, where he could work with Maria on the case. He put his own feelings aside, knowing that delaying the news wouldn't help Lana in the slightest.

"Lana, hi it's me." Lana launched into an excited tale of her day, detailing her progress in taming her friendly pigeons and her trip into the nearest village to stock up on fresh bread and milk. Munro couldn't bear to interrupt her; she sounded truly happy and carefree, and he knew he was about to ruin that for her. As she ran out of news, she turned to Stuart, asking how he was doing.

"He's been really brave about it all," Munro answered proudly. "His throat is a real mess, but he's resting and eating soft foods without complaining too much. He's desperate to get back to school but I think that will be a while yet." Munro sat forward and pressed his legs into the bench, literally and figuratively bracing himself for what he had to say.

"Lana, something has happened here. I don't want to worry you, but it is quite serious." He explained the visit from the police, the extraordinary compulsory treatment order, and what would happen if they found her. "They said they had already been to see your parents as well; I can drop in on them if you like? Maria and I agree that you should stay away, if possible. Tell no one where you are, and don't answer the door to anyone you don't know, especially policemen. If you could call your solicitor tomorrow as well and give him permission to talk with us: we'll be better able to defend you if we're working together. I'm so sorry to dump this on you when you're on your own; I should be there with you, but I can help better from here and while Stuart is ill my hands are tied..."

Lana interrupted him suddenly. "No, Munro please don't say that. None of this is your fault, and Stuart needs you. I'll be fine. Only you know where I am, and although some people have the phone number, I doubt they will give that to the police. I can't stay here forever, but if you think Maria and my solicitor can get this fixed before I come home to be committed, then that's what I'll do."

She amazed Munro by laughing lightly. He couldn't understand why she wasn't taking this seriously and quizzed her. "Lana, are you okay? Have you understood what I'm saying? Do you realise how serious this is?"

She laughed again, this time with a bitter twist. "Oh, yes, I totally understand. But Munro, don't you see? I've been worrying about exactly this since I received the first threats in their letter. This is the worst-case scenario I've been waiting for; sometimes it pays to be a cynic," she joked bitterly. "Don't worry, I'm not losing my marbles. I'm just... okay with it. I'm in the best possible place right now, well out of the way. If we can fix this without me spending some time in a hospital arguing about taking these meds, I'll be pleasantly surprised. And to be honest, it's wonderful here. I miss you, and my family, but even with all of this going on I still feel happier here than I have for a long while. I can stay here in hiding, can't I?" she asked.

"Of course, you can stay there as long as you want. In the long-term you'll need to come home, but there's no rush." He focused briefly on practicalities, distracting himself from his guilt and her ordeal. "I'll order a grocery delivery from the store in Stranraer, let me know what you need... you should probably get enough for another couple of weeks, just to be safe. I often get them to deliver to the woodstore, for when we arrive, so you won't need to see anyone." He shook his head at their surreal conversation. "I can't believe how calm you are about all this," Munro admitted. "You're the most amazing woman, Lana."

They couldn't stay on the phone; Munro needed to go home to Stuart and Lana wanted to call her parents and let them know their plan. As he said goodbye and started his brisk yomp home, he envied Lana's strength and calm acceptance, knowing he would be far weaker. He knew then that he wouldn't fully relax until he had solved Lana's problems, whatever it took.

Chapter 37 – Saturday 15th November

The car park was dark and quiet at this early hour, empty of the usual families and couples locking their cars and heading towards the vast shopping mall. Munro had left Stuart at home with Laurie for the weekend, saying he had to visit his parents on a family matter; his son had briefly complained but still wasn't well enough to put real energy into it. Now, he sat in his car, waiting and mulling over the last week.

He and Maria had worked tirelessly with Lana's solicitor, determining the full extent of Lana's situation and preparing her defence. They had finally discovered that the use of legal agreements prior to the Bryant-Cargill Factorisation analysis had resulted in a de facto amendment to the Mental Health Act: factorisation patients were effectively signing away their rights to fair representation without their knowledge. The GP community was up in arms, their representative bodies challenging the worrying precedent. Lana's solicitor was attempting to have her appeal expedited but was yet unable to have the enforcement order rescinded.

This left Lana at risk of being committed to in-patient mental health care if she was found, where she would be forced to take medications and give up her freedom until the legal battle was won. Munro couldn't cope with the uncertainty of it all; last night, in a moment of near panic, he had finally thrown aside his selfishness and called Bev Cargill, pleading for her help. Bev and Peter had been completely unaware of the situation, sitting too high in the hierarchy of doctors; owning the process but not the patient relationships or day to day management. As Munro told her the full story, she was at first disbelieving, and then appalled. This sort of misuse of their analysis was exactly what she had feared most during her work; that this had happened in her home country infuriated her. They had agreed to meet this morning and visit Lana, so that Bev could assess Lana's condition without medication, and determine a plan for the best way forward. "Don't worry, Munro, I can get her out of this mess: I have authority over the clinicians in my team and can push that through. But we need to be sure we do it smartly so we can stop this change of policy in its tracks. This is a crucial degradation of patient rights, and I think Lana deserves a say in how we fight it." Munro wished he could be as confident: the last few weeks had unnerved him. He glanced at the clock, realising he had been lost in his thoughts; they had agreed to rendezvous and drive down together, and it was now time to meet Bev.

As they reached Ayr, Bev pulled into a supermarket petrol station to fill up her diesel tank. Her car was luxuriously large and comfortable, but far from economical. She had laughingly explained her irresolute morning at the dealership, and the resulting impulsive decision to treat herself. She admitted that she regretted her choice in most car parks and high streets, although she loved driving it on motorways.

"Do you think we should pick up some food or anything?" she asked. "I don't like to turn up anywhere empty-handed, especially when I'm staying overnight."

Munro shook his head. "There should be plenty there; there was a grocery delivery yesterday. And don't expect too much; there's no spare bedroom," he reminded her before reverting to their previous discussion, "I can't understand why I can't get hold of her. We spoke on Thursday evening, but yesterday and this morning the phone is just ringing and ringing. I hope she's fine."

Bev smiled mischievously at him. "I'm sure she is. You've spent last night and this morning describing how hardy she is. Maybe she's been out, or the phone is wonky. We should be there in a couple of hours, shouldn't we?"

Munro nodded as she hopped out of the car and headed for the pump. He was eager to see Lana again, but worried that he hadn't been able to warn her about Bev's visit. He'd had no chance to admit that he knew the team responsible for factorisation. His residual guilt for encouraging Lana into the process was exacerbated by a fear that his connection to Bev may have influenced their decision to see her. Would Lana blame him for her predicament? Would she ever forgive him for not calling Bev sooner? As they pulled back out onto the main road south, anxiety gnawed at his soul.

"What I saw of Lana doesn't tie with her documented results at all," Bev confessed. "I read her full report last night. I'll need to find out where the factorisation went wrong - we'll have to halt consultations in the meantime. I'd like to get Lana's thoughts on it all, her debrief notes aren't very detailed. We can leave most of that for another day, though, if you're worried about it?" Bev looked to Munro as they turned off the road and onto the private driveway.

Munro was hesitant to agree. "Perhaps if we have theories as to why the results have been wrong it will be easier to refute them? That might help with pushing for an investigation, and feed the argument against the move away from full mental health tribunals?" He was glad to see Bev nodding thoughtfully. "We have plenty time over the weekend, we can certainly discuss it with her," he suggested.

They cleared the stands of trees and came into the parking area, both stiff after such a long drive. Munro sat for a moment, hoping this would truly be the end of Lana's ordeal but unable to discard his unabating disquiet. Bev was stretching and admiring the views. "This is wonderful. No wonder you and Stuart love it so much, it's perfect," she offered.

Munro moved around to the front door and found it locked. Bev looked questioningly at him as he headed to the back of the cottage and grinned. "She must be out. Luckily, we keep a spare back door key hidden: it's not terribly secure but saves a long drive if we forget the keys," he laughed as he lifted a trough planter and retrieved the key.

Bev had already reached the door. "It's open," she surprised him, pushing it wider. "Oh! Oh Lana, are you okay?"

They rushed into the kitchen, horrified to find Lana huddled against the units, arms wrapped protectively around her middle and tears standing in her eyes. She turned to Munro with devastated betrayal clear in her gaze. "You told me I had to stay hidden, they would hospitalise me," she gasped. "Why would you bring them here?"

As Munro realised how awful this must look, he scrambled for the right words to explain the situation, momentarily dumbfounded in the burden of her accusation.

Bev was quicker to react, raising her hands in submission, and responding softly. "It's okay, Lana. I'm here to help. There are some things you don't know about me; I've known Munro since we were students. I had no idea what was happening to you. We're here to help," she repeated, pouring deep sincerity into her voice.

Lana looked at them both, first doubtfully then angrily. "You two are friends?" she asked. "Why wouldn't you mention that?" she demanded of Munro.

"I felt so bad, Lana," he tried to explain. "I was so keen to see factorisation at work. I'd recommended the analysis, and it turned out so badly for you. Bev had called me when she accepted you; I wasn't sure if she'd brought you in as a favour." Munro glanced at Bev, glad to see she wasn't offended. "At first I didn't mention it because I didn't want you to think I was pushing you into it. Then later, I felt so responsible for the mess you were in: I didn't want you to blame me. I kept hoping we could fix this without having to admit to it all, and then when I hadn't told you at first it would look so bad if I ever did. I'm so sorry, Lana, I should have told you."

Lana wiped the tears from her eyes, staring at the floor for a few quiet moments before rising slowly. "Yes, you cloddy should have. I should be furious with you," she glared, breath jagging. "But that does make some sense, I guess. God, I don't know whether I should be angry or relieved or what." She shook her head and visibly dismissed the thought. "But I still don't understand why you're both here; why didn't you call me to explain? I was terrified when I saw who was driving. I nearly ran," she confessed, gesturing at her bag and the open door.

"Munro tried to call," Bev explained. "He couldn't get through. I know this has been a shock, but... We're here to plan how we sort out this mess. I can help you reverse the results and prescriptions, Lana. I wanted to meet you again first, to make sure you were as well as Munro described. And..." she shrugged, "I was being selfish. I want to know how we got things so wrong. But maybe the most important thing is that we've found out that my process is being used as a backdoor to allowing enforced treatment without due diligence, and we need to be able to stop that. We'll need your help with that, I suspect."

Lana looked doubtfully from Munro to Bev, recognising their good intentions and forcibly calming herself. "You'd better shut the door and I'll get the stove and kettle on. I think you'll need to explain this quite a bit more."

The day passed in a blur of discussion, Munro occasionally rising to prepare food and drinks as the two women compared notes and debated how best to proceed. He watched Lana considering Bev's proposals, adding suggestions and detailing her concerns. Their intellects were well matched as they debated, Bev clearly warming to Lana's transparency and desire to protect the greater good as well as her own position. As he added another log to the fire, he spotted the old blanket box, painstakingly restored and boasting a beautiful new tea tray, painted and lacquered to gleaming perfection.

"Lana, these are amazing," he interrupted the women. "I can't believe how well this old box looks. Is this one of the broken picture frames, too?"

Bev and Lana both came over into the living area, Lana smiling at Munro's pleasure. "Yes, it is. I used an old piece of veneer instead of the cardboard picture backing, painting it the same shade as I used for the frame and adding the gold paisley pattern before lacquering it all and replacing the glass into the frame. I thought it would save the box getting ring marked again," she teased. "I've nearly finished fixing up the little coffee table, too. It was such a cool 1950s shape, I couldn't resist. I've mended the legs and split wood; I'm finishing it in a sea foam shade with a matt finish to bring out the brass shoes on the legs."

"These are beautiful," Bev agreed with Munro. "There are stores in Edinburgh that would sell these for a fortune. Is this what you're going to do for a living now? Munro told me about your job."

Lana flushed. "Maybe. I'd have to see if there was a market for things, and I wasn't sure if they were good enough; I'd have to see how it went," she repeated. "I wondered about offering a renovation service as well as selling items. Lots of people have these sorts of pieces at home and just don't know how to bring them back to life. I think it might be something I could really enjoy doing."

"Well, let's work on getting you home so you can get that underway," Bev replied firmly. "Munro, I think we may have a plan." She led them back to the table, and her notes there. "It's clear that the factorisation analysis process we're trialling in the UK is still flawed. We've adapted it since it was rolled out in other countries, and that's caused some of the issues – but not all. A few points of note. Firstly, the baselining of responses to stimuli wasn't failproof – most likely because Lana was extremely familiar with two of the films that were used. Secondly, when Lana was interviewed, she was already extremely fatigued, leading to muted reactions and a tendency to agree with the interviewers. I believe the intensive in-patient scenario may lead to a hint of Stockholm syndrome," she laughed. "It sounds implausible, but that's what I think we're seeing. Thirdly, the analysis of the results was not confirmed through further talking therapy and testing; no second or third opinions were sought. Lastly, the analysis was performed by two of my most cautious clinicians – we need to factor in the risk aversion of those performing the analysis." Bev looked to Munro and Lana, who both nodded their understanding.

"Good. This is clearly enough to bring the current format of Bryant-Cargill in the UK into question, especially in Lana's case where she has displayed no evidence of suffering the problems prognosed. We can use that to revert her results and free her from this ridiculous pursuit by Central Care. I have the authority to do that as soon as I have access to my systems on Monday."

Munro felt giddy, felt his limbs lighten as if they might float, but stamped down hard on the elation. "Is that absolutely definite?" he asked. "Is there any chance that could fail?" Lana grasped his hand in mutual understanding.

"I could do it right now if we were in Edinburgh," Bev assured them both. "This is my programme; it is clearly at fault. No one can countermand my decision here."

Munro turned to see tears of joy coursing down Lana's features as he shuddered a breath of utter relief. Bev was giving them no time for celebration, though, and continued.

"I will also be halting the analysis of patients immediately and ordering a review of all patients we have seen. Some will have been appropriately treated – maybe all of them but Lana have been okay – but I cannot leave those stones unturned. I will also be working with the General Practitioners Committee and the other organisations to try to close this backdoor they've used to achieve enforced compulsory treatment without due process." Here, Bev sighed. "Depending on who is behind that, and the politics involved, we may not have much success. In fact, it's possible the factorisation analysis could be taken out of my hands and restarted as a programme. But if that happens, we can continue to lobby government as independents. It might be a bit of a battle."

Bev shook off her worries and returned to her plan. "Munro, Lana has agreed to let me use her case as an example of where this has gone wrong. There will be reports to draw up, we will need her assistance. She may need to testify. But if we possibly can, we will stop this happening to anyone else."

"I feel like some sort of revolutionary conspirator," Lana joked weakly. "It all seems so surreal. Thank you for coming to help, Bev. Thank you for taking this on. I'll help you any way I can; we both will."

Munro marvelled at the two women before him, their strength and determination to do the right thing for others. He wondered what the next few months would bring, and suddenly realised that whatever the future held, he and Lana would contend with it together. It felt wonderful.

Lana was smiling now, almost unrecognisable from the distraught woman they had first seen sitting on the floor. "Well, if we're finished for the day, and you're both staying over, would you like a glass of wine? We have plenty food, anyway," she laughed. "Munro bought enough for weeks. Thank God that wasn't necessary."

Chapter 38 – Sunday December 14th

Munro ushered Stuart out of the way, shouting, "Coming through! Beep Beep! Trees before boys, buster!"

Stuart giggled and ran down the hall and halfway up the stairs, thoroughly enjoying the drama. "I told you it was too big, Dad! I told you and you wouldn't listen! We'll never get Maurice on top of that!"

Munro stopped and parodied a glare at his son. "We'll have no more rebellion in the ranks, or it'll be stale bread rather than mince pies!" he joked. "Go and pop the oven on at 160 before I change my mind." Laying the tree down on the hall floor, he realised its base was not yet fully through the front door. "Oh. Maybe we did get a bit carried away," he admitted.

"Never!" Lana denied. "This ceiling is massive, it'll be perfect. And if we put it just here, Stuart can add Maurice from the stairs," she added, pointing to a spot where the hall was wide enough for everyone to pass by. Lana had just learned that instead of the usual fairy or star tree-topper, the Alexanders had Maurice, a foot high plastic mole wearing a checked waistcoat and scarf. She thought she'd handled this news quite well, considering. Stuart came back out into the hall, shyly grinning at her as he took off his coat and hat. They had met quite a few times now, but he was still a little hesitant when it came to asking questions. Lana waited patiently, giving him time to choose his words.

"Lana," he braved, "will you be here on Christmas Day, maybe?" He looked across at his dad, unsure whether he had said the wrong thing. Munro smiled and shrugged lightly, looking to Lana to answer.

"Looks like I'm not getting a steer from your dad," she smiled in response. "I would really like that, Stuart. I said I would spend Christmas Eve and the morning with my sister and her baby, and have lunch with my family, but maybe I could come around mid-afternoon. Just in time for Christmas cake, hopefully!"

"That would be perfect," Munro answered, ruffling Stuart's hair affectionately and finding pine needles lurking on his crown already. "We eat around lunchtime, too. It's just the two of us: Laurie sees her family and my parents don't do Christmas," he explained. "Stuart and I always start to get a little peckish again about 5 or 6. If you're lucky Stuart will make you one of his famous Christmas toasties."

Lana smiled as Stuart began describing a turkey, pig-in-blanket, cranberry and cheese toastie, but interrupted him. "That sounds lovely for tea-time. But it's such a shame that you two will be here alone for lunch. Why don't you come to my parents' instead? They always make plenty, and there's loads of room. They'd love to have you. We can still bring some leftovers back here for the toasties," she hurried to reassure an uncertain Stuart.

"What do you think, Stuart? Do you fancy a wee change to our routine?" Munro asked. Stuart beamed and nodded his reply, and the deal was struck.

Later, the tree decked in tinsel and lights, and the large lounge cheerful with decorations, Lana and Munro settled into the sofa and admired their efforts. Lana had never seen so many sets of fairy lights, nor this number of woodland creatures dressed in their big coats and scarves. Lana had initially felt awkward, helping to unpack Christmas decorations which had been so carefully collated by Ann, but as she unwrapped each one, she felt a little closer to the woman with whom she shared her love. It surprised her to find that she didn't mind living with Munro's history at all. His past was his own to treasure, and she would honour that; their future was their own. The front garden was secluded, so Munro rarely shut the curtains, and tonight the lights and candles reflected gleamingly against the dark backdrop. Lana stared into the spectacle, her eyes comfortably unfocused.

"Penny for them?" Munro interrupted her reverie.

She smiled and shook her head. "I was just thinking how different this is to last year. So much has changed... all for the better!" she reassured him. "Last year I was in my little flat with my little tree in the window and just a few bits and pieces; lunch with Mum and Dad and then a walk with Todd before heading home on my own. Now Jen has the flat; it's done up like a silver and blue themed winter wonderland," she laughed. "I'm staying back at my parents' and having Christmas with you and Stuart; it'll be lovely to have so many more people to share it all with."

Munro kissed her gently. "How are you feeling about it all, all the changes. You've had an incredibly difficult year."

Lana shrugged and smiled shyly. "It was awful at the time, but a lot of good has come out of it. You," she prodded him lightly in the ribs. "Getting away from the bank, starting to work more on the furniture, setting up my own business. That's a load of improvement." She paused to think. "I'm a lot happier with myself, too: I don't doubt myself so much, you know. Maybe none of that would have happened without the awful stuff as well." She looked at Munro, serious. "I'm glad it all happened; it's made me stronger, and it's brought us together. Next year might be a little tough as well, starting the business from scratch and helping Bev and Maria with their legal challenge. But I know I'm up to it, now. And I have you; I'm so grateful to have met you."

Munro minutely nodded his understanding. "I love you, too," he whispered, leaning his forehead gently on hers. "But..." he glanced out into the hall. "I don't think Stuart is going to wait much longer to get started on the T-Rex fossil skeleton Lego you brought him." He rose and offered her his hand, leading her through to the kitchen table, where the remains of mince pies sat surrounded by bags of plastic bricks.

They had just finished bag three when the doorbell rang, Lana raising an eyebrow and Munro shrugging as he headed into the hall. She heard the surprise in his tone as he greeted the visitor, and the door shut again. She turned as an enormous poinsettia entered the room, carried by a warmly dressed Lind.

"I know I should have thought of a better excuse," they announced, looking around, "but to be honest, I just wanted a nosey at this magnificent house! Hello, you must be Stuart. Where do you think we should put this?"

Stuart was looking wary and uncertain; Lana smiled at him and explained, "This is my best friend Lind, come with a present. Where do you guys still have room for one last Christmas decoration?"

Stuart beamed and rose from his seat, looking around excitedly. "There, in the big window ledge," he pointed. "It's too empty since the herbs all died."

Lind smiled, a vision in fuchsia lipstick and smoky eyeshadow, cheeks strongly defined, and hair slicked back into a tight ponytail. Leaning over the sink and into the deep window, they moved the herb pots to ensure the poinsettia was shown to its best advantage. "Perfect! Merry Christmas, and "God Bless Us, Every One!"" they quoted with a flourish and a grin.

Munro thanked Lind for the plant and offered a seat and something to drink, enjoying the sudden party spirit Lind had swept into his home. He was busy opening red wine and gathering glasses, when Stuart raised his eyes from the Lego once more. "Excuse me, but are you a man or a lady?" he asked forthrightly. Lana felt her eyes widen, knowing that Lind wasn't particularly used to children.

To her delight, Lind let loose a natural laugh, and leaned forward covertly before whispering behind their hand, "Neither!"

Stuart grinned back, happy with this answer. "That's brilliant!" he decided. "You get to do anything you want, then! Are you any good at Lego?"

Lana, heart molten and happier than she had felt in years, looked across from Stuart to both Lind and Munro and breathed, "Oh yes, Lind is absolutely the best."

Her phone started to ring beside her on the table, a backdrop of Jen holding Robbie flashing along with the Christmas lights. She smiled first at her sister's image, and then at everyone in the room. "You all are. You're perfect. This is going to be the perfect Christmas."

Afterword

Lana, Munro, and their friends will return in Insurrections, as they campaign with civil rights groups and take up the fight against medical control. If you have enjoyed this first novel in The Factors series, you can find *Insurrections* on Amazon from summer 2022.

This novel is set in my hometown, although the detailed locations are fictional. I've also drawn on some of my own past experiences, but the storyline and all characters and organisations are purely fictional. I thought carefully about how and where to end this novel but finally chose to end on a high note: I think we all need something heart-warming.

Please do leave a review on Amazon, I love to learn from all feedback and your opinions are so valuable for my future writing.

Thanks to my readers, especially Carolyn, Jon and Lisa: any flaws in this book are entirely my fault, their input was invaluable. Thanks also to Alison for her advice on promoting my work. Lastly, but certainly not least, I am most grateful for Alistair and Lyall, who believe in me enough to make me believe in myself.

Sally.

About the Author

Sal Hunter lives on the east coast of Scotland and has spent her life reading too much and ignoring her ambitions. Find out more on her Amazon author page.

Printed in Great Britain
by Amazon